"What can I get you today?" Kim asked.

"A smile would be nice" was the reply.

Tucking an escaped strand of hair into the tight twist she wore at the back of her head, Kim complied with a brief, self-conscious smile. "We have chocolate, coconut cream, lemon meringue, pecan and cherry pies today," she recited.

"You really should concentrate a little harder on your work," Zach suggested. "All this small talk and foolishness is such a waste of time."

Kim stiffened, and she didn't know what to say. When Zach's penetrating blue eyes settled on her, she could almost feel her mind empty of any intelligent thought.

She didn't think for a minute that he was interested in her. More likely, he got a laugh out of watching her squirm.

"What kind of pie can I get you?" she asked. *And would you like that on a plate or in your face?*

Dear Reader,

What better way to enjoy the last lingering days of summer than to revel in romance? And Special Edition's lineup for August will surely turn your thoughts to love!

This month's THAT'S MY BABY! title will tug your heartstrings. Brought to you by Ginna Gray, *Alissa's Miracle* is about a woman who marries the man of her dreams—even though he doesn't want children. But when she unexpectedly becomes pregnant, their love is put to the ultimate test.

Sometimes love comes when we least expect it—and that's what's in store for the heroines of the next three books. *Mother Nature's Hidden Agenda* by award-winning author Kate Freiman is about a self-assured woman who thinks she has everything...until a sexy horse breeder and his precocious daughter enter the picture! Another heroine rediscovers love the second time around in Gail Link's *Lone Star Lover.* And don't miss *Seven Reasons Why,* Neesa Hart's modern-day fairy tale about a brood of rascals who help their foster mom find happily-ever-after in the arms of a mysterious stranger!

Reader favorite Susan Mallery launches TRIPLE TROUBLE, her miniseries about identical triplets destined for love. In *The Girl of His Dreams,* the heroine will go to unbelievable lengths to avoid her feelings for her very best friend. The second and third titles of the series will be coming your way in September and October.

Finally, we're thrilled to bring you book two in our FROM BUD TO BLOSSOM theme series. Gina Wilkins returns with *It Could Happen To You,* a captivating tale about an overly cautious heroine who learns to take the greatest risk of all—love.

I hope you enjoy each and every story to come!

Sincerely,

Tara Gavin,
Senior Editor

GINA WILKINS

IT COULD HAPPEN TO YOU

Silhouette®

SPECIAL EDITION®

Published by Silhouette Books

America's Publisher of Contemporary Romance

My thanks to Bill Allen of the Jacksonville, Arkansas, Fire Department, who has been a good friend to me for more than twenty years—and to my husband for even longer. Somehow we've survived ski trips and weddings, babies and now teenagers...and I will always value your friendship.

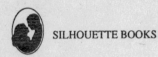

SILHOUETTE BOOKS

ISBN 0-373-24119-4

IT COULD HAPPEN TO YOU

This edition published by arrangement with Harlequin Books S.A.

Printed in U.S.A.

Books by Gina Wilkins

Silhouette Special Edition

The Father Next Door #1082
It Could Happen To You #1119

Previously published as Gina Ferris

Silhouette Special Edition

Healing Sympathy #496
Lady Beware #549
In From the Rain #677
Prodigal Father #711
**Full of Grace* #793
**Hardworking Man* #806
**Fair and Wise* #819
**Far To Go* #862
**Loving and Giving* #879
Babies on Board #913

*Family Found

Previously published as Gina Ferris Wilkins

Silhouette Special Edition

†*A Man for Mom* #955
†*A Match for Celia* #967
†*A Home for Adam* #980
†*Cody's Fiancée* #1006

†The Family Way

Silhouette Books

Mother's Day Collection 1995
Three Mothers & a Cradle
"Beginnings"

GINA WILKINS

declares that she is Southern by birth and by choice, and she has chosen to set many of her books in the South, where she finds a rich treasury of characters and settings. She particularly loves the Ozark mountain region of northern Arkansas and southern Missouri, and the proudly unique people who reside there. She and her husband, John, live in Arkansas, with their three children, Courtney, Kerry and David.

Dear Reader,

There have been many brave rescue workers, men and women, featured in the news during the past couple of years, and their stories fascinate me. They share a love for adventure, a genuine desire to help, a healthy ego and a great wealth of courage. The more I read about them, the more that little voice inside me that haunts all writers kept asking, "What if…?"

What if a man who fears nothing falls for a woman who is afraid of everything?

Raised by a timid aunt, Kim Berry is trying to build her courage a bit at a time. When she meets local hero Zach McCain, a firefighter renowned for his acts of bravery, she thinks no two people could be more different. To her surprise, she discovers that they actually have a great deal in common. But she is still afraid….

Zach has never found anything he fears, until he meets Kim and is faced for the first time with the danger of having his heart broken. This time he worries that he has met a challenge even he can't conquer….

Somehow, these two young lovers have to find the courage to face the future, whatever it may hold. Together.

I hope you enjoy the story that derived from my "What if…?" After all, we fans of romance understand better than most the magical, transforming power of love!

Gina Wilkins

Chapter One

Even with her back turned to the door, Kim Berry always knew when "they" walked into the Red Hog Diner on the outskirts of Fayetteville, Arkansas. She couldn't explain it, exactly, but it happened almost every time. She'd get a funny, tingly feeling, and she'd look around—and there they would be.

The golden boys. The local heroes.

Balancing a tray of empty coffee cups between her hands, she turned just in time to watch them saunter through the glass doors.

Zach McCain entered first, thumbs hooked in the belt loops of his low-slung jeans, dark hair tumbling boyishly over his tanned forehead, his wicked smile anything but boyish. His bright blue eyes made a quick sweep of the room, and Kim knew he had taken note of everything and everyone there—herself included.

Tom Lowery followed Zach. He was blond and bronzed,

a couple of inches shorter than Zach, but just as lean and fit. Just as cocky, Kim thought with a stifled sigh.

Kim assumed that most people would know just by looking at them that these were not ordinary men. Professional firefighters and volunteer rescue workers, they had an impressive and renowned record of saving lives in this part of northwest Arkansas, which was popular for daring outdoor sports such as white-water rafting, rock climbing, hiking and spelunking.

They seemed to be always in pursuit of a new adventure—or, Kim suspected, a new woman. Not that either of them had ever made a play for her, of course.

Maggie Warner, owner of the diner and Kim's employer, looked up from the cash register and, in her typically gruff manner, snapped, "Get a move on, Kim. The boys want their pie and coffee."

Kim shook her head as she deposited the tray in the kitchen, snatched up a pot of fresh-brewed and headed for the booth where "the boys" had settled. Since both of them were in their late twenties, she thought it was ridiculous to call them boys—regardless of their sometimes juvenile humor.

"What can I get you today?" she asked, filling their mugs without being asked.

"A smile would be a nice start," Tom replied promptly, flashing one of his own.

"Make that two," Zach seconded.

Tucking an escaped strand of brown hair into the tight twist she wore at the back of her head, Kim complied with a brief, self-conscious smile. "We have chocolate, coconut cream, lemon meringue, pecan and cherry pies today," she recited. "We just ran out of apple."

"You really should concentrate a little harder on your work," Zach suggested with a mock-serious expression. "All this small talk and foolishness is such a waste of time."

Tom laughed.

Kim reacted to their teasing as she always did; she stiffened, and her fingers tightened around the pencil poised above her order pad. She didn't know what to say, or how to act when they carried on like this. She occasionally bantered with other customers—not often, but sometimes—but these two always made her freeze up.

Especially Zach McCain. When those penetrating blue eyes of his settled on her, she could almost feel her mind empty of intelligent thought. She didn't for a minute think he was personally interested in her. More likely, he got a laugh out of watching her squirm.

"What kind of pie can I get you?" she persisted. *And would you like that on a plate or in your face?* she would have loved to have the courage to add.

Zach and Tom exchanged shrugs and wry looks that made Kim cringe inside. And then they grinned.

"Coconut," Zach said.

Tom asked for chocolate.

Kim nodded, turned on one sensible heel and walked stiffly toward the counter. She heard them laughing and talking behind her. And even as she told herself she disliked both of them, she secretly wished she was the sort of woman who could make them laugh *with* her, rather than at her.

Kim had to work a long shift that last Wednesday in August, since one of the evening employees called in sick. She didn't mind the extra work so much; she could use the money. She didn't like leaving that late, though. It was almost 9:00 p.m. when she finally got away.

The moon was hidden behind clouds, which meant that it was quite dark by the time she stepped out of the diner. A light rain had begun to fall, just enough to mist her hair as she hurried through the nearly deserted parking lot toward her car. Even as she started the engine, the rain grew heavier, promising to evolve into a real gully-washer before she reached her apartment.

She locked the doors, fastened her seat belt and pulled carefully out of her parking space, peering between the thumping windshield wipers and hoping her old Ford's temperamental engine wouldn't choose that particular evening to act up.

Aware of the nervous path her thoughts had taken, she made a face at herself in the rearview mirror. Honestly, sometimes she more resembled the timid little aunt who'd raised her than an independent twenty-four-year-old woman.

No wonder Zach and Tom found her so amusing. Men like those two, who feared nothing, would never understand someone who was afraid of *everything.*

She wondered what it would be like to possess the kind of reckless, daredevil courage that made one boldly pursue adventures, foolishly defy gravity, arrogantly taunt fate. She couldn't even imagine behaving that way.

For as far back as she could remember, Kim had been afraid. Head-under-the-covers afraid. Afraid of being hurt, physically or emotionally. Afraid of being lost. Afraid of bugs and spiders and dogs and wild animals. Afraid of being publicly humiliated.

Name it, and she feared it.

And she hated herself for it.

Oh, sure, she'd come a long way in the past few years. She'd moved from St. Louis to Fayetteville, where she'd known not a soul, after her aunt's death a couple of years ago. She'd moved into a tiny rented house in the safest neighborhood she'd been able to afford. She'd enrolled in morning classes at the University of Arkansas, where she was studying accounting. She'd found the job at the diner, forcing herself into daily contact with an often demanding and impatient public. She'd even stood up to crabby old

Maggie a time or two, which had taken all the meager courage inside her.

But it was still a daily struggle, fear still a constant, unwelcome companion. She wondered if she would ever free herself of it.

She turned onto the long stretch of dark, unpopulated, woods-lined road that led to her side of town. Fortunately, the Ford's cranky engine seemed to be running smoothly this evening, so she allowed herself to relax and enjoy the pretty song playing on the radio. Since there was no one around to hear her, she sang along during the chorus, raising her voice over the steady drumming of the rain against her windshield wipers.

She was taken completely by surprise when her back right tire blew out. The car swerved dangerously on the wet pavement. Kim's heart was hammering in her throat by the time she brought it under control. There was hardly any shoulder to park on, only a narrow strip of gravel separating the road from the woods.

The windshield wipers stopped halfway across their path when she turned off the engine. The radio went silent. The only sound was the rain pounding against the roof and Kim's deep, heartfelt groan of dismay.

She wrapped her shaking hands around the top of the wheel and rested her forehead against them. She had never changed a tire in her life. She had a vague idea how to go about it, but the thought of getting out in the pouring rain and fumbling around with a jack and a lug wrench—neither of which she'd ever used—was dismaying, to say the least.

There was an all-night convenience store at the next intersection—which was at least half a mile away. The idea of getting out and walking down a dark country road terrified her. She thought of lightning, wild animals, serial killers…any of which could be out there waiting for her, as far as she knew.

Better if she just waited in the car, she decided. This road wasn't a major thoroughfare, but it was used often enough that someone would have to come along eventually. Ideally, that someone would be a police officer.

But what if it wasn't?

She'd heard of the monsters who preyed on people in trouble. The women who simply disappeared, never to be seen alive again, leaving their cars parked mutely on the roadsides. Aunt Pearl had rarely missed an opportunity to read those articles to Kim from the daily newspaper as a warning of all the dangers that awaited a woman who ventured out into the world alone.

"You are being ridiculous," she told herself sternly. "This is a nice town. You know nearly everyone who lives in the area. They're good people. You're perfectly safe."

Had those unfortunate missing women told themselves the same thing? Kim gulped.

And then she nearly jumped out of her skin when someone suddenly tapped on the driver's side window.

Her squeak of alarm still echoing inside the little car, she peered anxiously through the rain pouring down the glass. A large, dark figure loomed outside. Obviously a man—but was he friend or foe?

He leaned closer to the window, shining a flashlight on his face to identify himself. Neither friend *nor* foe, Kim realized, recognizing him immediately. It was Zach McCain.

She cranked down the manually powered window an inch to hear him over the rain.

"Kim?" he asked, bending to peer in at her. "I thought I recognized your car. Are you okay?"

Wondering how he'd possibly known what her car looked like, she answered, "I think my back tire blew out."

"You're lucky you didn't lose control," Zach said,

seemingly oblivious to the heavy rain running down his face and drenching the rest of him.

She nodded, her heart still pounding from the frightening incident.

"Do you have a trunk release inside the car or do I need a key to get to the spare?" Zach asked.

"It takes a key," she answered automatically, and then realized that he intended to change the tire for her. "But you're getting soaked," she protested.

He shrugged. "I'm already wet now. I won't melt."

Thoroughly embarrassed, Kim slipped the trunk key off her key ring and handed it to him. Why had it been Zach who'd found her in this predicament? Why couldn't it have been kindly old Officer Beeman, or Reverend Cunningham? Someone who wouldn't make her feel so darned awkward and tongue-tied, the way Zach McCain always did.

"I'll help you," she said, reaching for the door handle.

"Forget it. There's no need for both of us to get soaked. I'm used to this sort of thing."

He loped around to the back of the car, and Kim rolled the window back up, wondering how in the world she could ever repay him for this. Maybe she'd buy his pie for him the next few times he came into the diner. Or would he think she was flirting with him if she did? She'd seen the way other women had done everything but climb in his lap to get his attention, and she certainly didn't want to be mistaken for one of his drooling admirers!

He was back at the window sooner than she'd expected. Shaking wet hair out of his face, he tapped on the glass. She quickly rolled the window down, instinctively flinching as a spray of cool rain blew through the two-inch crack.

"Kim," Zach said a bit wryly, "when was the last time you checked your spare tire?"

"I—er. I'm supposed to check it?" She'd always just

accepted that it was there, a rarely noticed precaution against an unfortunate incident such as this.

His sigh was barely audible above the heavy rain. "It's flat," he said. "As in pancake. Didn't even bounce when I took it out and dropped it on the pavement."

"Oh, dear."

"I'll call from my truck for someone to come take care of it for you," he offered.

She nodded her acceptance. "I really appreciate your help."

"No problem. Be right back." He was gone before she could say anything else.

Kim shivered and cranked the window back up, feeling guilty for being dry and relatively warm while Zach sloshed back and forth in the chilly rain. And she wondered how anyone could look so darned gorgeous even soaking wet.

Had *she* been the one out in the rain, she'd look like a soggy, pathetic mess. That wasn't at all the case with Zach, she mused as his handsome, wet face reappeared at her window.

"They're on the way," he called out. "I'll hang around until they arrive."

She started to tell him that wasn't necessary, that she would be fine waiting alone. She swallowed the words, because she suspected he wouldn't listen, anyway—and maybe because she didn't really want to wait alone.

On an impulse, she opened the door and scooted over on the bench seat, moving closer to the passenger door. "Get in."

He leaned over and eyed the worn fabric seat, then shook his head. "I'd get your upholstery wet. I'll wait in the truck."

She reached down to the floorboard and picked up a silver thermos. "Coffee," she explained. "Still hot."

His eyes locked greedily on the insulated container. He

seemed unaware of the slight shiver that rippled through him as another blast of wind hurled rain against his back and down the collar of his drenched denim shirt. "Coffee?"

She opened the lid, letting the strong aroma waft toward him on a wisp of steam. "Hot coffee," she repeated enticingly.

With one last, apologetic look toward her upholstery, he slid behind the wheel and closed the door. Kim then snapped on the interior light. The inside of the car seemed suddenly quiet and cozy with the rain closed outside and Zach taking up so much room inside.

"Remember that this was your idea. Don't blame me when you have to drive home with a damp backside," he quipped as a glittering raindrop danced down the right side of his face to caress the faint dimple beside his mouth.

She cleared her throat and carefully poured coffee into the plastic lid that also served as a cup. "Here you are," she said, shyly meeting his eyes.

Their fingertips brushed when he took the cup. Her whole arm seemed to go numb in reaction. "Thanks," he murmured. "I needed this."

He lifted the cup to his sexy lips, his gaze holding hers. She felt her own mouth go dry as she watched him take the first sip.

Get a grip, Kim.

Zach's throat worked with his swallow. He murmured his pleasure as the warmth spread through him. His faint shivers stopped.

"Do you always carry coffee in your car?" he asked, smiling at her in a way that made her breathing hitch in her chest.

He smiles at every female that way, Kim, she reminded herself almost angrily. *Even Maggie. So stop acting like a silly schoolgirl.*

She tried to speak coherently. "There was almost a

whole pot of coffee left when we closed the diner. Maggie was going to throw it out, but I asked if I could have it. I hated to waste it. I often bring home coffee from the diner to warm in my microwave, since it's easier than making a fresh pot just for myself in the mornings.''

She was babbling. She pressed her lips together and told herself to shut up.

A sudden clap of thunder rattled the windows and made Kim jump. The rain intensified, hammering furiously against the top of the car.

''It's okay,'' Zach murmured. ''Just thunder. You aren't afraid of storms, are you?''

''No,'' she lied. ''The thunder took me by surprise.''

He drained the plastic cup and handed it back to her. ''That was great.''

She thought it said something about the quality of the coffee he usually drank if he thought the hours-old brew tasted ''great.'' Since she had also grown accustomed to somewhat-less-than-fresh coffee, she didn't comment, except to nod and say, ''You're welcome. Would you like some more?''

''No, thanks.'' He reached up to turn off the interior light. ''Don't want a dead battery as well as a flat tire,'' he explained.

She concentrated on screwing the lid cup tightly back onto the thermos. The darkness added a new degree of intimacy to their circumstances, and though she knew it was stupid, she couldn't help being flustered.

''I really appreciate your help,'' she said. ''You've been very kind.''

''I'm glad I came along. There's not much traffic tonight in this weather. I don't like to think how long you'd have sat here before someone else came by.''

''I was trying to decide whether to get out and walk for help,'' she admitted. ''I've never changed a tire before, and this didn't seem like the best time to try to learn how.''

Another crash of thunder underscored her words.

Zach frowned. "Walking wouldn't have been the best choice. Better to stay in your car with the doors locked. You should think about getting a cellular phone. They're great for situations like this one."

She merely nodded, as though considering his advice.

A large truck drew up beside them, then pulled ahead and parked on the narrow shoulder in front of Kim's car. Zach reached for the door handle.

"That's the guy I called," he said. "We'll have you on your way in a few minutes."

She started to open her own door. He put a damp hand on her shoulder and smiled at her. "Sit tight," he said. "There's nothing you can do out there."

A moment later he slid out, into the rain. He shut the door behind him, leaving her sitting in the darkness and the sound of falling rain, her heart doing flip-flops in her chest. All because Zach McCain had touched her and smiled at her.

You really are an idiot, aren't you, Kim?

Zach followed her home. Telling herself he was only being courteous—who said chivalry was dead?—she tried not to make too much of it. She drove into her tiny covered carport and waved, expecting him to drive on. Instead, he pulled in to the driveway behind her.

She waited in the carport while he climbed out of his truck and dashed through the still-heavy rain toward her. She shook her head. The guy seemed determined to ensure that not an inch of him was left dry.

Grinning crookedly, he dug into the front right pocket of his jeans when he reached the shelter of the carport. "Your trunk key," he explained, holding it out to her. "I forgot to give it back to you. I remembered it just as you drove off."

She had known, of course, not to read any personal

meaning into his following her home. Now she had her explanation. She took the key without meeting his eyes. "Thank you. I'm sorry you had to go to so much trouble on my behalf."

"No problem," he assured her airily, running a hand through his wet black hair. "Glad I could help."

She wondered if she should invite him in. Because of her, he was wet and chilled and there was a streak of mud on the left leg of his jeans. She had no dry clothing to offer him, of course—but she could at least offer another hot drink. Fighting an attack of nerves at the thought of bringing this man into her house, she opened her mouth to extend the invitation.

But Zach was already moving toward his truck. "See you later, Kim," he said over his shoulder. "Have that spare repaired, okay?"

"Yes, I will. Er—thank you," she called after him.

She waited as he sauntered unhurriedly through the downpour to his truck. He reached the door, then looked back at her, apparently oblivious to the rain.

"Hey, Kim?"

"Yes?"

"Want to go out sometime?"

There was a rumble of thunder midway through his words. She told herself she couldn't possibly have understood him correctly. "Excuse me?"

He spoke a little louder. "Go out. With me. You know—a date?"

She had to make a serious effort to keep her jaw from dropping. Zach McCain was asking *her* for a date?

They'd known each other for months through her job at the diner, and he'd never given the least indication that he was interested in her. Nor had she expected him to. She'd seen the striking young women he and Tom occasionally brought into the diner, and face it, Kim was hardly his type.

She twisted her hands around the handle of her purse. Though she knew few other women her age would understand, the thought of accepting a date with Zach terrified her. What if she embarrassed herself? What if she bored him? What if he talked about her to his friends? What if she was foolish enough to let him hurt her?

"Kim?" There was an undercurrent of amusement in his raised voice. "I'm drowning out here."

Okay, Kim, you've wanted to conquer your fears and be like other women your age. How many of them do you think would turn down a date with Zach McCain?

She drew a deep breath. "Okay," she said.

"What was that?"

"Okay," she almost yelled.

His soft laugh carried to her on a gust of rain-soaked wind. "Great. I'll call you."

She swallowed hard and nodded.

With a cocky wave, he climbed into his truck. A moment later he'd started the engine. He waited until she unlocked and opened her door before he drove away.

Kim walked into her little rented house, tossed her purse onto a table and covered her face with her hands, wondering whose behavior had been the most astonishing—Zach's, when he'd asked her out, or hers, when she had accepted.

She reminded herself that he hadn't been specific, hadn't actually committed himself to a date or time. There was still a chance he would never follow up on the overture. That he would never mention it again.

The guy was an inveterate flirt, a compulsive tease. She wouldn't hold her breath waiting for him to ask her again, she decided. But she would take just a bit of pride in knowing that she'd actually found the nerve to take him up on his challenge—at least this one time.

She was definitely coming along in her effort to grow a backbone.

* * *

"Well, it's about time you—whoa. What have you been doing, swimming in all your clothes?"

Zach ran a hand through his dripping hair. "What are you doing in my living room?" he asked of the man who'd greeted him when he'd walked through his front door.

Looking completely at home, Tom Lowery lounged on Zach's couch, a bag of Zach's pretzels at his side, one of Zach's soft drinks in his hand, Zach's television remote on his knee. "I let myself in with my key. We were going to watch the game tonight, remember? It started over an hour ago."

Zach grimaced. "I'd forgotten," he admitted. "Mom had asked me to stop by for a few minutes on my way home, and she kept me there a while talking. Then I found Kim Berry stranded on the side of the road and I stopped to give her a hand. The game completely slipped my mind."

"It's a snoozer, anyway," Tom commented, turning down the volume and setting the remote aside. "What happened to Kim?"

"Tire blew out."

"Is she okay?"

"Yeah. She was sitting in her car looking scared half to death when I found her. She's never changed a tire in her life."

"So you got out in the rain and changed the lady's tire for her." Tom hefted his swiped soda in a mock salute. "Chalk up another rescue to Super Zach."

Zach was wet, tired and still a little bemused by his own earlier behavior. He was in no mood to be ribbed, even by his best friend.

"I'm going to take a hot shower," he said abruptly, heading for his bedroom. "You can watch the rest of the game if you want."

"Think I'll have a sandwich," Tom mused, unperturbed

by his friend's curtness. "Want me to make you a couple?"

"I ate at Mom's. But feel free to help yourself to my groceries."

Tom grinned. "Thanks. I will."

Zach almost moaned in gratitude when he stepped into the hot shower. He stood without moving for several long moments, letting the warmth penetrate his chilled skin. He'd been colder and wetter than he'd gotten tonight, but these days he found he preferred being warm and dry.

He didn't like to think his growing taste for physical comfort had anything to do with getting older.

He was facing his thirtieth birthday soon and he wasn't particularly looking forward to it. He'd had a great time in his twenties. He wasn't quite ready to leave them behind.

He didn't want to think of his birthday now. He lathered soap over his chest and thought about Kim Berry instead. He was still finding it hard to believe he'd finally asked her out—and that she'd accepted.

He was aware that he hadn't mentioned to Tom that he'd asked her out after "rescuing" her from the roadside. Though he and Tom rarely kept secrets from each other, especially when it came to their social lives, he didn't think he would mention his upcoming date with Kim just yet. He didn't want Tom kidding him about dating the shy waitress who'd amused them both so often with the expressively quelling looks she gave them when they teased her at the diner.

Kim had intrigued Zach from the day she'd started working at the diner next door to the fire station where he spent so much of his time, on and off duty. He'd always had a weakness for big brown eyes. Kim's dark eyes seemed to dominate her heart-shaped face. Her skin was fair and nearly flawless, and she had a sweetly curved, lush-looking mouth that seemed oddly out of character for someone so shy and serious.

A sinner's mouth in a saint's face, he'd thought fancifully.

He'd never been interested in saints. But he'd been attracted to Kim from the beginning.

He'd been tempted to ask her out immediately. It hadn't taken him long to realize that doing so would probably be a mistake. She was hardly his type, and he doubted seriously that he was hers. She always seemed vaguely disapproving of him and his friends, a bit bewildered by their antics and humor.

Despite the attraction, he'd talked himself out of pursuing her acquaintance, telling himself there was no need to waste his time. He'd never been a glutton for rejection—had rarely had to deal with it. When he wanted a date, there were a number of willing prospects to call. He wasn't interested in a serious relationship right now, anyway, so why even start anything with a woman who often looked at him as though he'd come from another planet, and she wouldn't mind if he returned there?

And yet, he still watched Kim every time he went into the diner, almost every day. He admired her big dark eyes and invitingly sexy mouth, wondered what thoughts lay behind that pretty, wary face. He'd seen flashes of spirit that surprised and intrigued him, making him suspect she wasn't quite as meek and mousy as she appeared. And he'd wondered what it would take to get past her barriers and discover what hidden fires burned inside.

Chapter Two

It began very much like any other date. Kim agonized over what to wear, finally settling on a simple red knit dress she'd been told was flattering to her. And then she paced for half an hour, chewing her nails and worrying.

Not that she'd had that many dates to compare this with. She'd been so shy and quiet in high school that few boys had even noticed her. She'd been so busy since that there'd been little time for a social life—or so she'd told herself.

She had a feeling that Zach McCain, accomplished flirt that he was, would be startled—and probably dismayed—if he were to learn how little experience Kim actually had with the opposite gender.

It was Saturday, three days after Zach had found her stranded by the roadside. She hadn't seen him since. He'd called after she'd gotten home from work Thursday evening and made the arrangements for this date. They hadn't chatted long. Kim had been so surprised that he'd actually called that she'd found herself speaking in monosyllables.

She was quite sure Zach had ended the conversation wondering why he'd asked her out in the first place. She'd half expected him to call again with an excuse to cancel. But, promptly at 7:00 p.m., the time they'd arranged, her doorbell rang.

She drew a deep breath and opened the door. She took one look at Zach and wondered what in the world she was doing going out with this man.

He was, quite simply, incredible. Just looking at him made her breath catch in her throat.

He was wearing a black shirt and black slacks with a charcoal jacket and a black-and-gray geometric tie. It was the first time she'd seen him when he wasn't dressed in denim or his fire department uniform. She was flattered that he'd made such an effort to look nice this evening, though she warned herself not to read too much into it. He probably always dressed this way for dinner dates.

His nearly black hair was neatly brushed away from his face, and he'd obviously recently shaved. There was a small nick on his chin. Even that slight imperfection looked good on him.

"You look very nice," he said when she only stood there, trying to regain her voice. "I like you in red."

She silently cleared her throat. "Thank you," she murmured, and she was grateful that the words did not come out as a croak. "So do you. Um...look nice, I mean."

And wasn't *that* an understatement?

"Would you like to come in?" she added belatedly, stepping back from the doorway. She tried to remember dating protocol. "I have soda or juice, if you'd like something to drink."

Zach glanced at his watch. "Thanks, but I made reservations for seven-thirty at that Italian place in Tontitown, so we'd better be on our way. I hope you like Italian food."

"Yes, very much."

She reached for her purse, which she'd left on a table near the door. And then she gave him a forced smile. "I'm ready," she said, knowing she lied.

She wasn't at all ready for this evening.

Zach glanced out of the corner of his eye and wondered wryly if Kim was trying to meld with the passenger door of his truck. If she scooted any closer to it, she was going to end up on the outside of the vehicle! He was curious if all men intimidated her, or if it was just him. He couldn't think of anything he'd done to make her treat him so warily.

Ever since she'd opened the door for him, she'd eyed him as though she didn't know quite what to make of him. As if he really were that alien he'd always suspected she imagined him to be.

Why had she agreed to have dinner with him if he made her so nervous?

Knowing the drive to Tontitown was going to seem endless if they made the entire trip in silence, he initiated a conversation. "How long have you worked at the diner now, Kim?"

She seemed startled by the sound of his voice. "Um...almost six months. Before that I worked at a department store in the mall, but they weren't as flexible with my hours as Maggie has been. I take morning classes at the university, and Maggie's been good about letting me work around my school schedule."

"You like working for Maggie?"

Kim hesitated only a beat. "I have no complaints," she said circumspectly.

Zach was amused by her tact. "She can be a grouch at times, but she's got a good heart. I've known her all my life."

"She told me she's a friend of your mother's."

He chuckled. "They've known each other since their

school days. Still fuss like a couple of old hens every time they get together. They both seem to like it that way."

"Maggie does seem to enjoy arguing just for the sake of it," Kim agreed with a slight smile.

"Are you kidding? It's her favorite pastime."

And that seemed to be the end of that topic. They fell silent again. Zach glanced at the purse Kim gripped in her lap, and saw how whitely her knuckles gleamed against the dark leather. He was pretty sure if he yelled "boo," she'd jump right through the roof of his truck.

It was going to be a very long evening.

He racked his brain for something else to say. "You didn't grow up here in Fayetteville, did you?" he asked.

"No. I'm from St. Louis, originally. I moved here just over a year ago to start classes at UA. I was a transfer student. I attended St. Louis University for two years, taking a few classes each semester while I supported myself waiting tables."

"Does your family still live in St. Louis?"

"My mother died when I was two. I was raised by an aunt, who passed away only a few months before I moved here. That's another reason it's taking me so long to earn my degree. Aunt Pearl became ill during my senior year of high school and I spent the next few years taking care of her as she grew weaker."

"And your father?" Zach hoped he wasn't stepping over the boundaries of privacy, but he was desperate to keep the conversation going. And, besides, he was curious.

"My parents separated when I was a toddler. I haven't seen my father since." There was little emotion in Kim's voice as she matter-of-factly answered Zach's personal questions in more detail than he'd expected.

Zach was startled. "You don't even know if he's still living?"

"No. He never tried to contact me after he left. I always

had the impression that his split with my mother was very unpleasant."

Zach shook his head. "That may be, but I still can't believe he wouldn't want to see his daughter."

The son of a man who loved his family more than life itself, Zach couldn't even imagine a man who would willingly walk away from his own child.

Kim shrugged. "Apparently he didn't. Since I don't even remember him, I haven't missed him. Aunt Pearl was very good to me. I had a safe and happy childhood."

Zach was getting a clearer picture of Kim's background now. "Your aunt wasn't married?"

"No, she never married. I think she was engaged once when she was in her early twenties, but she never talked about it. She was quite a bit older than her sister, my mother. Aunt Pearl had just turned fifty when I moved in with her after my mother died unexpectedly. She supported herself by giving private piano lessons in a little studio in her home, a wonderful old house she'd inherited from her parents. I hated having to sell it after she died, but it was necessary," Kim added, still in that prosaic tone that Zach suspected was her way of camouflaging her real emotions. "Aunt Pearl's medical bills really piled up during the last two years of her illness. Selling the house allowed me to pay them off."

Zach didn't want to risk embarrassing her or making her uncomfortable with further prying questions. And, besides, he thought he had a fairly clear picture of her background now, and could better understand her shyness.

He and Kim Berry couldn't be more different—in experiences, in personality, in *anything*. It was something he'd suspected from the first time he'd seen her, but he'd let his attraction to her big brown eyes and lush mouth overcome his better judgment.

She'd gone quiet again. He wondered if they were going to have to spend the entire evening with him asking questions and her answering them. She didn't seem to mind that, but she had yet to introduce a topic of her own. Since she didn't seem inclined to ask questions, he decided to give her some answers without prompting. If nothing else, his voice filled the awkward silence.

"I grew up in these parts," he began. "My parents still live here. I have two older sisters, both married, both with kids of their own. One lives in Springdale and the other in Rogers, so we're all together quite a bit."

"So you're the baby of the family. And the only son," Kim murmured.

Zach wondered if he'd only imagined a silent "ah-hah," as if his explanation about his background told her as much about him as he'd learned from *her* remarks. "Yeah," he said a bit wryly. "I was just a tad indulged as a kid."

"Mmm. Now, why doesn't that surprise me?"

He smiled in response to her teasing remark, hopeful that she was finally beginning to relax with him. But then she blushed and looked hastily away from him, as though she regretted the lapse. Maybe she was afraid she'd offended him.

He hurried to reassure her that she had not. "Gee, I don't know. Maybe you're psychic or something."

She only murmured something unintelligible.

Zach almost sighed.

It was *definitely* going to be a long evening.

Why don't you just smack the guy over the head with a two-by-four, Kim? It would be a lot faster and kinder than boring him into unconsciousness.

Kim was furious with herself for the way she'd behaved so far on this ill-advised outing. Her mind had gone blank the moment she'd climbed into his fancy, new-looking pickup. It was one of those extended cab models, and the area behind the front seat was crammed with what appeared to be the tools of his profession and avocations, nothing recognizable to her, everything looking technical and slightly dangerous.

She'd realized right then that she had no business getting involved—even casually—with this dashing, adventurous man.

He was trying hard. He'd pretended interest in her background by asking questions, then listened politely when she'd babbled answers that were probably more detailed than he'd wanted or expected.

And then, when he'd shared a bit of his own life with her, she'd practically accused him of being spoiled and pampered by his family. Fortunately, he hadn't taken offense at her comments, but she didn't know what in the world had gotten into her. She usually kept her dry comments about others to herself, amusing only herself with her wisecracks. Zach just had a way of keeping her off guard.

It was going to be an interminable evening if she didn't start behaving as though she had a brain in her silly head. Zach was probably already wondering why on earth he'd asked her out.

She glanced out the passenger window, hardly noticing the landmarks they passed on their way out of Fayetteville and toward nearby Tontitown. Zach wasn't taking the usual, well-traveled route, but a rural, back road that was more interesting and maybe a bit shorter. Usually Kim enjoyed looking at the surrounding hillsides and hollows of this area renowned for its natural beauty. But her attention at the moment was focused entirely on the man behind the wheel.

He had filled the silence by asking questions. She decided to follow his example.

"How long have you been a fireman?" she asked.

"Almost five years. I worked at another job for a while after I graduated from the university."

She hadn't realized he'd earned his degree. She turned her head to look at him. "What was your major?"

"Business administration," he replied with a wry grimace that made her smile. "I worked for a bank for nearly a year before I realized that I was never going to be able to sit behind a desk for eight hours a day. What are you majoring in?"

"Accounting." Her smile deepened wryly. "After six months on my feet as a waitress, there's nothing I'd rather do than sit behind a desk for eight hours a day."

He chuckled. "To each his own. Or hers, as the case may be."

He was really spectacular when he smiled, Kim couldn't help noticing. His teeth flashed white against his tanned face, and there was just a hint of a dimple in his cheek. She would bet that women had been falling in love with him since he'd entered puberty. Not that she had any intention of following their example, of course. She couldn't imagine anything more pathetic than herself being lovesick over Zach McCain.

"Anyway," Zach went on, "my buddy Tom had joined the fire department a couple of years earlier, and he talked me into giving it a try. I tried it, and I liked it. Now we've both taken courses in rescue operations and we're volunteer members of the Washington County Search and Rescue Team. That's why I carry a pager," he added, motioning toward the small plastic box clipped to his belt. "In case I'm needed."

"So you're on call twenty-four hours a day, seven days a week?"

He shrugged. "I'm a volunteer, of course, but yeah, that's pretty much the way it turns out. Keeps us busy during the most active outdoor months—spring through fall. Seems like there's always someone falling off a mountain or clinging to a branch in a white-water stream, or parachuting into the top of a tree or something. When that happens, we see what we can do to help. I take courses whenever I get a chance. I'm going to Florida in the spring for a class on team management and logistics. Metro-Dade Fire Rescue is sort of like a model for rescue teams all over the country.''

An adventurer, she thought again as he started telling her about his interest in working with FEMA—the Federal Emergency Management Agency. She was sure he was genuinely concerned about the people he rescued, but he also seemed to thrive on the challenge. She'd heard about his hobbies; everyone in town talked about Zach and Tom and how they were always risking their lives skydiving or rock climbing or white-water rafting or bungee jumping, for Pete's sake.

The most daring hobby Kim indulged in was needlepoint. She'd drawn blood occasionally by poking her finger with the needle. Somehow she didn't think Zach would be overly impressed.

She was just about to ask another question about his rescue work when a car coming too fast from the other direction skidded on a curve directly ahead of them and sailed off the road. A column of water seemed to explode into the air from the spot where the car disappeared. Stunned, Kim realized that the vehicle must have landed in a ditch flooded by the heavy rains they'd been having in this area for the past week.

Hissing a startled curse between his teeth, Zach jerked the truck to the side of the road, slammed the gearshift into Park and opened his door.

''Call 911,'' he ordered over his shoulder, already running toward the spot where the car had disappeared over the side of the road.

Kim shook off her momentary paralysis—a reaction Zach obviously hadn't suffered—and reached for his cellular phone. She frantically punched buttons, hoping she was using the instrument correctly, groping in her mind for adequate directions to give the dispatcher. All the while, she kept her eyes trained on the side of the road, where Zach, too, had now disappeared.

Moments later, her call completed, she jumped out of the truck and hurried across the road just as Zach struggled to the top of the embankment with a sobbing teenager in his arms. Both of them were covered with mud and weeds, and Kim couldn't tell if the girl was hurt.

"Stay with her," he said, gently depositing the girl on the grass next to the asphalt shoulder, in a spot illuminated by the headlights from his truck. "I'm going back down. There's someone else in the car."

Kim knelt on the grass beside the loudly crying girl, who looked to be in her late teens. She'd never done anything like this, but she knew she had to calm the girl down somehow. "My name is Kim," she said gently. "I've already called for help. Are you in pain?"

The teenager was crying too hard to answer. Kim could tell that she had been badly frightened. There was a trickle of blood on her neck. Kim touched it gently with her fingers to judge the depth of the cut. It seemed to be quite shallow. Kim thought that it had probably been caused by the seat belt tightening in response to the impact.

The girl was shaking now, her teeth chattering from shock. Kim wiped a damp strand of blond hair away from her face. "Can you tell me your name?"

"Car-Carla."

"Where do you hurt?"

"My car," Carla wailed. "I crashed my new car."

Kim shook her head, reminding herself that the girl was still very shaken. "Don't worry about your car. The only thing that matters is that you're all right."

Zach reappeared, another teenager in his arms. Kim saw that the second girl was a brunette, that she was alert and sitting up in Zach's arms, clinging to his neck. She was very quiet, her face pale and expressionless. She didn't seem to want to let go when he tried to lay her down next to her friend.

Zach gently loosened her grasp from around his neck. "Are you okay?" he asked her.

The girl nodded, her motions zombielike. She, too, was beginning to shake from being wet, cold and frightened.

"I'm going to the truck for some blankets," Zach said to Kim. "Luckily, neither of them seems to be hurt, but we have to watch them for shock. Did you call for help?"

"An ambulance is on its way."

"Thanks. Be right back."

He ran to the truck, leaving Kim sitting between Carla, who was now sobbing quietly, and the other girl, who lay much too still and quiet for Kim's peace of mind. She hoped the ambulance would arrive soon.

Gratefully, she heard sirens in the distance just as Zach tossed her a blanket. She wrapped it carefully around Carla, murmuring reassurances, knowing Zach was caring for the other girl.

Kim looked over her shoulder toward the car in the ditch. The vehicle had landed right side up in the mud and thigh-deep water. The girls had been very fortunate that they hadn't been badly injured.

A police car and an ambulance arrived almost simultaneously. Zach and Kim gratefully turned the girls over to the professionals. Kim heard Zach explain to a paramedic that he'd moved the girls out of their vehicle because Carla had been so hysterical that he'd been afraid she'd bolt out on her own if he didn't help her, and the second girl had begged him not to leave her in the car. He'd tried to make sure, he added, that neither of them had injuries that would have been worsened by moving them.

Zach then gave a statement to the police officer making out a report of the accident. "Both the girls were wearing seat belts," he added when he'd finished explaining what had happened.

"Lucky for them," the officer murmured, making a note on her report.

Both Zach and Kim were relieved when they were able to leave, knowing everything there was under control. Zach looked ruefully down at his formerly neat clothing, now liberally streaked with mud and gunk from wading in the rain-swollen ditch.

"This is why I have leather seats in my truck," he murmured, climbing behind the wheel. "Easier to clean than cloth."

Kim brushed at a spot of dirt on her skirt, where she'd knelt on the ground beside Carla. "You do seem to end up wet and muddy quite a lot," she commented.

"All the time," he agreed without apparent regret.

She released a long breath and snapped her seat belt, then pushed her hair away from her face. "That was a nerve-racking experience. I couldn't believe it when that car just flew off the road right in front of us."

"She was driving too fast. I was afraid the car had flipped upside down into the ditch. They could have drowned if that had happened. As it was, they were lucky to escape with only a few bruises. They're going to feel like someone beat them with a baseball bat tomorrow."

"You reacted so quickly. I was still sitting here stunned and you were already jumping out of the truck and running that way."

"It becomes instinct, after a while in this business," he admitted. "Someone told me once about a fiery plane crash at an air show. The crowd was so shocked and horrified that everyone froze, except the rescue-trained people, who started running straight for the flames. They were the only ones moving."

"I would think it would take a special sort of personality to go into your kind of work," she murmured. "A lot of courage."

"I'm told it takes a lot of ego," he answered with a

self-deprecating smile. "We tend to think we're indestructible."

She frowned a bit at that. That kind of confidence could get a person badly hurt—or worse, she thought. And she didn't think it was only her own fears making her think that way.

Zach started the truck, then glanced down at his clothes again with a grimace. "I'm afraid we're going to have to change our plans. No nice restaurant is going to let me in looking and smelling like I've crawled out of the Black Lagoon."

"That's okay," she assured him. "Another time, perhaps." *If* he still wanted to go out with her, of course, after this evening had gotten off to such a slow start—prior to the excitement of the accident.

"I'm still going to feed you," he said, his tone inviting no argument. "How does takeout grab you? We'll pick something up and take it to my place."

She bit her lower lip.

Zach shot her a quick glance. "You don't have to worry. I'm only suggesting dinner."

Her cheeks burned. "I wasn't—I didn't mean to—I, er..."

Zach laughed. "Chinese or pizza?"

She felt like sinking into the seat. He must really think she was an idiot. He was only being kind to offer to feed her, of course, since their earlier plans had fallen through. She was tempted to ask him just to take her home, but then he would probably think she didn't trust him not to attack her when they were alone in his home. And wouldn't he find *that* amusing?

"Pizza," she murmured, her voice a bit strained.

He nodded and reached for his phone. "I'll order now, so it'll be ready when we get there. What toppings do you like? Or should I go for the works?"

"Whatever you usually order. I like any kind of pizza. Er, you know the number?"

He flashed her a grin that was bright enough to make her blink. "Darlin', I'm a bachelor. I survive on pizza."

"Oh," she said inanely.

He probably calls everyone "darlin'," Kim. Start acting like you have half a brain, will you?

She was glumly certain that Zach would laugh about this evening with his friends for some time to come. The one and only night he dated the silly, tongue-tied waitress from the Red Hog Diner.

Chapter Three

Zach had given himself a mission for the remainder of his evening with Kim. He took pride in always making sure a woman had a nice time when she was out with him, and he was grimly determined that he was going to make Kim enjoy herself—no matter what.

Since flirting seemed to alarm her, he treated her as casually and easily as if she were another one of his sisters. Wisecracks made her smile, so he spouted them out with the dedication of a workaholic stand-up comic. She seemed to enjoy hearing about his work, so he regaled her with a string of anecdotes, liberally embellished to make them more entertaining.

He couldn't remember ever working this hard at a date. But by the time they'd reduced the pizza to a smear of grease and tomato sauce on the take-out box, Kim had relaxed enough to laugh with him, and even to make a few teasing remarks of her own. Every smile he drew from her was like a reward for his efforts, and he was rather bemused by how proud he was of each one of them.

When they'd arrived at his apartment, he'd left her in the den while he took the quickest shower in history and changed into black jeans and a long-sleeved, black-and-red striped pullover. He'd brushed his wet hair carelessly back from his face, and had left off his shoes, wearing only a pair of dark socks on his feet.

Kim didn't seem to mind his casual appearance; in fact, she acted more comfortable with him now than she had when he'd been turned out in his best jacket and tie. Or rather, what *had* been his best jacket and tie, he thought regretfully, remembering the mud and other stains that now liberally covered both.

He was secretly delighted when Kim slipped out of her own shoes during dinner, an action that seemed almost subconscious on her part, but indicated that she was beginning to feel more comfortable with him. He promptly refilled her wineglass, though she'd told him when he'd brought it out that she wasn't much of a wine drinker. That hadn't stopped her from having two glasses, and she didn't protest when he filled it again.

It wasn't that he was trying to get her drunk. Seduction was not what he had in mind, and he'd never used alcohol to that end, anyway. He just wanted her to relax. He had decided that Kim Berry was a woman who needed very badly to kick back and enjoy herself occasionally.

They were sitting on his couch, the now-empty pizza box on the coffee table in front of them, the now-empty bottle of wine lying on its side on the floor. Music played softly from the CD player in one corner of the room, a random collection of soft rock tunes.

Kim had half turned to face him, one stocking foot drawn beneath her. Her left arm rested on the back of the couch, hand supporting her head. She held her wineglass in her right hand, and absently sipped from it as she listened to yet another story of his exploits. She giggled when he finished.

"You know, of course, that I've only believed about half of what you've told me tonight," she accused him, smiling.

"That much?" He grinned. "Then you're even more gullible than I thought."

"Still," she said with a shake of her head, "I believe you lead a very adventurous life. What is it that draws you to such dangerous pursuits?"

He thought about it a moment. He'd been talking about his job, about his rescue work, about his hobbies of skydiving and climbing and rafting and biking. He supposed there was some risk involved in all of them, depending on circumstances, but he didn't really consider himself a daredevil.

"I like a challenge," he said finally, not knowing quite how else to explain.

And maybe, he mused, that was what drew him to Kim. She was possibly the most challenging woman he'd ever met. Just getting her to laugh was a feat that required his full concentration.

Perhaps he *had* become a bit spoiled. He was accustomed to having women encourage his pursuit, even to pursue him. He hadn't taken advantage of every opportunity, and there'd been the occasional woman who simply hadn't been interested—but Kim was unique.

He just hadn't quite determined why.

She shook her head again, her soft brown hair waving gently around her pretty face. Her chocolate eyes were pensive.

"You're an adventurer," she murmured. "I've always admired people who are brave. I'm not, you know."

He reached out to brush a strand of hair away from the corner of her mouth. "You aren't?" he asked, his tone encouraging her to continue. He'd been doing almost all the talking that evening.

She sighed. "No. I'm afraid."

"Of what?" He kept his tone soft, not wanting to risk startling her into silence again.

"Everything. Name it, I'm afraid of it."

"Heights?"

"Yup."

"Water?"

"Of course."

"Animals?"

"Deathly."

"Flying?"

She shuddered. "Can't even talk about it."

"Insects."

She looked around as though fearing one might be crawling on her as they spoke. "Bugs. All bugs."

Somehow his fingers had strayed back to her cheek. He found her admission of vulnerability rather endearing, though he couldn't say he totally understood. How could anyone be afraid of *everything?*

A drop of wine glistened on her full lower lip. He brushed it away with his thumb. Her mouth felt as soft as it looked, he discovered. "Kim?"

She seemed to be holding her breath. Her wineglass tilted precariously in her right hand. "Hmm?"

"Are you afraid of *me?*"

She swallowed. "Er..."

He saw the answer in her eyes just before she quickly drew out of his reach and frowned at her half-empty wineglass. "I told you I can't drink," she complained. "How much of this have I had?"

He took the glass out of her hand and set it on the table. "Not enough to worry about," he assured her.

Avoiding his eyes, she looked at her watch. "It's getting late. I'd better be going."

It wasn't even ten o'clock. Only a toddler would consider it late. But Zach didn't want to argue with her. He was still mulling over her silent admission that he unnerved her. And wondering why.

He would have liked to kiss her. Just to satisfy his curiosity as to the taste of that amazing mouth of hers, he assured himself. He decided to wait to see how amenable she acted when he walked her to her door.

One kiss, he thought. And then he could bring the evening to an end, write it off as an interesting experience and go back to a friendly-professional relationship with Kim Berry, the pretty but unapproachable waitress.

He stood. "I'll get my shoes."

She looked down at her own feet, as though surprised to find them bare. "I suppose I'd better put mine on, too."

He smiled and held out a hand to her. "That might be best."

After only a momentary hesitation, she placed her hand in his and allowed him to help her off the couch. She stumbled.

He steadied her, his grin deepening. "You really don't drink very often, do you?"

"I told you I don't," she chided him, appearing to be torn between amusement and exasperation.

"Don't tell me. You're afraid of grapes."

He'd startled her into a laugh. "Probably," she agreed.

He wasn't sure he was going to be able to wait until they reached her doorstep before he kissed her. Especially when she was looking at him like this, her dark eyes gleaming, her mouth curved into an inviting smile.

He dipped his head toward hers, slowly, trying to gauge her reaction.

The front door opened.

"Oops. Sorry. I didn't know you were..." Halfway into the room, Tom suddenly stopped talking and stared. "Oh."

Zach swallowed a curse of frustration. Kim had sprung away from him as though they'd been caught doing something illegal. And, darn it, he hadn't intended Tom to know anything about this date. Now he'd never hear the end of it.

Tom was already eyeing them in open curiosity, his gaze darting from Kim's flushed face to Zach's grim one, from their bare feet to the empty wine bottle on the floor. Zach could just imagine what was going through his friend's dirty mind.

"When are you going to stop treating my apartment as if it were your own?" he griped, planting his hands on his hips and taking the offensive. "The least you could do is ring the bell occasionally."

"Didn't know you were home," Tom answered with a shrug, still looking at Kim. "You said you had plans for tonight."

"So you decided to practice breaking and entering?"

"Nah. I wanted to borrow your Room of Doom video game. My neighbor's kid and I want to play it this evening."

"It's in the cabinet," Zach said with a cross sigh. He was going to have to talk to Tom later about overstepping the bounds of friendship. Had things been a bit different between him and Kim, this could have been very embarrassing for all of them.

Tom made no move toward the cabinet. "Hi, Kim," he said. "How's it going?"

She had already stepped into her shoes, her movements exaggeratedly careful. "Fine, thank you," she said primly.

"Nice weather this evening, hmm?" His tone was sober enough, but his green eyes were glittering with private amusement. Zach thought semiseriously about killing him.

Kim didn't seem to know how to respond to Tom's insouciant manner. "Er, yes. Very nice. I, um, I was just leaving."

"Don't rush out on my account."

"Tom," Zach murmured to his grinning friend, "get the game and get lost, will you?"

"Sure, Zach." But Tom was still looking at Kim. "You look very nice tonight," he told her. "Red is definitely your color."

Red was certainly the color of her cheeks. She looked imploringly at Zach, who nodded reassuringly to her. Tom's incessant smart-aleck remarks were sometimes hard for even Zach to take, and he and Tom had been closer than most brothers since grade school.

"I'll get my shoes and drive you home," Zach said to Kim. "And I'll hurry," he added when her gaze darted nervously to Tom.

"Hey, I'll drive her home," Tom called after him. "My pleasure."

"Go away, Lowery," Zach retorted over his shoulder.

For Kim's sake, he donned his shoes hastily. When he returned, Tom and Kim were chatting, though Kim was still not as relaxed as she'd been before Tom arrived.

"You still here, Lowery?" Zach asked pointedly.

"I was just leaving," Tom said, finally reading the warning in Zach's eyes. "Kim was telling me about your daring rescue earlier this evening. Super Zach struck again, huh?"

Aware that Kim's gaze had shot to his face in response to the facetious nickname, Zach cleared his throat. "Just happened to be in the right place at the right time, I guess."

"Amazing how often that happens," Tom murmured. "Trying to make the papers again?"

"God forbid." Zach had never been particularly fond of seeing his name or photo in the newspaper. Publicity wasn't the reason he'd chosen a career in public service.

He turned to Kim. "Ready to go?"

"Yes, whenever you are."

"Lock up when you leave, Tom."

"Yeah, sure. See you around, Kim."

"Yes. Good night."

Zach and Tom shared a look that promised a very long conversation later, both of them having a few things they wanted to say. And then Zach motioned for Kim to precede him out the door.

"Super Zach?" Kim murmured the words when she and Zach were alone in his truck, headed toward her place.

His eyes on the road, Zach cleared his throat and looked a bit embarrassed. "He calls me that sometimes. It's just a joke."

"You didn't tell Tom about our date, did you?" The question had been bothering her ever since she'd caught the look of surprise in Tom's eyes when he'd seen her and Zach together.

"No," Zach admitted.

"Why not?"

He shrugged. "It just never came up."

Kim suspected the two close friends usually shared such information with each other. So why hadn't Zach told Tom about this? None of the possibilities that came to mind were particularly flattering to her.

"It's no big deal," Zach said, apparently trying to read her silence. "Tom and I aren't really joined at the hip. We're just friends and co-workers. Sometimes I want a little privacy."

"Of course," she murmured, pretending to understand.

Neither of them said anything else for the duration of the short drive. Reaching her house, Zach turned into her driveway, shoved the gearshift into Park and killed the engine. He opened his door just as Kim reached for her own door handle.

Though it hadn't exactly been a typical date, Kim knew what the usual procedure was at this point. She doubted that Zach expected her to ask him in, but most dates ended with a kiss. Did he want to kiss her? Should she turn to him invitingly at the door, indicating her willingness to follow through with the tradition? Should she offer him her hand, instead?

She wished she'd had just a bit more experience at this sort of thing so she wouldn't feel quite so awkward and stupid now.

He stood nearby while she put her key in the lock and turned it. The dim yellow bulb in her porch light was their only illumination and there was little traffic on this street at night, so there was a sense of intimacy surrounding them that made Kim even more nervous.

Drawing a deep breath, she turned and managed a semblance of a smile. "It's been a very...interesting evening," she said.

His own smile was a bit crooked. "Didn't turn out exactly the way we planned it, did it?"

"No. But I'm sure Carla and her friend are very grateful you were there when they needed you."

"Yeah, well..."

If he'd been a schoolboy, he'd be worrying a stone with his toe. As it was, she found his aw-shucks-ma'am manner much too endearing. Was he aware of its effect? Probably.

He shifted a bit closer to her. "Kim?"

"Yes?" she asked, trying not to sound too wary.

"You never did answer my question."

She frowned, but didn't back up when he moved even nearer. "What question?"

He touched his thumb to her lower lip, the way he had earlier when he'd brushed away the drop of wine. It affected her now much as it had then—all the way to her toes.

"*Are* you afraid of me?" he asked quietly.

She could have lied. But she doubted that he would believe her. "Yes," she whispered.

"Why?"

Candor could go only so far. She had no intention of telling him that she was afraid of falling for him, afraid of being hurt by him, afraid of making a fool of herself over him. She settled for saying, "I don't know."

His blue eyes gleamed in the soft porch light as he lowered his head. "Trust me," he murmured. "I'm not in the least dangerous."

She might have laughed aloud...had his mouth not closed over hers at precisely that moment. Any amusement she might have felt immediately dissipated.

Somehow her hands had become trapped between them, palms flattened on his chest. She could feel his heart beating beneath his shirt, and she wondered if its rate was always that rapid. She knew hers was racing like a Formula One car.

He kissed her softly at first, gently, as if he were trying not to give her further reason to fear him. Lured by the illusion of safety, she allowed herself to respond, to tentatively kiss him back.

He murmured his approval and increased the pressure of the kiss, just enough to make her instinctively part her lips. He touched just the tip of his tongue to her lower lip, as if sampling her taste. She shivered in response.

"See?" he murmured, lifting his head only an inch. "Nothing to be afraid of."

Before she could reply, he was kissing her again, and this time he made no allowances for apprehension.

Admittedly, Kim hadn't been kissed all that often. But she had *never* been kissed like this. The closest comparison in her limited experience was the time a friend had somehow talked her into riding the big roller coaster at the Six Flags amusement park just outside St. Louis. She'd been both terrified and exhilarated by the ride, the only roller coaster she'd ever ridden, since Aunt Pearl had never encouraged such daring entertainment. She hadn't done anything like that since, but she'd never quite forgotten the rush.

Kissing Zach McCain was like riding that roller coaster. Thrilling. Breathtaking. Just a little dangerous.

She liked it just a bit too much.

Afraid that she was on the verge of making that embarrassing gaffe she'd dreaded all evening, she pulled her mouth away from his and slid her hands—which had somehow ended up clenching his shoulders—down his forearms to hold him away. "Zach, I..."

He stepped back. "I'd better be going," he said, his voice sounding just a bit odd. "It's getting late."

"Good night, Zach."

"I'll, er, see you around."

"Of course." She turned away from him and opened her door, not wanting him to see the confusion in her eyes in response to his suddenly abrupt manner.

She felt him hesitate, and then he turned and walked to his truck. He didn't quite run.

Kim let herself into the house, closed the door behind her and sagged against it without bothering to turn on the lights. Her mouth still tingling, she listened as the roar of Zach's truck faded to silence.

And that, she thought, was that.

Zach was determined that there would be no awkwardness between them when he saw Kim again. After all, he and Tom and the other firefighters were frequent patrons at the diner. He would see her often. He'd managed to remain friendly with other women he'd dated once or twice and decided not to see again, for one reason or another. He could do the same with Kim.

He'd told himself all weekend following their date that it would be a mistake to ask her out again. They were so obviously mismatched. He usually dated women who enjoyed the same activities he did. As for Kim—well, she was terrified of all his favorite activities. What could they do together other than go out to eat or see an occasional movie? Those quiet pastimes were fine on occasion, but a steady routine of them would bore him senseless.

Suddenly reminded of the kisses they'd shared at her door, a thought flashed through his mind of something *else* he and Kim could do to pass time together, a very pleasurable pursuit, indeed. But no. Remembering the little he'd learned about Kim during their evening together, he suspected that a relationship based on nothing more than sex would hardly appeal to her.

She was probably as afraid of sex as she was of everything else, he thought wryly.

Better for both of them if they left things as they were—casual acquaintances, nothing more.

But, damn, that last kiss lingered in his mind like a nagging ache that just wouldn't go away. And he couldn't for the life of him decide why.

It was a few days after their date when he saw her again. He and Tom and a couple of their other off-duty friends from the station were taking an afternoon pie break at the diner. Zach had thought about coming up with an excuse not to join them, but told himself that was stupid. He had no intention of avoiding Kim forever, and besides, Tom would really rib him about it.

Zach had told Tom that he'd asked Kim to dinner somewhat impulsively, that, despite the disruption, they'd had a pleasant enough time, that Kim seemed like a very nice woman, and that no, they probably wouldn't go out again. No matter how Tom had pried, Zach had refused to go into further detail.

Zach knew Tom was watching him when Kim approached their table to take their orders. As far as he knew, none of the others was aware that Kim and Zach had ever been on a date.

He gave her a friendly, casual smile. "Hi, Kim. How's it going?"

She nodded. "Fine, thank you, Zach. What will you have today?"

Exactly, he thought, as if she'd never seen him outside the diner. As if he were just another of her regular customers. And that was exactly the way he'd wanted her to act, wasn't it? So why was her detached expression annoying him so much?

"What do you recommend?" he asked her, watching her face for any expression other than indifference.

"Everyone's been complimenting the pecan pie today."

"Then I'll have that. With coffee."

Without meeting his eyes, she nodded and wrote down his order.

"Sounds good. Make mine the same," Chris Patton said from her seat beside Zach in the booth.

A rookie firefighter who'd been with the department less than six months, twenty-one-year-old Chris had quickly become a favorite with her co-workers. Even those dinosaurs still doubtful about women firefighters soon fell for Chris's jovial manner, her spirited responses and her unquestionable dedication to her work. Not only that, Zach thought, she was damned good at it.

She was also newly engaged to a linebacker on the Arkansas Razorbacks football team, a hulk of a young man about the size of a city bus. Since the guys Chris worked with possessed healthy instincts for self-preservation, none of them had dared to give her too hard a time, though she insisted she'd have been able to handle it on her own, had they tried. Zach, for one, believed her.

Tom and Sherm Gilbert, their other friend from the department, placed their orders and then returned to the spirited political discussion they'd begun as soon as they'd taken their seats. Ignoring their good-natured arguing, Zach watched Kim as she walked toward the kitchen.

The jeans she wore with her Red Hog Diner T-shirt molded faithfully to her gently swaying hips. He hadn't really noticed before how gracefully she walked—like a dancer or something, he thought fancifully. He suddenly realized that he wasn't the only one watching her; a thick-necked biker type across the room was also eyeing her backside in those slim-fitting jeans.

Zach glared at the guy. Didn't he know it was rude to leer at a woman? Couldn't he see that Kim wasn't the type who would welcome his insulting scrutiny?

"Isn't that right, Zach?"

Zach blinked in response to his name. "Er, what was that, Sherm?"

Sherm sighed. "Man, where is your head today? I've asked you twice if you agree with my opinion of the new safety inspection policies."

Zach could feel Tom's gaze on him, and knew his friend was probably grinning like an idiot, suspecting where Zach's attention had wandered. He cleared his throat. He had no idea *what* Sherm's opinions were of the new policies—and didn't particularly care at the moment. He tried to think of some way to phrase that tactfully, but fortunately he was saved from having to comment when Kim returned with a tray holding their pies and coffee.

She efficiently distributed the desserts, sliding Zach's in front of him last. "Can I get you anything else?"

For once, Zach couldn't come up with a witty reply. He merely shook his head, ignoring what might have been a chuckle from Tom's direction.

Kim left the table and moved on to refill Thick-Neck's cup. Watching covertly, Zach noticed that she stayed well out of range of the guy's roaming hands. She moved as if she had experience in fending off unwelcome advances. And yet, he thought in bemusement, she seemed to have little idea of how attractive she really was. Talk about naive...

"She seems nice," Chris commented.

Zach turned his head to look at her. "Who?"

"Kim," she replied, nodding in Kim's direction. "Every time I come in, she's polite and efficient and pleasant. No matter how busy it gets in here, nothing seems to ruffle her particularly. You know, Tom, you should ask her out."

Zach frowned.

Tom's eyes widened in surprise at Chris's out-of-the-blue suggestion. "Why should *I* ask her out?"

Chris shrugged. "I don't know. She just seems like maybe she'd be your type."

Tom cocked his head, apparently giving her advice some thought. Zach thought about kicking him under the table to let him know he didn't want this conversation to go any further. Before he could move, Tom asked Chris, "What about Zach? Don't you think she might be his type, instead?"

Chris and Sherm both laughed.

"Zach?" Chris said. "Hardly."

Zach concentrated grimly on his pie, refusing to be drawn in to the stupid discussion.

"How come?" Tom asked, to Zach's annoyance.

"It's obvious that Kim's a *nice* girl. Home and hearth and all that stuff. Zach...well..." Chris paused impishly.

Zach gave her a cool look. "Would you care to finish that observation?"

She giggled. "I just can't see you tied down to a steady relationship with a nice girl. A guy like you wants a good time with no strings attached."

Zach didn't know whether to be amused or rather stung. He found that amusement was difficult to summon.

"I suppose you're speaking from your own vast experience?" he inquired, subtly pointing out her youth.

"A girl learns to spot your type before she finishes

grade school,'' Chris needled him. ''Heartache on the hoof.''

''Hey, I think I resent this conversation,'' Tom complained. ''You didn't call *me* heartache on the hoof. You act like I'm about as ordinary as white bread.''

''Hate to tell you this, pal, but you're about as white bread as they come,'' Sherm quipped, flashing a mocking grin at Tom. ''Every mama in town wants her little girl to go out with a nice young man like you.''

''I'll have you know there are several large, hairy guys in town who have forbidden me to date their sisters,'' Tom boasted.

Sherm snorted. ''Yeah, but that's only because you're ugly. Got nothing to do with you being a heartbreaker.''

Chris was laughing. ''Face it, Tom, you're just a sweetheart of a guy. You pay your bills, take good care of your mother, mentor fatherless boys. You'll probably even floss after you finish that pie.''

''So I think good dental hygiene is important. But I can be a rebel. I once chewed a whole pack of gum in one day. And it wasn't even sugarless gum,'' he bragged, getting into the spirit of the nonsense.

Ignoring them, Zach was watching Kim again, though he tried not to make it too obvious. As far as he could tell, she hadn't glanced at him once while she went about her duties. Had she so easily forgotten the kisses that he was having so much trouble putting out of his mind?

''So, what do you think, Zach?'' Tom asked, his tone deceptively innocuous.

Why did people keep asking him that today? ''About what?'' Zach repeated.

''Should I ask Kim out?''

Zach stared at his friend across the table. ''I don't think that would be such a good idea.''

Tom's expression was as innocent as a choirboy's. ''How come?''

Because then I'd have to hurt you. But Zach said only, "I just doubt that you're her type."

"And who do you think is her type?"

Drop it, Lowery. "Now, how would I know that?" he asked.

"Well, you're the one—"

Tom fell abruptly silent when Kim suddenly appeared at the table to refill their coffee cups. Chris swallowed a giggle, masking it as a sudden cough.

Kim looked quickly, suspiciously at Zach, and he knew she thought he had been talking about her. He gave her a look meant to reassure her that he had not—not intentionally, at least—but she only laid their ticket on the table and turned away, carrying the coffee carafe to the next table.

"Personally, I think this whole conversation is academic," Sherm pronounced. "Doesn't look to me as though she's interested in either of you."

"You're right," Chris conceded. "She probably goes for the classy, intellectual type. And that leaves out both of our friends here, huh, Sherm?"

Sherm grinned. "You got that straight."

Swallowing a frustrated curse, Zach threw some money on the table. "I don't know about the rest of you loafers, but I've got stuff to do this afternoon. I'd better get to it."

To his relief, the others stood without further comment about Kim. As he left the diner, Zach glanced over his shoulder one last time, but Kim was still pointedly not looking at him.

Better to leave it this way, he told himself again. He wasn't the only one who thought they were mismatched. No matter what happened when they kissed.

Chapter Four

Kim had been home only an hour that evening when her telephone rang. She looked up from the textbook she'd been studying and reached for the receiver, telling herself it was probably only a telemarketer or a friend from church. *It's not Zach,* she told her pulse, *so settle down.*

But it was Zach. And her pulse doubled its rate.

He didn't even have to identify himself. "Hi" was all he said when she answered.

"Hi." She tucked a strand of hair behind her ear, picturing him as he'd looked at the diner that afternoon, surrounded by his friends. He hadn't seemed to be in a very good mood, though the others had laughed and chattered happily enough. She'd wondered what had been bothering Zach. And if it had anything to do with her.

She remembered that moment when she'd approached his table to refill coffee cups, when he and his friends had fallen into an abrupt, loaded silence. She'd suspected then that they'd been talking about her, laughing at her, perhaps. She'd called herself paranoid and juvenile to be so concerned, but she'd still felt terribly awkward with them.

"I hope I'm not interrupting anything."

She pushed the textbook aside. "Nothing that can't wait."

"Um, how are you?"

Her eyebrow lifted. He sounded uncharacteristically hesitant, even a bit awkward. As if he didn't know what to say now that he'd called her. So why *had* he called her?

"I'm fine, thank you." She cleared her throat, trying to think of something else to say.

He seemed to grow suddenly impatient with the stilted small talk. "Listen, Tom and I are going to the Razorback game Saturday afternoon, and then we're meeting some friends afterward for a party. I've got an extra ticket for the game. Would you like to go with me?"

She pictured herself spending time with Zach and his friends—the same friends who'd abruptly stopped talking and laughing when she'd appeared beside their table to serve them coffee. "I...er—"

"Don't tell me. You're afraid of football players," Zach interrupted teasingly, obviously trying to set her at ease.

"No," she retorted, "cheerleaders."

He laughed. She felt a faint glimmer of pride that she'd made him laugh with her for once, even if it was at her own expense.

"So, will you go?" he asked.

Well, Kim? Are you brave enough to join a nice group of people for a pleasant Saturday afternoon? Or are you really such a coward you'd rather hide in your house alone?

"Yes, I'd like to go," she said in defiance of that doubting little voice inside her.

"Great. I'll let you know what time I'll pick you up, okay?"

"That will be fine. Goodbye."

She hung up with a confused shake of her head. And then she found herself laughing, though she couldn't have said whether her amusement was directed at Zach, herself, or both of them.

He'd asked her out again. He hadn't exactly intended to, but he'd gotten to thinking about the game, and how he'd meant all along to invite a date, and how there wasn't anyone else in particular he wanted to go out with at the moment. And he'd known full well that none of those reasons had as much to do with his call to Kim as had his annoyance that she'd treated him like just another customer of the Red Hog Diner.

He called himself an idiot. An arrogant jerk. What did he think, that any woman should fall for him after she'd sampled his kisses? Of course not. But they *had* been pretty terrific kisses. And then she'd looked at him today as though she had some difficulty recalling his name. Treated him much the same way as she had the thick-necked biker with the insolent leer.

So maybe he'd asked her because he was trying to figure out why it was so easy for her to forget all about their one evening together when he was having a hard time putting it out of his mind. Or maybe he just liked being around her. No big deal, right? He had lots of women friends.

A tiny voice somewhere inside him murmured that there was something different about Kim. That he didn't think of her the same way he did his other women friends.

He told that tiny voice to shut up.

Kim was leaving her Intermediate Accounting II class Friday morning when she heard her name called from behind her. There was a brisk breeze blowing, tossing fallen leaves across the sidewalks engraved with the names of the more than one hundred thousand graduates of the University of Arkansas. Kim looked forward to the day when her own name would be etched into concrete on this beautiful campus, when she would finally have the college degree she'd been working so hard to obtain.

Pushing her hair away from her face, she turned to find a friend from the class hurrying toward her. Kim had met Dawn Lester in a class she'd taken the year before. Both of them were slightly older than most of the others in their classes, both were working their way through school on their own, both were out of the loop when it came to the campus social life. They'd been drawn together by their similarities and had remained friends despite their differences.

Breathless, Dawn was laughing when she finally caught up with Kim. "I've been hollering your name," she chided. "Where is your mind?"

Kim smiled apologetically. "Sorry. Guess I was thinking about that test Monday."

"Actually, that's what I wanted to talk to you about. Can you get together to study this afternoon, around three?"

Kim shook her head. "I have to work. How about later tonight?"

"Can't. I'm working late shift." Her round, mocha-toned face creased in thought, Dawn said, "What about tomorrow afternoon? Are you working then?"

"No. I, er, have a date."

Dawn's eyebrows rose sharply. "Excuse me? Did I just hear you say you have a date for tomorrow?"

Kim cleared her throat and nodded. Since Dawn had been good-naturedly fussing at her for months about getting a more active social life—*any* type of social life, actually—she understood why her friend looked so surprised. "Yeah. We're going to the game."

"The game? But you don't even like football."

"I thought it might be interesting," Kim said lamely.

"Uh-huh. So who are you going with? Anyone I know?"

"I doubt it. His name is Zach McCain. He's—"

"Zach McCain?" Dawn interrupted incredulously. "You're going out with Zach McCain?"

Had *everyone* in this town heard of him? Kim nodded. "Yes."

"The firefighter and rescue guy? The one who dove into Beaver Lake this summer and saved that whole family whose boat had capsized? The same one who carried the little old lady from a burning house last year? And then went back in to save her cat?"

Kim wished Dawn would stop listing Zach's amazing accomplishments. It served only to reinforce what an unlikely couple she and Zach made.

Zach McCain. Otherwise known as "Super Zach." And he was going out for the second time with Kim Berry. "Scaredy-cat Kim," as a boy in school had once called her. No wonder Dawn had wondered if she'd heard her correctly.

"That's the guy," Kim muttered.

"Wow. My cousin, Faye, is married to a fireman in Springdale. They act like the guy's a hero. You'd think Alonzo would be jealous of all the attention Zach gets, but he really likes him. Says everyone does."

"So I hear." Uncomfortable now, Kim shifted her books to her other arm and spoke briskly. "I'm free Sunday afternoon. Would you like to study then?"

"You bet I would. I'll want to hear all the juicy details of your date with Zach McCain...er, if you want to share them, of course," Dawn added.

Kim smiled weakly. "I doubt that there will be any juicy details. We're only going to a football game with some of his friends."

"Well, if he has any other interesting, single, hero-type

friends, you keep me in mind, okay? That's what friends are for, right?''

Kim's smile wavered, but she managed to hold on to it. ''I'd better be going. See you Sunday.''

''Have fun tomorrow.''

Kim wasn't making any bets on how much fun she would have, especially if everyone who saw her with Zach acted as startled as Dawn had been. But, she told herself in determination, she was certainly going to try. That was the whole point of this thing, wasn't it? An afternoon of fun?

It wasn't as if she was expecting anything more momentous from Zach.

Kim had talked herself into an optimistic mood by the time Zach arrived to pick her up the next afternoon. Since red was the only color to wear to a Razorbacks game, she'd splurged and bought herself a new red bomber-style jacket, which she wore with a white T-shirt, black jeans and black lace-up half boots. The bold colors cheered her when she looked in the mirror. And, besides, she couldn't help thinking, Zach had said he liked her in red.

She left her hair down, turned under softly just below her collar. Freshly washed, it gleamed in the light. Not an exotic shade, she thought critically, studying her reflection in the mirror. Just brown. But she'd always thought it suited her well enough.

She opened the door to Zach with a breezy confidence she'd had to work hard to attain. ''Hi,'' she said.

''Hi, yourself. You look great.''

Pleased that he'd noticed her efforts, she smiled. ''Thank you.''

He, too, had worn black jeans, pairing them with a white-and-red Razorbacks T-shirt. Even today, she noticed, he wore his pager clipped discreetly to his belt. With a quick glance downward, Kim decided that black denim could well have been invented with Zach McCain in mind.

Of course, she'd yet to see him look bad in anything, even soaking wet.

"Do you like football?" Zach asked when they were under way.

"I don't dislike it," she answered tactfully. "I just don't know that much about it. I know what a touchdown is, of course, and a tackle and a fumble and an interception—but the penalties always confuse me."

"Sounds like you've got a basic idea of the game. But here's the really important question—can you call the hogs?"

"No one could live in this town for almost two years—or work at a place called the Red Hog Diner—without learning woo-pig-sooie," she answered dryly.

Zach laughed.

"Just don't ask me to wear one of those plastic hog hats," she added. "That's where I draw the line."

"Nothing worse than hog-hat hair, is there?" he commiserated.

They carried on in that light vein for the remainder of the drive past the dozens of motels and apartment complexes that made up the university-centered town. Traffic grew heavy as they got closer to the stadium, but Zach navigated it competently, setting Kim at ease with his driving skill. Not that she'd doubted it. She couldn't imagine that Zach did anything badly.

They had to park some distance away from the entrance gate. To keep from being separated by the crowds pouring into the stadium, Zach took Kim's hand. Even as her fingers tingled wildly in his grasp, she told herself not to make too big a deal of it. It was only a friendly gesture.

An air of excitement and expectation surrounded them. Razorback fans tended to be exuberant and fanatically loyal. Many of them, Kim decided, had gotten a head start on the celebration, judging from their overbright eyes and noisy manner. Still, their enthusiasm was proving contagious. She looked at Zach and smiled. He grinned down at her and tightened his grasp on her hand.

Tom was already in his seat when Zach and Kim arrived. Zach seemed in no hurry to release Kim's hand as he towed her down the crowded passageway toward the two empty places next to his friend. Kim noted the quick glance Tom gave their linked hands, but his smile was friendly when he stood and greeted her. He didn't seem overly surprised to see her.

She'd expected Tom to have a date, and was a bit surprised to find that he'd come alone. She wondered how he really felt about Zach including her on their outing.

"Are you a football fan, Kim?" Tom asked her when she'd been seated between him and Zach.

"I don't know that much about it," she explained, as she had to Zach. "But I'm looking forward to this game. Do you think we'll win?"

Tom shrugged. "Maybe. Odds are about even. Myself, I just come to watch the cheerleaders."

Zach and Kim exchanged a quick glance and a chuckle. "Don't worry, Kim," Zach murmured. "I'll protect you from those scary pom-pom girls."

Tom lifted an eyebrow in question. Zach shook his head. "Private joke," he explained.

"Oh." Again Tom looked a bit speculatively from Kim to Zach. She cleared her throat and looked toward the field, where the cheerleaders in question were preparing to lead the crowd in a rousing "hog call."

Once the game began, Zach and Tom split their attention evenly between the action on the field, teasing Kim and cheerfully insulting each other. Kim responded easily enough to Zach's quips, and a bit shyly, but increasingly comfortably, to Tom.

It would have been impossible not to relax around these

two, with their constant banter. Kim was struck by the genuine affection between the men, though she suspected that it was an unspoken bond that they had long taken for granted.

She would have liked to have a friend she felt that close to, she thought a bit wistfully. She'd met quite a few people through work and school since moving to this area, and had become quite friendly with several of them—Dawn, for example. But there was no one who knew her and understood her as well as Zach and Tom seemed to know and understand each other.

Zach and Tom got into a good-natured argument about who would fetch snacks at halftime. Zach lost. Telling Tom to behave himself with Kim, Zach left them together with obvious reluctance.

"So," Tom commented after he and Kim had chatted about inconsequentials for a few minutes, "you and Zach seem to be getting along well."

Trying to read his expression, Kim shrugged lightly. "It isn't hard to get along with him."

Tom chuckled. "You obviously haven't seen his temper yet. He can be moody, but it's usually easy enough to tease him into a good mood."

Kim remembered her impression that Zach had been a bit grumpy when he'd come into the diner with his friends earlier in the week. "I suppose everyone has good days and bad."

Tom nodded. "Despite all the insults we throw around, Zach and I have been good friends for a long time," he said, his gaze on the field below where the marching band was making intricate formations.

Wondering where he was leading with this topic, Kim merely said, "Yes, I know."

"He's really a great guy. A little cocky, but that's just his way."

"Yes." She was aware that her voice had risen slightly

with the word, making it a question. Just what *was* Tom trying to tell her?

He looked at her then, his bright green eyes unusually serious. "There's something I think you should know about him. Zach's never been able to resist a challenge. The more difficult a task seems to him, the more determined he becomes, you know? And then, once he conquers it, he moves on to the next."

Still confused, Kim nodded slowly. "I'd already figured that out about him."

"Yeah, well, that's the way he is. Put up a wall and he's just got to climb over it. Dig a moat and he's got to swim it. Hide behind a dragon and he'll either slay it or tame it—probably the latter. Set up a line of guns and he'll find himself a tank. Build a—"

Smiling, Kim held up a hand to shush him. "I get the picture. But what does this have to do with me?"

Tom shrugged and looked innocent. The expression didn't work very well for him. "Just thought you might be interested. I've always expected Zach to come up against a challenge someday that might hold his interest longer than the others have. When that happens, he won't be in such a hurry to move on to the next. And I think it will be good for him."

She had definitely lost the thread of this conversation. Was he warning her off Zach, or encouraging her to work at holding Zach's interest? Either way, he was reading more into this date than he should be, she thought. It wasn't that big a deal.

Before she could decide what to say, Zach rejoined them, carefully balancing a cardboard container that held three drinks and five hot dogs. "Food," he announced. "Two dogs each for me and Tom, one for you, Kim. You're sure that will be enough?"

She assured him that it would be. He distributed the snacks, then took his seat again. "So, what have you two been talking about?'' he asked, glancing suspiciously from Tom to Kim.

Tom shrugged. ''Politics. Are you aware that you're spending the afternoon with an anarchist, McCain? She's been spouting all this propaganda about blowing up the White House and taking over control of Congress. She thinks waitresses should rule the world.''

''Who brings you an extra-big slice of Maggie's chocolate pie when you're suffering withdrawal symptoms, hmm?'' Kim asked him sternly. ''Be very careful, or we might just 'accidentally' be out of it next time you're craving it.''

Tom widened his eyes humorously. ''You can't keep me from Maggie's chocolate pie. That would be cruel and unusual punishment. I'll concede your power.''

''And so you should,'' she declared, smiling at him.

Zach grinned at their nonsense, then casually scooted a bit closer to Kim on the metal bleacher bench. ''Okay, you two, knock it off. The game's about to start again.''

Her entire left side tingling in response to Zach's proximity, Kim concentrated on eating her hot dog without choking on it. Her reactions to Zach were definitely different from the way she felt about Tom, she thought again. She only wished she could believe that there would ever be a time when Zach could smile at her without making her silly heart pound.

After the game was the part of the outing that Kim had been dreading. She'd been comfortable enough with Zach and Tom at the game, considering, but the idea of spending time with Zach's friends was a bit daunting.

She was tempted to suggest that Zach drop her off at her place on his way to Sherm's house, where the party was to be held. She managed not to do so.

''Is there a purpose for this party, or is it just a get-together?'' she asked Zach in his truck, trying to work up her nerve.

''It's sort of an engagement party for Chris and Burle. Burle Montgomery,'' he added. ''The star linebacker in today's game.''

Kim nodded to indicate that she remembered him pointing the player out to her. ''And Chris is your redhead friend from the fire department, right?''

''Right. Chris Patton. Hell of a firefighter.''

Kim thought that was probably high praise, coming from Zach. She glanced over her shoulder, noting that Tom was following them in his black sport utility vehicle. ''Tom doesn't have a date for the party?''

Zach shook his head. ''He broke up with someone a couple of months ago and hasn't gotten back into dating much yet. He's still stinging a little, I think.''

Kim frowned, picturing Tom's bright smile and easy laugh. She didn't like to think he'd been hurt.

''Hey, it's okay,'' Zach said, apparently reading the concern in her eyes. ''He got his pride hurt more than anything else. He wasn't planning marriage, or anything.''

''Tom isn't interested in getting married?''

''Let's just say he's not in any hurry.'' Zach made it sound as though Tom weren't the only one with an aversion to that sort of commitment.

After a moment Zach cleared his throat and said, ''You and Tom seemed to get along pretty well at the game.''

''I like him,'' Kim said simply. ''He's a lot of fun.''

She noted the slight frown that appeared between Zach's brows. ''Yeah, he's a great guy,'' he murmured, then abruptly changed the subject. ''So how are you doing with your classes? How much longer until you get your degree?''

Kim went along with the change of subject, telling him about the big test coming up on Monday, and how she was a bit worried about it. ''I'm studying with a friend tomorrow,'' she added, ''and that should help, but it's going to be a tough one.''

''I'm sure you'll do fine on it,'' Zach said with a confidence she wished she felt. ''Er, who's the friend? Anyone I know?''

''Her name's Dawn Lester. She has a cousin whose husband is a fireman in Springdale. I think she said his name is Alonzo.''

''Alonzo Carter? Great guy.''

Kim wondered if there was anyone Zach didn't like. He seemed to have a knack for making friends. Again she found herself envying him. Brave, outgoing, popular, admired—he was everything she'd always wanted to be.

And here she was going as his date to a party. She shook her head in amazement, wondering how this had happened.

There were already several cars and trucks crowding the curb in front of the neat, yellow-sided house Zach pointed out as their destination. It was in a modest new development on the east side of town, and had a nice-sized yard fenced in chain link.

''Sherm and Sami—his wife—are hoping to start a family soon,'' Zach explained. ''They bought this house a few months ago. We've been teasing Sherm about his nesting instincts kicking in, but it's a nice place.''

They had to park some distance down the cul-de-sac. Tom pulled in behind them and the three of them walked together to the front gate. Tom reached for the gate latch. Just as he did so, two very large and very shaggy yellow dogs came running around the side of the house, barking loudly and wagging their tails.

Kim instinctively gasped and shrank back. Zach slung an arm around her shoulders. ''Sorry,'' he said. ''I forgot to warn you about the dogs. But they're a couple of marshmallows, I promise. They like everyone.''

''You afraid of dogs, Kim?'' Tom asked, cocking his

head as he looked at her over his shoulder, his hand still resting on the latch.

Embarrassed, and keeping her eyes on the massive-looking animals, Kim nodded. "A little. It's silly, I know, but—"

"My mom's afraid of dogs," Tom said understandingly. "Got a real phobia about them. Zach's right about these two being harmless, but I'll have Sherm put them in their pen in the backyard if it will make you more comfortable. He won't mind."

"No, please don't do that." Kim hated to meet Zach's friends under those circumstances. "I'll be fine, really."

Still keeping an arm around her, Zach drew her forward, through the open gate. She pressed close to him, holding her breath, hoping he'd get her inside quickly. Instead, he paused.

"Hold out your hand," he said.

She stared at him. "Why?"

He gave her an encouraging smile. "That's the way you introduce yourself to a dog. You let him sniff you."

"What if he decides I smell tasty?" she asked weakly.

Zach's smile deepened. "Hey, I've thought that about you all along and I haven't bitten you yet, have I?"

"Yeah, but you're not a dog."

"I know a few people who might argue with that," Tom murmured, closing the gate behind him. Obviously recognizing an old friend, the dogs crowded close to him, tails frantically beating the air as they competed to lick his face.

Tom laughed and knelt to pet them. "Zach, I'll keep the dogs busy while you take Kim inside."

That sounded like a very good idea to Kim. But Zach shook his head. "Come on, Kim, hold out your hand," he said again. "Let me introduce you to them. They're great dogs. You'll be friends in no time."

"I'm really just not a dog person. I—"

He took her hand, gently. "Give it a try?" he asked enticingly.

"Don't force her, Zach," Tom chided. "Phobias are nothing to fool around with. Or to be ashamed of," he added for Kim's benefit.

She was grateful for his championing her, but something in Zach's expression made her want to try.

"It's not really a phobia," she murmured, fully aware of the difference between a serious, debilitating fear and her own general wariness. "I just haven't been around many dogs."

The approval in Zach's eyes in response to her brave words gave her the courage to hold out her hand, though she was acutely conscious of the tremors that shook it, and knew both men had to be equally aware of them.

One of the dogs left Tom to thrust his cold, wet nose into her palm. Kim flinched, but managed to keep her hand in place. A moment later a wet tongue lapped at her fingers. And then the other dog joined the first, both of them seemingly eager to meet this new friend.

She couldn't exactly say she liked the experience, but she was relieved to discover that her fear was abating. As Zach and Tom had assured her, these animals seemed friendly enough. She risked patting the nearest shaggy head. The dog seemed to smile up at her in response. She softened a bit more.

"What are their names?" she asked in a voice that was only a little higher than normal.

"Killer and Bruiser," Zach answered wryly.

She snatched back her hand.

Zach laughed at her expression. "Sherm's idea of a joke," he told her hastily. "I swear, they wouldn't hurt a fly. They welcome burglars with open paws. They even like mail carriers."

Despite her successful meeting with the fearsomely named pets, Kim was glad that Zach and Tom stayed on either side of her as they moved toward the front porch, the dogs staying behind to roll happily in the autumn-dried grass of the front lawn. She felt a glow of pride that she'd successfully met that challenge.

She heard the noise and laughter from inside the house as Zach reached out to ring the doorbell, and was suddenly hit by another attack of nerves. She wondered how Zach and Tom would react if she told them that she was as nervous about entering this house and facing their friends as she had been about the dogs.

They would probably be amazed to discover just how big a coward Kim Berry really was.

Chapter Five

Sherm's wife opened the door. Her exotically attractive face lit up when she recognized the new arrivals.

"Zach, Tom, I'm so glad you both could come," she said. "And who is this?"

"Samiya Gilbert, this is Kim Berry," Zach said.

"Call me Sami," the woman, who appeared to be in her late twenties, said, holding out a hand to Kim. "It's very nice to meet you. Come on in and meet my husband and our friends."

"Kim already knows Sherm and some of the others," Zach explained as they entered. "She works for Maggie at the diner."

Sami laughed and wrinkled her nose. "You guys and your pie breaks. Sherm's gained ten pounds since he started working with you all."

"They all love Maggie's pies," Kim agreed with a smile. "She does make wonderful ones."

"I'll have to come in and try a slice sometime." Sami

led the way into a medium-sized den made to look small by the number of people milling around in it.

The first familiar face Kim spotted was Chris Patton's. The perky redhead looked startled at first to see Kim entering with Zach and Tom, then pleased. She hurried toward them.

"Kim, what a nice surprise." She winked at Tom. "Took my advice, did you?"

Kim wondered what she'd meant by that, especially when Tom cleared his throat and murmured, "Er—"

With a sudden frown, Zach moved closer to Kim. "Kim's with me, Chris."

Kim wasn't particularly flattered by the way Chris's eyes widened. "A...oh," she stammered. "Sorry, I—" She broke off to give Zach a look that Kim thought was a bit reproachful.

What *were* these people talking about?

Chris waved a hand to dismiss the confusion. "Anyway, it's nice to see you here, Kim. Come on in and meet everyone."

"Everyone" turned out to be a group of firefighters and their spouses, for the most part. Some of them Kim had met before, others were strangers to her. She found herself fighting that old, lamentable shyness as the others chatted easily and spiritedly, tossing around inside jokes and insults bred of long familiarity. She would have given anything to be the type of person who could walk into a roomful of strangers and join right in, who didn't have to fight a tendency to blush and stammer whenever attention was turned her way.

It was almost as if she were transported straight back to her teen years, when she'd been the awkward, shy, studious girl being quietly raised by an overprotective aunt. She told herself in irritation that she'd matured and changed since those days. She could hold her own in a conversation. She no longer worried about wearing the "right" clothing or fitting in to the "right" crowd. She was an intelligent adult, making her own way in the world, and she had nothing to be shy or self-conscious about.

But she was, anyway, darn it.

It didn't help that those who knew her from the diner seemed either surprised or amused, or both, to learn that she was Zach's date. Or that there were a couple of women in the room who looked as though they would gladly trade places with her—no matter what it would take.

Even though she was aware that she was being paranoid, she suspected that more than one person at the party was wondering what on earth Zach saw in her.

To give Zach credit, he was a very attentive date. Even when he was engaged in lively conversation with his friends, he made sure Kim stayed nearby. He looked at her and smiled at her often, frequently asked if she wanted another soda or snack, asked her opinion about various topics of discussion. He touched her easily, taking her hand, slipping an arm around her waist, brushing a strand of hair away from her face.

He was a toucher, she told herself. It didn't really mean anything to him. Even if those touches threatened to melt her kneecaps.

An appropriate fuss was made over Chris and Burle's engagement, as well as his victory in the stadium that afternoon. Everyone teased Burle about being in such a hurry to get married. A lighthearted debate began about the relative merits of being married or single. Kim would have been interested in what Zach had to say on that topic—just for curiosity, of course—but he and Tom were involved in a discussion about a new fiber-optic camera for locating disaster victims buried under rubble. Neither seemed interested in talking about marriage.

The party was beginning to break up when someone spoke to Zach about an outing the group had apparently had planned for some time. "You haven't forgotten, have you?"

Zach shook his head. "Are you kidding? I'm counting the days."

He glanced at Kim. "A group of us are going skydiving in November," he explained. "We've chartered a plane for a Sunday afternoon. It was the first date all of us who were interested were free on the same day."

"Skydiving?" she repeated weakly, and shivered. "Um, have fun."

"You should go with us, Kim," Chris said eagerly. "It'll be my first time, and I can't wait."

Kim managed a smile. Okay, she thought, here it was. Everyone would find out what a coward she was, how poorly she fit in to this adventurous crowd. "I think I'll pass on skydiving."

"Me, too," Burle-the-bulky-linebacker agreed heartily. "I'd rather single-handedly take on a whole pride of lions than jump out of an airplane with nothing more than a bedsheet on strings to keep me from splatting on the ground."

Everyone laughed. A few teased Burle about being a chicken—but those who did stayed well out of range of his very large arms. Kim was grateful to him for taking the attention off her.

"Tell you what, Kim. You and me'll stay on the ground with a couple of comfortable chairs and a bottle of good champagne and we'll watch," Burle offered. "We'll see who enjoys the afternoon the most."

Kim smiled and murmured something noncommittal. The skydiving outing was a couple of months away. She knew better than to commit to anything involving Zach that far in the future.

"Who knows," Zach said lightly. "Maybe by then I'll have talked her into going up with us. I think she'd look good in a parachute, don't you, Tom?"

"I think Kim would look good in a paper bag," Tom answered with a grin, "but judging from the look she just gave you it'll be a cold day in hell before you see her in a parachute."

"Hell could freeze over and you wouldn't see me in a parachute," Kim agreed.

"It's really quite safe, Kim," Chris assured her, her big eyes sincere. "No more risky than driving on the freeway."

"I have no intention of jumping out of a moving car, either," Kim retorted, making the others chuckle.

Kim was grateful that someone changed the subject then. Though she'd managed to joke about it, she was very uncomfortable at having her fears brought out in front of this group. Sure, Burle shared her aversion to jumping out of airplanes, but he regularly faced a line of very large young men who wanted to flatten him, so he wasn't an all-around coward the way Kim was.

He fit in to the group. She didn't. It was as simple as that, she told herself glumly.

Kim stayed very close to Zach as they left the Gilberts' house and passed the enthusiastic dogs. Zach didn't pause this time to commune with the animals, to Kim's relief. One innocuous encounter had not transformed her into a dog lover.

Tom separated from them at the vehicles. "It's been fun, Kim," he said with a friendly smile that gleamed in the rapidly falling darkness. "See you at the diner, okay?"

"I'll save you a slice of pie," she promised.

"A woman after my own heart," he said with an exaggerated sigh.

"Get lost, Lowery," Zach growled, opening Kim's door for her.

Tom laughed. "Always nice to be around you, too, buddy. See you later."

"Are you hungry?" Zach asked Kim when they were under way. "Would you like to stop somewhere for something to eat?"

She shook her head. "Thanks, but Sami filled me up with so many snacks and finger sandwiches that I won't need anything else until morning."

"Yeah, me, too," he admitted. "Getting that last pecan brownie down was tough, but I hated to hurt her feelings by refusing it."

Kim wrinkled her nose. "I could tell what a sacrifice it was for you."

"That's me. Genuine, all-around, unselfish nice guy."

"And modest, too."

"That's one of my more attractive attributes," he acknowledged.

She laughed and leaned back against the seat. Only now that they were alone and relaxed again did she realize how tense she'd been all afternoon. She was rather tired from being on guard for so long.

She and Zach made small talk during the remainder of the drive to her house. He pulled in to her driveway, killed the engine and said, "I'll walk you to the door."

Kim immediately tensed again.

It was an unseasonably cool evening, probably due to all the rain they'd been having lately. Kim shivered a bit as they stepped onto her porch, into the soft yellow light. Zach turned to her, smiled and touched a fingertip to the end of her nose. "Your nose is turning pink."

"Nights like this remind me that winter isn't far away," she commented, rubbing her forearms with her hands.

He nodded. "We stay busier at the fire department in the winter. Space heaters, fireplaces, Christmas trees, woodstoves—seems like someone's always being careless with something combustible."

"Are you working tomorrow?" Kim knew that Zach worked the standard twenty-four-hours-on, forty-eight-hours-off schedule, and she wondered how any of them kept up with their days. Several firefighters, she knew, worked extra, part-time jobs during their two days off duty.

He shook his head. "I go back on duty Monday morning. Would you like to see a movie with me tomorrow afternoon?"

She hoped he hadn't thought she was hinting for him to spend more time with her. She hastily reminded him, "I'm studying with my friend Dawn tomorrow. Remember—the big test Monday?"

"Oh, yeah. I'd forgotten." He sounded just a bit chagrined, and she didn't know whether it was because of his memory lapse, or because she'd turned down another opportunity to go out with him.

But then he smiled and shrugged. "Some other time, then. Good luck with your test."

"Thanks. I'm probably going to need it."

"I'm sure you'll do fine. Something tells me you can do anything that you really want to do."

She wrinkled her nose. "I wish I had your confidence."

"Bet you could even jump out of an airplane with a parachute if you just made an effort," he added, tongue in cheek.

She groaned. "I am *not* jumping out of an airplane, Zach McCain. Nothing you can say will change my mind."

"That certainly sounds like a challenge," he murmured.

She knew how he felt about challenges. "Don't even think about it."

"There's *nothing* I can do to talk you into it?" he asked, moving closer to her, a wicked expression on his too-handsome face.

She backed up against her door, eyeing him suspiciously. "Nothing at all," she assured him. "I told you, I'm a first-class coward. You might get me to let a dog lick my fingers, but no way am I risking life and limb by skydiving.''

He planted a hand on the door on either side of her, trapping her between his arms. ''I don't think you're nearly as much a coward as you pretend to be, Kim Berry. I think that's just your excuse to keep from doing things you don't want to do.''

She knew better, but didn't bother to argue that point. ''Maybe. But I definitely do not want to jump out of a plane.''

Zach's breath was warm on her face when he leaned close and murmured, ''It's really not all that dangerous. Not if you have someone with you who knows what he's doing.''

She cleared her suddenly hoarse throat. ''No.''

''Chris has never done it, either, but she's willing to try. She knows we'd never let anything happen to her.''

''No.''

He rubbed the end of his nose against hers, and she felt the heat begin to collect in the pit of her stomach. ''I'd even hold your hand.''

''No.'' The syllable came out as a shaky exhale rather than the firm refusal she'd tried for.

He brushed a kiss against the corner of her mouth. ''I'll buy you dinner afterward.''

''I can buy my own dinners,'' she managed to say, telling herself she really should stop this now. It wasn't like her to let a man stand this close to her, to let him nibble on her face the way Zach was doing. It wasn't at all like her…but, oh, it felt nice!

''I'll give you a dollar.''

She couldn't help giggling a little, the giddy, high-pitched sound surprising her. ''Not even for a million dollars.''

''Did anyone ever tell you you're cute when you smile and scowl all at the same time?'' he asked whimsically.

"No. But flattery won't work, either. I am *not* going to—"

He smothered the rest of her adamant refusal beneath his lips. And Kim promptly forgot whatever it was they'd been arguing about.

He didn't kiss her tentatively. It wasn't the kiss of a first date—or even a second. It wasn't a casual embrace between friends. It was a kiss that curled her toes inside her boots. Made a shiver start somewhere deep inside her and ripple its way through her entire body. Made her knees go weak and her fingers go numb, her pulse pound and her breathing stop.

It was the kind of kiss that could almost make a girl want to jump out of a plane for a guy.

She broke away before she could do something really stupid—like tell him so.

She gulped in a breath of air and tried to speak coherently. "Good night, Zach. It's been a very nice day. Thank you for inviting me."

He looked at her as though he wasn't sure he'd heard her correctly. And then he blinked, as though his mind was slowly clearing—had the kiss really affected him as strongly as it had her, or was he just surprised that she wasn't begging him to kiss her again?—and said, "Er, yeah, sure. Good night, Kim."

She escaped inside her house with a haste that might have been funny had her knees not given way the moment she closed the door behind her. She fell gracelessly into the nearest chair, fanning her face with her hands and asking herself what in the world she thought she was doing.

When it came to Zach McCain, she was playing with fire. And she had always been so very careful about not being burned.

Kim was having trouble getting her study partner to concentrate on the advanced principles of accounting on Sunday afternoon. Dawn seemed to be more interested in trying to counsel Kim about her social life.

"I've been talking to some friends about Zach McCain," Dawn admitted. "And, Kim, I think you'd better be very careful with this guy."

For at least the dozenth time Kim dragged her attention away from her notes and textbooks. She sighed. "Why do you say that, Dawn?"

Dawn shook her head, making her treasured new hair-weave bob wave softly around her pleasant face. "Everyone agrees that he's really great—"

"Oh, yes, that *does* sound dangerous."

Dawn ignored Kim's facetious interruption. "He certainly doesn't have a reputation as a deliberate heartbreaker or anything—"

"Nice to hear."

"But," Dawn said meaningfully, raising her voice slightly to drown out Kim's comments, "he breaks hearts, anyway. My cousin told me there could be a thriving support group for all the women who have tried to land that man, only to be disappointed when he got away."

"For one thing," Kim replied dryly, "I'm not fishing for a man, so I have no interest in landing Zach McCain. And for another, you aren't telling me anything I haven't already figured out for myself. I'm not setting myself up for heartbreak, Dawn. I've just gone out with him a couple of times for fun, okay?"

"I can understand wanting to have fun with a guy like that," Dawn acknowledged. "But you take everything so seriously, Kim. Are you sure you aren't—well, getting in over your head?"

"I'm quite sure. I'm not even expecting Zach to call for another date. If he does, I may or may not accept, depending on whether I have anything better to do. Okay?" She hoped she'd sounded worldly enough and casual enough to convince her concerned friend that she was hardly so naive as to to fall for a man like Zach.

Dawn blinked a few times, obviously trying to decide whether Kim was really as nonchalant about the subject as she'd sounded, and whether any further warnings were necessary. And then she smiled.

"Okay," she agreed. "That's the spirit. Enjoy it while it lasts and then move on. Who knows, maybe you'll be the one to finally break Zach McCain's heart."

Kim managed a laugh. "Oh, yeah, sure."

"Hey, it could happen."

"And so could failing this course if we don't start studying for the test tomorrow."

Dawn sighed loudly and reached for the canned soda she'd been sipping while they tried to study. "You're right. But—well, isn't there anything juicy you can tell me about this legendary Zach guy?"

Kim thought a moment, then shrugged. "He looks really good wet—especially right out of the shower," she murmured wickedly.

Dawn's eyes widened. She choked dramatically on her drink. "Kim! Now you *have* to tell me more."

"No," Kim said sweetly, "I don't. What's the answer to study question number seven, Dawn?"

Groaning her frustration, Dawn obligingly looked down at her notebook. "It's either '75.3' or 'Nebraska.'"

Kim laughed and shook her head. "I think we'd better get back to studying."

"What's this I hear about you going out with Zach McCain?" Maggie Warner demanded the moment Kim reported for work Monday afternoon.

"Hello to you, too, Maggie." Kim wasn't really surprised that her employer had heard about her date with Zach. Listening to gossip was Maggie's second-favorite pastime—after arguing, of course.

Maggie shook her head of stiff, iron gray curls. "Bad idea, Kim. You and Zach—well, I just can't see the two of you together for very long."

Kim swallowed a sigh as she tied her apron over her jeans. Was everyone going to warn her off Zach? So far his best friend and hers had tried, and now even her grouchy employer felt the need to put in her two cents worth. "Zach and I are only friends, Maggie. He has a lot of friends, you know."

"Yeah, but I can't really see you fitting in to that group. They're a party crowd, you know. A shy, serious little thing like you is liable to get left in their dust."

Annoyed, Kim lifted an eyebrow. She didn't particularly like being referred to as a "shy, serious little thing." Nor did she appreciate Maggie's implication that she wasn't perfectly capable of looking out for herself.

"Thank you for your advice," she said coolly, "but I know what I'm doing."

Maggie exhaled sharply through her thin, rather pointed nose. "Just don't come crying to me when you get your feelings hurt or your heart broke."

"Believe me. Even if either of those things happen, I won't come crying to you."

Maggie gave a bark of laughter. "No, you wouldn't, would you? Handle everything yourself, don't you?"

"I certainly try." Kim pulled out her order pad. "Now, if you'll excuse me, there are customers waiting for me."

Maggie nodded. Kim thought she saw a gleam of approval in the older woman's gray eyes. Maggie always seemed to like it when someone stood up to her or talked back to her, which Kim was just getting the courage to do after all these months of working for the old battle-ax. She supposed she should be flattered that her employer had cared enough about her to offer advice intended to prevent heartache, but it still annoyed her that no one seemed to think she was capable of dealing with Zach McCain.

Maybe their opinions bothered her so badly because there was a secret part of her that tended to agree with them. A tiny voice that kept telling her to run before it was too late.

Zach called her again that night.

"Aren't you working?" she asked.

"Yeah," Zach replied. "But there's nothing much going on right now. Everyone else is watching some stupid made-for-TV movie. I made it through about fifteen minutes of it before I had to leave the room or put a foot through the TV screen."

"That bad, huh?"

"Worse. But, actually, I wanted to ask about your test. How did it go?"

She couldn't help but be pleased that he'd remembered. "Pretty well, I think. Dawn and I studied very hard yesterday." Once she'd gotten Dawn to stop asking about Zach, of course.

"Hey, that's great. Any other big tests coming up this week?"

"No, but I have a paper due Wednesday morning. I was just working on it when you called."

"Does that mean you won't be free to go out with me tomorrow night? I was sort of hoping we could take in a movie. A *good* one," he added, obviously referring scornfully to the one his co-workers were currently watching.

She hesitated. She wished she knew exactly why he kept asking her out. Tom had implied that Zach saw her as a challenge, but that explanation didn't quite seem to fit. She'd even wondered if Zach thought he was doing her some sort of favor—adding a bit of excitement to Kim Berry's dull social life—but that wouldn't explain why he kept calling. Charity could be taken only so far, after all.

Maybe, she thought hesitantly, he simply enjoyed being with her. The way she enjoyed being with him. And maybe it was possible for her to savor his company without making too much of it. Of course, he would have to stop kissing her the way he had. As far as she knew, casual friends didn't kiss like that. Not in her experience, anyway. And she knew it would be safer all around for her and Zach to remain just that—casual friends. She doubted that he would argue that point.

"Kim? You still there? Couldn't you sort of breathe loudly or something, so I'd know you haven't hung up on me?"

She smiled in response to his deliberately plaintive tone. "Sorry, Zach. I'm afraid I got distracted."

"Not very flattering, you know," he complained. "A guy asks you out and you start thinking about something else."

"I'd be happy to see a movie with you," she said. "On one condition."

"What condition?" he asked suspiciously.

"Promise you won't try again to talk me into jumping out of an airplane."

"I can't even try to talk you into it?"

"No," she said firmly, but still smiling. "The subject is closed."

"Mmm."

"Zach." She didn't trust that noncommittal murmur for a moment. "You haven't promised yet."

He sighed heavily. "Okay."

"Okay, what?"

He laughed. "You don't trust me an inch, do you?"

"Let's just say I've been warned about you," she answered lightly. *Boy, have I been warned about you!* she almost added.

"Okay, Kim. I promise I won't try to talk you into jumping out of an airplane. But if you should decide on your own that you'd like to do so, I'd be happy to offer my assistance."

Giggling, she assured him that she was more likely to sprout wings and take off on her own than to ever decide to jump out of a plane.

Zach concluded the call a moment later, after setting a time for their movie date. "Good night, Kim," he said. "Sleep well."

"Thanks. You, too."

"Oh, I intend to. I'll be dreaming of a certain brown-eyed angel."

She knew better than to take his flattery seriously. "Forget it, Zach. I'm *still* not jumping."

He laughed. "I'm looking forward to our date," he said, and hung up.

Kim was smiling when she replaced her own receiver in its cradle. She'd made Zach laugh, she thought contentedly. At himself, that time.

Despite all those dire warnings, she thought Zach McCain was good for her. As long as she kept her silly fantasies in check, of course. And she'd always been very good at that.

It started raining again just as Zach turned onto Kim's street at the end of their date Tuesday evening. By the time he pulled in to her driveway, it was pouring, much as it had been the night of her blowout. Still in a good mood from the clever comedy they'd seen, they both started laughing as Zach killed the engine and stared wryly at the torrents of rain falling between his truck and her house.

"Boy, does this look familiar," he said. "And would you believe, out of all this stuff I carry around with me, I don't have an umbrella?"

She giggled. "Don't real men use umbrellas?"

"Sure they do. But this one tends to leave his wherever he uses it last," he admitted with a grin. "I buy them by the dozen, then immediately lose them all."

Then it's a good thing you look so good wet, isn't it? Kim thought. She bit her tongue to keep the quip to herself. Somehow, it didn't seem like the just-friends type of comment that would fit the tone of the evening thus far.

Zach glanced out again as the rain seemed to increase in intensity, pounding the top of his truck with an almost deafening rhythm. "Maybe we should just sit here a few minutes," he suggested. "This has to let up soon."

Kim laced her fingers in her lap. Funny, but the deeply shadowed interior of his truck seemed suddenly as intimate as a bedroom, with the rain falling in thick curtains around them, and no one else in sight. The light from the street lamps filtered in through the wet windows just enough for her to see the gleam of Zach's smile as he turned to her, and the glitter of his bright blue eyes.

She gulped. "Um, I can make a run for it," she said. "There's no need for you to get out."

He caught her arm when she moved toward her door handle. "There's no hurry, is there? If you step out there now, you'll be drenched before you reach your porch."

He was right, of course. Telling herself she was being silly, she tried to relax. "I suppose I can wait a few minutes, if you don't mind sitting here that long."

"Mind?" He flashed her another dazzling smile and, still holding her arm, drew her a bit closer to him. "No, I don't mind this at all."

Sensing what was coming, she cleared her throat. "Er, Zach..."

"Mmm, Kim." He lowered his head, brushed his mouth across hers.

She jerked back as though he'd stung her. "You know, I think the rain has let up," she said breathlessly. "I'd better go on in. Good night."

"But—"

She opened her door.

"Wait, I'll walk you—"

"No, that's not necessary. No need for both of us to get soaked. Good night."

She was out in the rain, the truck door slammed closed behind her, before he could say another word. She made a dash for her front door, both to escape the rain and to prevent Zach from coming after her.

He waited until she was inside the house before he drove away.

Kim called herself every kind of an idiot for the way she'd acted, but she simply hadn't been able to sit in that truck and—well, and make out with Zach, if that's what it was still called these days. She was determined to keep their relationship friendly and nonthreatening, and she couldn't do that if he kept on kissing her.

He was a toucher, she reminded herself. Kissing was something that came easily to him, a pleasant way to relax and pass time. It was possible he felt the same way about sex. Kim did not.

She would already miss him if he stopped calling her. She had already become accustomed to his friendship, and had grown comfortable talking to him about a variety of subjects—her job, her schooling, her career plans, their mutual acquaintances. He made her relax and laugh in a way that no one ever had before. But she could still recover if he suddenly stopped calling, stopped asking her out, started avoiding her for some reason. It was what she'd expected all along, right?

But if she was ever foolish enough to make love with him—and for her, it would be much more than sex—it wouldn't be so easy when it ended. That was exactly why she'd been so wary about getting involved with him in the first place. High on the list of the many things Kim was afraid of was the long-lasting pain of a broken heart. And Zach was definitely the guy who could break hers if she wasn't very careful.

She pushed her hand through her damp hair and headed

for her bedroom to change. As she turned on her bedroom light, she caught a glimpse of herself in the mirror over her dresser. The rain had made her hair go limp, and had left makeup streaks on her face. The end of her nose was reddened from the cool, wet air.

She definitely did not look as good wet as Zach did, she thought glumly. She doubted that he would even *want* to kiss her if he saw her looking like this.

That thought made her feel a bit like crying.

Chapter Six

"So, how are things going between you and Kim?" Tom asked Zach as they sat in a boat on Beaver Lake, enjoying a lazy afternoon on the pretext of fishing.

Zach had been expecting this question. In fact, he was surprised Tom had waited so long to get around to it. To give him a moment to decide how to answer, he cast his lure toward a likely looking spot near the brushy bank. "We saw a movie together last night. We had a good time."

Lounging against the seat, his booted feet propped against the side of the bass boat, Tom seemed to be concentrating on his own line, though Zach knew his absent manner was deceptive. Tom was more interested in the conversation than he pretended to be. "Seeing quite a bit of each other, aren't you?"

Zach shrugged. "It was only our third date."

"In—what—a week?"

"Couple of weeks. Hey, did I tell you that Elaine's expecting again? Just announced it yesterday."

"Congratulations. You'll be an uncle for the fifth time. Maybe your mom will finally get a granddaughter."

Pleased that his conversational bait had been taken, Zach was able to relax a bit and concentrate on his fishing. He thought he'd just felt a nibble at his lure. "That's what she's hoping for. She's probably out shopping for pink booties today, just in case."

"Have you introduced Kim to your family yet?"

Zach jerked his rod too quickly, lost the strike and swore beneath his breath. Tom seemed to have a one-track mind today, for some reason.

"No," he said, reeling in his lure. "I haven't. Kim and I are just friends, Tom. Don't make a big deal out of it, okay?"

"Just friends."

"Right. I like her. She's got a sharp sense of humor behind that innocent-looking face."

"I noticed that," Tom said with a grin. "She gets in a few zingers against you, doesn't she?"

"She can hold her own," Zach agreed, wincing as he remembered a few of those zingers from last night. The more comfortable Kim became around him, the more easily she returned his verbal volleys. She'd caught him off guard several times with unexpectedly wicked comments made with such sweetly innocent expressions that he couldn't help laughing out loud.

He really did like being with her. But he'd convinced himself that was all there was to it. Kim had made it clear enough that friendship was all she was interested in. When he'd tried to kiss her in his truck last night, she'd bolted as if he'd threatened to bite her, or something. She'd jumped out into the pouring rain rather than linger in the cozy truck with him.

Zach wasn't used to having women go to quite such lengths to avoid his kisses.

"So, how would you feel if I ask her out sometime?"

Zach swore and nearly took the end of his thumb off with a fishhook. He glared at his friend. "Why would you want to ask her out?"

Tom didn't do innocent nearly as well as Kim did, though he made an obvious effort. "Like you said, she's fun to be with. Nice sense of humor. I just thought I might take her to dinner or something sometime."

"You never said anything about this before."

"I've thought about asking her," Tom admitted. "I just never actually got around to it."

"So you waited until *I* started going out with her to decide to get around to it?" Zach asked testily.

"Going out with her?" Tom repeated, his voice as bland as his expression. "I thought you said you were just friends."

Zach narrowed his eyes. "What the hell is this, anyway?"

Tom shrugged. "Just trying to define your idea of friendship. Obviously you don't much care for the idea of me asking out your newest 'friend.'"

"No," Zach snapped. "I don't."

"So, what if someone else asks her out? Mike Henry was feeling me out about it yesterday, wondering if you'd mind if he got to know her a little better."

Zach couldn't believe it. Kim had been working at the diner next to the station for six months. Yet none of the guys seemed to have noticed her until Zach, himself, had shown an interest. He couldn't exactly call their imitation flattering. "You're kidding."

"He asked if I thought you'd get mad."

"And what did you tell him?"

"I told him you'd probably take his head off if he got

anywhere near Kim. And, obviously, I was right,'' Tom said smugly, eyeing Zach's scowl.

''Tom—''

''Just friends, my left ear,'' his buddy muttered. ''You've had your eye on Kim Berry since the day you first spotted her at the diner. I was beginning to think you were never going to do anything about it.''

''I, er—''

''And you think I wasn't watching the two of you Saturday? I thought you were going to swallow your tongue every time she turned those big brown eyes on you and smiled. You're hooked, McCain. Just like this fish,'' he added, snapping his rod to set his hook and beginning to reel in his catch.

Zach couldn't help laughing when the feisty crappie managed to get away just as Tom was about to bring him into the boat. ''Want to make any more comparisons?''

''Yeah, well, keep dragging your feet, pal. But don't say I didn't warn you when you see Kim out with some other 'friend.'''

Zach thought of Tom's warning when he entered the diner the following Tuesday afternoon. He'd been off duty for hours, but had hung around the station with one excuse or another until he knew it was time for Kim to report to work. And then he'd decided he was hungry.

Still wearing his dark blue polo shirt with the Fayetteville Fire Department logo and the navy Nomex slacks that made up the rest of his uniform, he sauntered into the diner alone. He hadn't asked anyone else to join him. He was just going to have a quick lunch, and then be on his way.

Or so he told himself.

He took a booth in the back of the diner. He spotted Kim immediately, taking orders from a table of six gray-haired ladies who seemed to be having some difficulty deciding what they wanted. Zach's mouth twisted wryly.

The menu here was hardly extensive; how long could it take to decide between the five daily lunch specials?

Kim seemed to be incredibly patient with her dithering customers. In fact, she was smiling sweetly at them and appeared to be offering suggestions. Zach could tell the ladies were responding to her. A couple of them looked as though they were thinking about adopting her, he thought with a glimmer of amusement.

It seemed that a lot of people found themselves drawn to Kim.

The diner was rather crowded today. He glanced around the room, noticing in disapproval how many of the men seemed to be watching Kim. Had this been going on the whole time she'd worked here? And if so, why hadn't he noticed before that her pretty face and slender figure garnered so much covert attention?

He set his menu aside, unopened, and watched Kim go about her work. And he considered the disclaimer he'd given to Tom during their fishing trip. He'd assured Tom repeatedly that he and Kim were just friends.

Friends hung out together. Enjoyed being together. Swapped stories about their experiences, shared their thoughts, laughed at each other's jokes. They offered hugs and support, advice and encouragement. Zach had other women friends.

None of them made him feel the way Kim did.

Having finally turned in the gray-haired contingent's orders, Kim was free to wait on her other customers. She spotted Zach and broke into a quick, spontaneous smile accompanied by what might have been a very faint blush. And his heart kicked suddenly against the wall of his chest. All because Kim Berry had smiled at him.

His mouth felt suddenly dry.

"I'm sorry you were kept waiting," she said, hurrying to his table. "What would you like?"

"Lunch," he replied, forcing a smile. "I'm starved."

She cocked her head. "Any preference?"

Yes. You. He cleared his throat. "I, er, whatever's good today."

"That would be either the baked chicken or grilled pork chop. Both seem to be popular today."

She was treating him like a customer again, darn it. He didn't know why that annoyed him so much when he *was,* in fact, a customer—but it did.

"Baked chicken," he said. "And a glass of iced tea."

She nodded. "It won't take long."

He caught her wrist when she would have hurried away. "You look very pretty today," he said, just to see her blush.

Her cheeks went pink, and she touched her neatly twisted hair with her free hand, the gesture seemingly automatic. Her smile was shy again, her eyes warm. "Thank you," she said softly.

Satisfied, for the moment, he released her hand and sat back in the booth to wait for his lunch.

He braced himself again when Maggie Warner made her way to his booth a few minutes later. "How you doing, Zach?" she inquired, sliding onto the other bench without waiting for an invitation.

He eyed the older woman warily. Anytime Maggie was wearing that bland, fake smile, those who knew her prepared for trouble. "Just fine, thanks."

"Your mama doin' all right? I haven't seen her in a while."

"Yes, she's fine. She's been busy with her hospital volunteer work."

"I hear your sister Elaine's going to have another baby. What is she now, thirty-four? Thirty-five?"

"Thirty-four. She and Mark will probably stop after this one, even if it's another boy."

"I should hope so," Maggie, always one to offer an

opinion, said with a huff. "Three young'uns is enough for anyone."

Zach wasn't really aware that his gaze had drifted back to Kim, who was busily setting plates in front of the ladies across the room. Maggie noticed, however. "Rumor has it that you and Kim are an item these days," she said.

Zach cleared his throat. "We're..."

He'd started to give her his usual just-friends line. But then he shrugged and said, "We've been out a few times."

Maggie frowned. "Kim's a nice girl."

"And what am I, an ax murderer?" Zach asked crossly.

"Just be careful with her, you hear?"

Before Zach could answer, or even decide what he would have said, Kim appeared with his lunch. She looked warily at Maggie as she slid the well-filled plate in front of him.

Maggie stood abruptly. "I'll let you enjoy your lunch," she said to Zach. "You tell your mama I said to give me a call, you hear? She won two dollars off me at gin rummy last time and I want a chance to get it back."

"I'll tell her." Zach waited until Maggie had stalked across the room, barking gruff greetings to her regular customers along the way, and then he smiled wryly up at Kim. "Boy, she's in a mood today."

Kim made a face. "Tell me about it. She's kept everyone hopping. Do you need anything else?"

He shook his head. "No, I'm fine. Go take care of your other customers."

"Okay. Give me a sign if there's anything you want."

He figured he'd been giving her signs for weeks now. Apparently, she hadn't read them very well.

Just friends?

He was beginning to understand that he'd always known there would be more than that between them. Maybe that was the reason he'd taken so long to ask her out in the first place.

* * *

Kim was sitting at her piano Saturday afternoon, having a wonderful time banging out a Scott Joplin ragtime number. Her fingers seemed to fly over the keys, and she laughed aloud when she hit one particularly difficult chord perfectly. She almost always blew that chord.

Aunt Pearl hadn't cared for ragtime, or for pop tunes. She'd discouraged Kim from playing anything but classical pieces. Since Aunt Pearl's death, Kim had purchased stacks of sheet music. Pop, ragtime, Broadway tunes, even—she could almost sense Aunt Pearl shuddering—country songs. Kim simply enjoyed playing for her own entertainment, and while she appreciated classical music, the contemporary pieces were more fun for her to play.

She ended with a crash of chords that reverberated in the small room. Though she rarely played in front of anyone else, she almost wished someone had been there to hear her that time. She thought she'd played the number better than she ever had before.

She was feeling so confident that she immediately launched into a new tune—and this time she sang along. In contrast to the cheery ragtime number, this one was a sad song, but one of her all-time favorites—"Is It Over Yet?" from Wynonna Judd's first solo album. Both the piano accompaniment and the lyrics were beautiful, in Kim's opinion.

Kim loved to sing, but rarely did so when anyone else was listening. Being alone gave her the confidence to pour emotion into the song of a woman who couldn't bear to watch her lover leave her.

She drew a long breath when she'd played the last note, fantasizing about the applause from an audience she'd never really have the nerve to perform for. And then, feeling unusually giddy, she stood and gave a flourishing bow to the empty room, her back to the door. "Thank you, thank you. You're much too kind," she said aloud.

From behind her, a deep voice responded. "Brava. Encore."

She nearly jumped out of her skin. Turning so fast she almost fell on her face, she found Zach McCain leaning against the frame of the doorway that led into her living room from the tiny entry hall. While she stared at him, he brought his hands lightly together in applause.

"Very nice," he said. "I liked the Joplin number, but I'm more of a country fan, myself."

She was torn between sinking through the floor or killing him. Maybe she'd kill him and *then* sink through the floor.

"What," she asked, bringing a shaking hand to her throat, "are you doing in my house?"

"Your front door was open," he said. "I rang the bell several times, but I guess you didn't hear it."

She'd left the front door open on that gorgeous autumn afternoon to let in some fresh air. She'd thought she'd locked the screen door, but obviously she hadn't. She'd become a bit lax about security while living in this quiet, virtually crime-free neighborhood. Aunt Pearl would have sternly disapproved.

"So you just let yourself in?" she asked coolly, crossing her arms over the chest of the comfortable blue fleece pullover she'd worn with an old, faded pair of jeans. She hadn't been expecting company.

Zach affected a concerned, sincere expression. "You could have been hurt," he explained gravely. "Lying on the floor injured, unable to answer the door. It was my civic duty to make sure you were okay."

"You didn't hear the piano?"

"Well, yeah. When I realized that you were playing, I hated to disturb you."

The word that erupted from her was both earthy and unexpected, surprising even her. She almost clapped a hand over her mouth. Aunt Pearl would have been running for the soap by now. Kim could only blame the lapse on still being rattled by Zach's unexpected appearance.

Zach laughed. "Why, Kim Berry. Who'd have thought someone who sings like an angel could swear like the devil?"

Her cheeks were on fire. She drew a deep breath, trying to make her still-reeling mind come up with something to say that didn't make her sound like a total idiot.

Zach grew suddenly serious. "I'm sorry, Kim. When I heard you playing and realized the door was unlocked, I came in by impulse. Didn't stop to think that it would frighten you. I guess that's a flaw of mine—being impulsive, I mean."

She tried not to be disarmed by the apology. "Gee, ya think?"

He winced. "Do you want me to leave?"

"No. Just, please, don't do that again."

He held up a hand. "Scout's honor."

She eyed him suspiciously. "*Were* you a Scout?"

He cleared his throat.

She sighed and shook her head. Darn it, it was hard to stay mad at the guy, no matter how much he deserved it. "I didn't think so," she muttered.

"I had no idea you were such a talented performer—singing and playing," Zach commented, nodding toward the piano. "Do you ever perform in public?"

She shook her head, her cheeks warming again. "Never. Aunt Pearl insisted that I learn to play, and I enjoy it just for myself, but I never had a desire to perform."

"That's a shame. You're really very good."

She shook her head. "Adequate at best. Would you like something to drink? I have juice or soda. Or I could make coffee." She figured since he was a guest in her home—uninvited though he might be—she should at least act the gracious hostess.

"Coffee sounds good." He was looking around her tiny

living room, studying the extensive accumulation of paperbacks on her bookshelves, the framed photographs of Kim's mother and her aunt Pearl, her simple, but tasteful furniture. He turned his attention to a curio cabinet in one corner of the room.

"Snails," he said, peering through the glass. He glanced at her with a smile. "Is this your collection?"

She nodded. It felt odd, having him in her home, looking over her things. Though she'd already been to his place, this was different, somehow. She couldn't have explained it had she tried. "I've been collecting them since I was sixteen."

Grinning, he studied the whimsical assortment. She had snails in porcelain and glass, in brass and pewter and plastic. Comic snails with funny faces and gaily painted shells, realistic-looking models no bigger than her thumb, one large snail carved of wood and finished to a rich, dark gloss. "Why snails?" he asked.

She shrugged self-consciously. "I don't know. Something about them just appeals to me."

She'd tried not to overanalyze her attachment to the slow-moving, cautious, shellbound little creatures. She'd told herself she liked her little figures only because they were clever and cute. Certainly not because she personally identified with them, or anything.

"I'll make the coffee," she said, moving toward the kitchen.

Zach followed her. After studying her minuscule yellow kitchen with the same apparent fascination with which he'd examined her living room, he pulled out one of the four oak bow-back chairs at her small, round pedestal table and sat down to watch her measure coffee into the basket. He propped his elbows on the table and rested his chin on his hands.

She was beginning to feel like an exhibit in a zoo, the way he kept watching her. "Um, was there a reason you dropped by today?'' she asked, trying to sound casual about it.

''I just wanted to see you,'' he answered with a slight shrug. ''Guess I should have called first, huh?''

Assuming the question was rhetorical—not to mention obvious—she lifted the lid of a cake plate and turned to show him its contents. ''Chocolate cake?''

His eyes lit up almost comically. ''You bet.''

He definitely had a sweet tooth. She wondered how he managed to stay so slim and fit looking, then decided it must have to do with his very active life-style. She cut him a generous slice of the cake, and a smaller portion for herself. By the time she'd set the plates on the table, the coffee was ready to pour.

''This is great,'' Zach said, digging in to the dessert with enthusiasm. ''Did you make it?''

She nodded. ''It was my aunt's recipe. She loved to bake. I guess she passed that trait to me.''

''My mom's a good cook. My sister Elaine does a lot of baking—cookies and pies and stuff—but that's about it. Patrice and her family tend to eat out a lot.''

''What about you? Do you cook?''

He grimaced. ''A little, but the results aren't always pretty.''

She smiled and sipped her coffee. She couldn't help wondering why he'd really stopped by. She found it hard to believe that he'd simply wanted to see her, as he'd said. Surely he had more interesting ways to pass a Saturday afternoon than to sit in her kitchen eating cake and swapping recipes.

He seemed to be about to say something else when her telephone rang, interrupting them. ''Excuse me,'' she said, standing to reach for the kitchen extension. ''Hello?''

''Kim? Hi, it's Tyler Murphy. You know, from your financial management class?''

She smiled. Tyler sat beside her in the class and had

always been very nice to her. He was a couple of years younger than she was, but they'd discovered some common interests during casual conversations before and after class. "Hi, Tyler. What's up?"

"I had to skip class yesterday to go to my grandmother's funeral. You suppose I could look over your notes sometime this weekend?"

"I'm very sorry about your grandmother," Kim said sympathetically. "And of course you may copy my notes. Actually, you didn't miss that much Friday. We got into one of those off-the-subject group discussions that ate up most of the class period."

"That's a relief. I really appreciate this, Kim. Er, maybe you'd let me buy you dinner tonight? We could look over the notes then."

"Dinner tonight?" she repeated, startled by the invitation. She and Tyler had never seen each other outside of the classroom. "Well, I—"

"You have plans," Zach said flatly, and loudly enough to be heard at the other end of the line. Kim jumped. She hadn't heard him get out of his chair and come to stand so close behind her.

She shot him a chiding look as Tyler stammered, "Oh, s-sorry. I didn't know you were, um—"

"That's all right, Tyler. Thank you for asking, but I'm afraid I have plans for the evening. You can stop by any time to pick up the notes. If I'm not here, I'll put them in a folder and leave them under my mat, okay?"

"Sure. Thanks."

Kim gave him her address, then hung up. She turned to find Zach frowning at her.

"You know, walking into my house without an invitation is one thing," she said sternly, "but now you're eavesdropping on my telephone calls. Just what makes you think—"

He pulled her into his arms and covered her mouth with his own.

Chapter Seven

Some time passed before Zach ended the kiss—or before Kim thought to pull back. When he finally lifted his head, he looked almost as stunned as she felt, as though he hadn't actually intended to kiss her until he'd found himself doing so.

And then he took a deep breath, locked his arms around her and kissed her again. And this time she would have sworn she felt the world tilt beneath her feet. She held on to Zach with both arms, just in case.

He'd kissed her before. But not like this. This, she thought dazedly, straining helplessly toward him, was the way he would kiss a woman he wanted. A woman he intended to have.

Her head was reeling by the time he broke the kiss—a combination of lack of oxygen and pure, overwhelming sensation. She gasped for breath, aware that her arms were still locked around Zach's neck, but unable, for the moment, to release him for fear of falling flat on her face without his support.

His own breathing was ragged, his arms tight around her as though he, too, needed balance.

Kim searched his face cautiously, noting his darkened, heavy-lidded eyes, the faint flush of color on his tanned cheeks, the slight strain around his mouth. She wasn't the only one who'd been deeply affected by the kiss, she thought in wonder. She was finding it hard to believe that it was she who had brought that dazed look to Zach McCain's face.

"What—" She had to stop to clear her throat. "What was that?"

"That," he said, his voice hoarse, "is what I've been trying to tell you for weeks now."

She caught her breath in response to the open desire burning in his eyes. "Try telling me again," she whispered, lifting her face to his once more.

She caught a glimpse of his flashing smile just before he eagerly, and thoroughly, complied.

A small voice inside her asked what on earth she thought she was doing. This wasn't at all like her. Or rather, not at all like the woman she'd been three weeks ago—before Zach McCain had found her at the side of a road and had made himself part of her life, at least for now.

The new Kim wanted to explore, wanted to experiment, wanted to savor the thrill of being with Zach for however long it lasted without worrying about the future. But the old Kim—the *real* Kim, she reminded herself—knew better than to think that would work for her.

As wonderful as it felt to be held in Zach's strong arms, as thrilling as it was to have him kissing her, stroking her back with his hand, touching her face and hair as though she was special to him, she couldn't let this continue. She couldn't expect it to last.

Zach abruptly lifted his head, framed her face between his hands and frowned down at her. "Don't do that."

She moistened her tender lips. "Don't do what?"

"You're trying to be afraid again. Don't."

She didn't like his wording. "I don't *try* to be afraid, Zach. I *am* afraid."

"No. You're simply in the habit of being afraid. Using fear as an excuse is easier than taking a risk."

He was making her head spin again, but this time from confusion rather than passion. How could he kiss her like that one minute, then criticize her the next? She tried to pull away from him. "I'm not—let me go."

"Not yet," he murmured, and brushed his lips across hers again. "Not until you admit that you know there's no reason for you to be afraid of me."

"It isn't that I'm afraid of you...exactly," she hedged.

Still frowning, he merely continued to look at her. Waiting.

"It's just that I don't think we should...well, g-get involved." She was aware that she was stammering, that she sounded like an idiot. But she struggled on, making an effort to convince him that there were sound reasons for her wariness. "Everyone thinks we're wrong together."

His frown deepened, pulling his dark brows into a stern V between his narrowed blue eyes. "Everyone?"

"Well, some people. Your friends—Tom and Chris. Maggie. My friend Dawn."

He looked stunned. "They've all talked to you about us? *Tom* said something to you?"

Realizing that he was stung by what might be perceived as betrayal by his friends, Kim quickly shook her head, even though Zach's hands still rested on either side of her face. "Tom didn't say anything specifically, and neither did Chris. I just got the impression that they were surprised you were dating me. And, of course, Maggie's a pessimist about everything, and Dawn doesn't even know you, but..."

Zach relaxed somewhere during that convoluted retraction. "You've just effectively wiped out that argument," he observed gently. "The others aren't involved here. So what *is* the problem?"

"It's us. You and me. We're just so different. You're—well, you're Zach McCain. And I'm—I'm just Kim. And—"

He irritated her greatly by laughing. "I'm sorry," he said, shaking his head, "but you really aren't making much sense. I don't really think our names have anything to do with this, and yes, I know we're different in some ways, but I don't happen to think those differences are all that important. I like being with you. I like talking to you. I think we have almost as many things in common as we do in contrast. I want to keep seeing you, Kim. And not just as friends, or pals or buddies. There's a lot more to it than that."

She bit her lip.

"I'm not trying to rush you into anything you aren't ready for," he assured her. "I'd just like to know that you won't be running away from me every time I try to kiss you—the way you did the other night, when it was raining. Because, if we continue to see each other, Kim, I *will* want to kiss you."

The heat in his voice nearly liquefied her knees. Oh, the way he could look at a woman and melt any obstacles she might have built against him. She didn't even want to think how much practice he'd had to become this very good at it.

"I suppose this whole thing has taken me by surprise," she admitted.

He laughed softly. "You and me both. You got into my head. I found myself waking up in the mornings thinking about you. Wondering what you were doing at odd times during the day. Looking forward to seeing you again. And then when the other guys started talking about asking you out, I—''

Kim frowned. ''Other guys?'' she broke in.

His mouth crooked into a cross between a smile and a grimace. ''I'm not the only man who thinks you're special, Kim. You're just too modest to notice.''

She frowned and pulled away from him, making his arms drop to his sides. ''You asked me out just because someone else wanted to?''

''No, of course not. I'm hardly that competitive.''

Wasn't he? Kim remembered Tom's veiled warning that Zach thrived on challenges. She eyed him suspiciously, thinking that he had suddenly had an urge to kiss her today only after Tyler had called and asked her for dinner. She hardly found it flattering to think that Zach was going out with her only to score macho points, or something along those lines.

Zach sighed ruefully. ''How long is it going to take before you learn to trust me?''

''I—''

''Never mind. You'll find that I can be very patient when it's something that matters to me.''

She almost melted again. It had been so long since she'd really mattered to anyone. She'd been alone for a long time. The intensity of her reaction to his words only reinforced her fear of becoming too attached to him.

''I don't want to be afraid, Zach.''

''Then don't be.''

''It isn't that easy.''

He touched her cheek. ''I know. But you'll try?''

She drew a deep breath and wondered if she'd lost her mind. ''I'll try.''

His quick grin was a sign of his approval. ''Great. So, when are we jumping out of that airplane?''

Kim felt her eyes go huge. She started to sputter an

absolute refusal, but Zach was laughing before she could get the words out.

"Sorry," he said, holding both hands up, palms out, in a sign of surrender. "I was only teasing. I promise, I won't try to talk you into anything you don't want to do—including skydiving. Deal?"

"Deal," she said forcefully. "Because, trust me on this, Zach, you will *never* get me to jump out of that plane."

His eyes glinted with the challenge, but he only smiled and kissed her cheek. "Where would you like me to take you for dinner this evening?"

She lifted an eyebrow. "I have plans for this evening. Didn't you hear me say that to Tyler?"

His frown had returned in full force. "I thought you meant you had plans with me."

She shook her head, taking a small pleasure in the jab at that inflated ego of his. "No. You hadn't asked me to dinner when I talked to Tyler, remember?"

"So, what *are* you doing?" he asked suspiciously.

"I told Maggie I'd cover the evening shift. Joanne's sick again."

"Oh, is that all? I bet if I call Maggie, she'd give you the evening off. She can find someone else to—"

"You'll do no such thing. Maggie has been very good to work with my class schedules. I'm not going to leave her in the lurch after promising to help her out this evening."

Zach sighed. "I suppose I should admire your sense of responsibility."

She tapped the pager on his belt. "Are you telling me that you would ignore this if it started beeping?"

A bit sheepishly, he shook his head. "No."

"My job might not involve saving lives, but it's important to me. It's letting me finish my education. I'm not going to risk losing it."

Zach shoved a hand through his hair. "Sorry. I keep

putting my foot in it today, don't I? I promise, I won't always come on this strong, Kim. I guess I'm just a little off balance today. I didn't really plan this conversation," he added with a candor that was as disarming as it was exasperating.

"Neither did I," she assured him fervently. And, as for being off balance, she had been ever since she'd looked up to find Zach McCain standing in her living room, watching her play the piano.

"When do you have to leave for work?"

She glanced at her watch. "In just over an hour."

"I suppose I'd better go, then. You'll want to get ready for work. Will you see me tomorrow?"

"I was planning to attend church in the morning."

"I'll call you afterward, then. We'll do something tomorrow afternoon. Okay?"

She nodded.

He leaned over to kiss her firmly. "Bye, Kim," he said when he released her. "Drive carefully this evening."

Feeling as though her brain had gone into overload, she could only nod again.

Looking rather pleased with himself, Zach sauntered to the door. He looked back over his shoulder before leaving. "Kim?"

She'd been admiring the way his snug jeans cupped his lean backside. She looked quickly up at his face, her cheeks flaming. "Yes?"

"In case your friend Tyler asks you to dinner again, you're going to have other plans for a long time."

She frowned and opened her mouth to inform him that he had no right to dictate her actions with Tyler or anyone else. But he was gone before she could say anything. She heard him whistling cheerily as he went down the hallway and outside, shutting the front door rather loudly behind him.

Kim sank into a chair at the kitchen table and buried her face in her hands with a heartfelt groan.

What on *earth* had happened here today? It had started out as an average Saturday, just her and her piano and a few chores on her to-be-done list. Then Zach had waltzed into her home without warning and now, somehow, it seemed that she was officially dating him.

Judging from his parting shot, he considered it an exclusive arrangement. He'd made it clear that he didn't want her having dinner with Tyler. Did that mean he had no plans to see anyone else, either? Because if he thought she was going to sit here and wait by her phone for him to call while he was out having a good time, then he had a lot to learn about her.

She was crazy to think this could work. She suspected that she could ask anyone and they would tell her the same thing. She could think of few less likely couples than herself and Zach. And yet…he'd told her she'd gotten into his head. And heaven only knew that he'd been inside hers for months. So, maybe…

Maybe she *was* crazy. And maybe she was going to get her heart broken. And maybe she would end up wishing she'd never moved to Fayetteville, Arkansas, or ever met Zach McCain. But she had met him, and for now, at least, he wanted to be with her. Wouldn't she spend the rest of her life regretting her cowardice if she didn't at least give it a chance?

He'd told her that being afraid had become a habit for her. That he believed she could get past it if she wanted to badly enough. She didn't want to be a coward. She had never wanted that. Now here was another opportunity for her to prove something. To Zach. And to herself.

She drew a deep breath and lifted her chin. She was going to do it, she thought with a surge of excitement. She was going to call Zach's bluff, find out just what he really wanted from her.

But, she told herself, her newfound confidence wavering for a moment, there was no way in hell that she was jumping out of that airplane. And not even "Super Zach" could change her mind about that!

Zach and Kim shared a picnic at the park on Sunday afternoon. It had been Zach's idea. He'd called her and told her, basically, that he was on his way to pick her up and that he would provide the food. He hadn't really given her a chance to say no…but she wouldn't have done so, anyway. She'd said she would give this a chance, and she intended to follow through.

Even if the thought of the possible consequences scared her spitless.

Zach had purchased a bucket of chicken and several side dishes. He'd also brought along paper plates, plastic forks, canned soft drinks, a tablecloth and a Frisbee. After they'd eaten all they could hold, he talked her into a game of catch, even though she tried to warn him she was lousy with Frisbees.

After she'd thrown the darned thing all over the park a few times, making him have to run after it, he'd had to admit that she was right. But he didn't seem to mind. And after he'd given her a few pointers, she found that she could sail it to within a few yards of him, which was a definite improvement. She even caught it quite a few times when he sailed it her way. Actually, he was so good at aiming it that it was either catch it or get hit by it.

It was a gorgeous day. They didn't have the park to themselves, but it wasn't overly crowded, either. She couldn't remember when she'd been so relaxed, or had laughed as much as she had this afternoon. Zach seemed to go all out to keep her entertained, and he succeeded. She was having a very nice time.

And then she saw a group of four adolescent boys tormenting a cat.

Zach had uncharacteristically overthrown the Frisbee, causing Kim to have to dash after it. Out of the corner of her eye she saw the cluster of boys beneath a stand of trees at the very edge of the park. She paid them little attention until a pitiful yowl made her frown and look around.

Realizing what was going on, she threw the Frisbee down and bolted toward the boys.

"Get away from that poor animal right this minute!" she ordered, skidding to a stop beside them. "What do you think you're doing?"

The cat was cowering in fear. Its legs had been tied together with string, so that it couldn't move, could only lie helplessly on the ground, shivering, as the boys did what they wanted to it. Fortunately, it didn't seem to be badly injured, so Kim assumed they had just gotten started.

One of the boys eyed Kim's slight build and flushed face and decided to show off his machismo. "Leave us alone, lady—this ain't none of your business."

She faced him down, her fists planted on her hips. "I'm not going to allow you to torture this cat. Now, go on and leave it alone before I call the authorities."

"It's just a flea-bit old stray," one of the other boys muttered. "Just dirtying up the park."

"It's a living creature with feelings," Kim retorted. "Look at it. It's frightened and in pain. What you were doing is cruel and heartless—and it's illegal. Now, get away and let me take care of it."

The first boy who'd challenged her, obviously the leader of the group, stepped forward belligerently, his dark eyes glinting with anger and rebellion. "Yeah? You think you can make us go if we don't want to?"

"If she can't, I can," Zach said. He'd approached quietly and was now standing only a few feet away, looking tough and a bit dangerous as he faced the punks with narrowed eyes and squared jaw.

Two of the boys immediately ran off. The other two hesitated.

"Get out of here," Zach growled.

The boys looked at each other, then at Kim, then at Zach. And they ran.

Kim was already kneeling beside the cat, stroking its head and crooning at it in an attempt to calm it as it flopped around, trying to escape its bonds. "Help me set him free, Zach."

He bent beside her. "Careful. He's scared. He's liable to claw your hand off."

She sneezed, then murmured, "He'd only be doing what comes naturally, wouldn't you, sweetie?"

Kim continued to talk softly to the animal while Zach carefully loosened the knots. "Bring me the tablecloth. We'll wrap him in that and take him to a vet."

Nodding, she ran for the cloth.

The angry cat didn't make it easy for them, but Zach and Kim managed to get it to a vet—who happened to be an attractive brunette friend of Zach's. Kim tried not to let their obvious familiarity bother her. Dr. Sanderson seemed very nice and was willing to take the cat in and find it a good home.

"Don't be such a stranger, Zach," she called out as Kim and Zach left her clinic, where she'd met them when Zach had called her.

"We really appreciate this, Stacy," Zach responded, slinging an arm around Kim's shoulders.

Kim sneezed, then nodded a grateful second. "Yes, we do. Thank you."

Looking speculatively from Kim to Zach, Dr. Sanderson assured them that it had been no trouble at all.

Kim was still sneezing when she and Zach climbed into his truck.

"You're allergic, right?"

She dug in her purse for a tissue. "Right."

"But not afraid of cats?"

"Certainly not cats that are tied up and helpless. Honestly, we should have reported those brats to the authorities. I would have, if I hadn't been so anxious to get the poor cat some attention."

"They were obnoxious, weren't they? And mean as young scorpions. For a shy little thing, you can be quite a tiger when you make an effort, can't you?" Zach's voice was warm with amusement and approval.

Her cheeks warmed. She still didn't care to be called a "shy little thing," but she only shrugged and looked out the side window. "It just makes me so mad when I see defenseless animals being mistreated. Or children. Or anyone, for that matter."

Zach reached over to stroke her cheek with the backs of his fingers. "Remind me to step carefully around you," he teased. "The way you looked at those boys had me shaking in my shoes."

Despite the chaos his tender touch set off inside her, Kim managed an inelegant snort. "Oh, I'm sure I scare you."

Zach's smile faded. "There are times when I think you do."

She decided she didn't want to question him too closely on that. She was almost relieved when another sneeze made it unnecessary for her to comment.

"You know," Zach said meditatively, "someone as brave as you were when you faced down those boys shouldn't have a bit of trouble jumping out of a plane...."

She groaned loudly. "Forget it, Zach."

He only laughed.

"I can't believe I'm doing this," Kim muttered, clutching her hands tightly in her lap.

Zach grinned over at her from behind the wheel of his truck. "Relax. Everything will be fine."

She shook her head. "Why did I let you talk me into it? I'm really just not comfortable with this, Zach."

"Calm down, okay? What could go wrong?"

"Everything."

He laughed. "You're really making too much of this. It's only dinner with my family. "

She groaned.

Zach reached over to cover her icy hands with his warm right hand. "Trust me. They're nice people. They aren't dangerous. They don't bite. Spending time with them doesn't cause cancer in laboratory mice."

She couldn't help chuckling.

He squeezed her hands. "That's better. Seriously, Kim, it's going to be a nice evening. I think you'll like my family."

"I'm sure they're very nice. I just—well, I'm not sure I'll fit in."

"You'll fit in great. Everyone's looking forward to meeting you."

She almost groaned again. Zach had taken her completely by surprise when he'd insisted she accompany him to this dinner party that was being held in honor of his father's sixty-fifth birthday. She'd tried to make excuses, but Zach wouldn't hear them. He'd decided he wanted her there with him, and if there was one thing she'd learned about Zach during the past few weeks, it was that he simply didn't recognize the word *no.* Apparently he hadn't encountered it enough during his charmed lifetime for it to have become a part of his vocabulary.

She was trying to teach him the meaning of the word. Two weeks had passed since that Saturday when he'd shown up unexpectedly at her house. They'd been out to dinner a couple of times, and had spent a lazy evening playing board games with Tom—which Kim had enjoyed thoroughly.

She and Zach would have been together even more during those two weeks had she not been resolute about having her schoolwork done and being available at the diner when she was needed. Zach tended to pout a bit when she told him she had other plans—or did men sulk, rather than pout?—but so far he'd been cooperative enough working with her schedule.

His own schedule was certainly complex. It was hard enough to keep up with his twenty-four on, forty-eight off working hours, but he was also active in several civic organizations, his volunteer rescue squad, a safety education program in the local grade schools, and who only knew what else. Zach liked staying busy, and spent few evenings home alone.

If he'd been dating anyone else recently, he hadn't mentioned it. And now he was taking her to meet his family.

She gulped. She wasn't at all sure she was ready for this.

Zach pulled in to the driveway of a rather large, Tudor-style house near the Fayetteville Country Club. "This is my sister Elaine's house. Looks like everyone else is already here. There's Dad's Oldsmobile, and the Suburban belongs to my sister Patrice and her husband, Eric."

Smoothing the slacks of her hunter green knit pantsuit, Kim eyed the nice home he'd brought her to. "This is a lovely place."

"Did I mention that Elaine's husband is a surgeon?" Zach asked wryly. "He's on the staff at Washington Regional."

"No. You didn't mention that."

"Don't tell me you're afraid of doctors."

She wrinkled her nose at him. Zach loved teasing her about that. Yet he teased so gently and so good-naturedly that she simply couldn't take offense at it. "As a matter of fact, I am,'' she muttered. ''But only if they're carrying needles or scalpels.''

''Well, since Mark rarely operates in his home, you should be safe this evening.''

She managed to smile. ''That's good to hear.''

''Elaine's a licensed family therapist. She works part-time at the clinic downtown, which allows her to be with her own family quite a bit.''

''Quite an accomplished group,'' Kim tried to say lightly.

Zach killed the engine and turned in his seat to face her, suddenly serious. He reached out to touch her cheek. ''Don't worry so much about it, Kim. It's only a dinner party, and it's only my family. It'll be fun.''

''You're right, of course,'' she said, feeling a bit foolish. ''It's not such a big deal. I'm sure you've brought other friends to occasions like this.''

''No,'' he said quietly. ''It's been years since I brought anyone to a family dinner. I was always afraid they'd read too much into it if I did.''

''And you're not concerned this time?'' Kim asked with a frown, wondering exactly how to take that.

He shook his head. ''This time they would probably be right,'' he said breezily. He leaned over to brush a kiss across her mouth, and then opened his door. ''Coming?'' he asked, sliding out of the truck.

Kim blinked rapidly a couple of times, told her suddenly racing heart to behave itself, and opened her own door.

Zach had accomplished one thing, she thought wryly as she joined him on the walkway to his sister's house. She was no longer worried about embarrassing herself at the dinner party.

He'd just given her an all-new set of potential catastrophes to worry about!

''Zach, she's lovely.''

Zach dragged his gaze away from Kim, who stood

across the room flirting lightly with his father, and turned his full attention to his mother, who was beaming happily at his side. "She is pretty, isn't she?" he agreed, thinking that Kim looked especially nice today in the dark green pantsuit that complemented her brown hair and eyes.

Nancy McCain nodded her salon-maintained ash blond head. "Yes, she's very attractive, but I was talking primarily about her personality. What a charming young woman. Such nice manners. And she's very good with the children, isn't she?" she added, referring to her four young grandsons, who were playing in another room at the moment.

Zach tapped his mother's tilted nose. "Subtle as a neon sign, Mom. I've only been dating her a few weeks. Don't start ordering wedding invitations just yet, okay?"

His mother smiled sheepishly. "Sorry, dear. It's just that it's been so long since you've brought anyone to meet us that I was beginning to wonder if you were turning into a workaholic."

Zach's sister Elaine had been standing close enough to overhear. She made a production of choking in disbelief. "Workaholic? Zach? Surely you jest."

Nancy frowned. "Zach's a very hard worker, Elaine. He's always either at the fire department or taking classes to improve his skills. And that rescue squad he's joined takes time, as well."

"Mmm. And all that rafting and climbing and biking and football and softball playing are such hard work, too, right, Zach?"

Zach ruffled his sister's dark hair. "You know what they say about all work and no play."

"Making Zach a dull boy?" Elaine made a face at him. "No danger of that."

"Thanks. I think."

Elaine glanced across her living room to where Kim and

George McCain were sitting so cozily on a love seat, chatting away. "Looks like Dad's getting along great with your new girlfriend, Zach."

While Zach contemplated how he felt about hearing Kim referred to as his "new girlfriend," Nancy sighed.

"Look at the old goat preen," she said affectionately of her husband of forty-two years. "He just loves talking to pretty young women."

A crashing sound came from the direction of the den. Elaine winced. "The boys are supposed to be playing a quiet board game in there," she said. "How can they make that much noise playing a game? Guess I'd better go check on them. Zach, I want to talk to you later."

Zach suspected that he knew what Elaine wanted to talk about. Kim. The whole family seemed fascinated by her, and consumed with curiosity about Zach's relationship with her.

He wondered why they'd reacted so strongly to her. Sure, it had been a while since he'd dated anyone steadily, even longer since he'd brought anyone to meet his family. He didn't really think they were all that surprised that he was dating someone now. But after watching him with Kim for a very short time this evening, they'd suddenly become intensely interested in his feelings for her.

He wondered what they'd seen in his expression when he'd introduced Kim.

Half his attention on his mother's lengthy description of a symphony performance she and Patrice had attended at Walton Arts Center the evening before, Zach glanced across the room toward Kim and his father. They really did seem to be getting along amazingly well. While Kim had been quite friendly to the rest of Zach's family, it was his father with whom she'd bonded almost immediately. Now they were chatting away like best friends. Zach wondered what they were talking about. Judging from the way his dad was grinning, it was something amusing.

Zach couldn't blame his father for being captivated by Kim's shy, sweet smile and her way of listening to his long-winded stories with her full attention and apparent appreciation. As for Kim, she seemed genuinely taken with Zach's jovial, garrulous, bighearted father. Zach thought sympathetically about her admission that she'd never known her own father.

Kim must have had a lonely childhood, he mused. No father, no siblings, her mother dying so young, her only family the aunt who'd taken her in. And yet she'd turned out quite nicely. A bit shy, a bit sheltered, somewhat anxious about many things, but bright and competent. She knew what she wanted and, in her own quiet way, she was going after it.

He was falling hard for her, and he knew it. It had taken him by surprise, but he wasn't trying to fight it. That thirtieth birthday was getting closer every day. Maybe it was time for him to settle down, try his hand at a serious relationship.

He and Kim had seemed very different at the beginning, but they found more in common each time they were together. He suspected that if he was patient and persistent enough he could introduce her to some of his other interests. She'd already vetoed skydiving; he wondered how she felt about hang gliding.

"Zach, are you listening to me?"

With a guilty start, Zach looked at his mother. "Sorry, Mom. I guess I drifted for a minute."

Glancing across the room, she smiled and patted his arm. "Go talk to Kim, dear. You and I can catch up later."

Knowing his smile was sheepish, he kissed her soft cheek. "You're a treasure, Mom."

Nancy beamed after him as he moved across the room toward Kim.

Chapter Eight

"You," Kim told Zach an hour later as they left his sister's home in Zach's truck, "are spoiled rotten."

Zach laughed. "What makes you say that?"

She rolled her eyes. "As if you didn't know. Your family thinks the sun rises and sets on you. Your parents, your nephews, even your sisters. What ever happened to sibling rivalry?"

"We had a few quarrels when we were growing up," he admitted. "But not many. On the whole, we got along unusually well. Maybe it's because of the age difference. Patrice is almost nine years older than I am, and Elaine's almost five years older. I was more of a new toy for them than a rival."

"Yes, I heard how much fun they had dressing you up and putting makeup on you," she murmured with a smile.

He grimaced. "Don't remind me. Patty still has photographs she's holding for blackmail purposes." There was one in particular. He'd been about seven, and they'd dressed him in a pink ruffled dress with a big bow clipped to his hair and makeup smeared all over his face. If Patrice ever pulled that out to show Kim, Zach would have to express his extreme displeasure. Physically, if necessary.

"You really do have a nice family, Zach," Kim said, and she sounded as though she was trying to keep envy from coloring her voice.

He immediately softened. "Yeah, I do. And I know how lucky I am," he added gently.

She nodded. "Very."

"They liked you, you know. They all want to see you again soon."

She murmured something noncommittal and looked out the side window of the truck, pretending a sudden interest in the passing scenery, even though it was pitch-dark outside.

Zach almost sighed. Every time he made even the most offhand comment about the future, Kim immediately retreated behind some invisible barrier. Why was it so difficult for her to look ahead with him? Was she still so convinced that their relationship was doomed? Everything had been going so well. What more did he have to do to prove that his interest in her was sincere, and not some passing fancy?

He was quiet as he turned into her driveway, pulled up behind her car and killed the engine. Their dates usually ended with a kiss at her door. When she asked him in for coffee, he stayed only a short while, leaving with a kiss at her door. He was growing impatient to progress a few steps beyond those very nice but unsatisfying kisses.

Maybe Kim was just waiting for him to make a move.

They opened their doors at almost the same moment. Zach slid out of the truck and caught up with Kim as she stepped onto her front porch.

She glanced sideways at him as she slipped her key into

the lock. She must have seen something in his expression, because she said, "Would you like to come in?"

"Yes," he said before she had a chance to change her mind.

She gave him a vaguely quizzical look—probably in response to the eagerness of his reply—then nodded and opened the door. "I'll make coffee, if you like."

He stepped into the house behind her, closed the door and reached for her. "Coffee isn't what I had in mind," he murmured.

He was pleased that she was smiling when she tilted her face up to meet his kiss.

He kissed her lightly at first. Almost lazily. He could feel her relaxing against him as her arms went slowly around his waist.

He eased into a deeper embrace. She tasted so good to him, sweet and spicy, making him hunger for more. He pulled her closer, allowing his hands to stray just a bit. She was slender, but nicely curved. Her hips flared gently from a tiny waist. He could feel her breasts pressing against his chest, small but firm. His palms itched to cup them. Very slowly he moved his right hand upward.

Kim stiffened for a moment, then went very still when he slipped his hand between them. Keeping her mouth occupied with his lips and tongue, he stroked the side of her left breast. When she made no move to draw away from him, he closed his hand more boldly over her softness. He felt a tremor ripple through her, but she didn't pull away. Her arms tightened and moved to his neck, bringing them into even closer contact.

Zach was wryly amused at his own kick of excitement. He felt rather like a nervous schoolboy with his first girlfriend. He had to remind himself that Kim wasn't the first woman he'd kissed, and hers wasn't the first breast he'd held. But that didn't seem to make any difference just now.

He could hardly remember any other woman when Kim was in his arms.

Kim was different from the others. He was different when he was with her. And he reacted to that realization with equal parts of pleasure and uneasiness.

Somehow they ended up on her couch. Her hunter green pantsuit was open to the waist and Zach was able to see for himself just how perfectly she was formed. Her breasts were creamy, pink tipped, soft. He nuzzled his cheek against her, murmuring his pleasure at the taste and feel of her.

Kim's fingers were clenched in his hair, and her heart pounded rapidly beneath his exploring fingers. Her glossy brown hair tumbled wildly around her flushed face. Her eyes were heavy lidded, so dark he could hardly distinguish the pupils from the irises. Her full, pouty mouth was slightly swollen and damp from his kisses.

He thought she'd never looked more beautiful.

"Kim." His voice was rough, husky. "Kim, I—"

He broke off with a groan of protest when a shrill beeping suddenly erupted from the vicinity of his belt.

He fumbled for the button that would silence the pager, almost groaning again when his movements brought certain inflamed parts of him into intimate contact with Kim. He heard her breath catch just before he forced himself to move off her.

He glanced at the number on the pager and drew a deep breath. "A search party's being formed. May I use your phone?"

She nodded. "Of course." Her voice was breathless, a half octave higher than usual.

Watching in regret as she rapidly rearranged her clothing and buttoned her top all the way to her throat, Zach placed the call from her living room extension. It didn't take him long. He hung up with a sigh of resignation.

"I have to go. An elderly man has wandered into the

Ozark Forest and he may not survive the night if he isn't found."

He saw the concern flash into her eyes—and something else. Relief? Or disappointment? "You should hurry," she urged him. "They need you."

It was the first time he'd ever hesitated to answer a call. He drew a deep breath, shoved a hand through his disheveled hair and leaned over to brush a quick kiss across her mouth. "I'll call you."

She nodded. She didn't quite meet his eyes. "Be careful."

He flashed her a smile. "Careful is my middle name."

He noticed that she looked decidedly skeptical as he left her on that quip.

Kim was in love. And it scared her half to death.

The being scared part was certainly nothing unusual for her. But being in love was definitely all new. She'd never been in love before. She'd fought like crazy to keep from falling this time.

Apparently she hadn't fought hard enough.

She had all the classic symptoms. She couldn't eat. Wasn't sleeping well. Was having trouble concentrating on her schoolwork. Found herself drifting into glazed-eyed daydreaming spells with no warning.

Being in love, she'd decided glumly, was a lot like having the flu.

Whenever she heard a siren pass by on the street—police car? ambulance? or fire truck?—she wondered if Zach was rushing into danger. She thought about Zach any time she heard about a daring rescue on the TV news. She thought of him each time she saw a bright blue sky, the same bright blue as his eyes. She thought of him every time it rained—or even looked as if it might.

She simply thought of him. Often.

She tried to decide what, exactly, it was about him that

she loved. His pretty face? His easy charm? His courage? His devotion to his family? His sense of humor? His success at teasing her out of her fears without making her feel foolish for having them? His confidence in her, even when she doubted herself? The way he had of seeming to understand her even when she struggled to express her thoughts or feelings? All of the above?

She tried to remind herself of the things about him she didn't like. Though it was harder to come up with that list, she managed to find a few. His cockiness. His refusal to accept even the possibility of defeat. His inability to believe in his own mortality. She worried that he was going to be seriously injured—or worse—by being overconfident during one of his rescues or stunts. He always laughed her off when she tried to tell him so, which irritated her.

She tried to keep their differences in mind, preparing herself for the worst if those differences should eventually split them up. His love of adventure, her need for security. His closeness to his family, her own lack of any family ties. His laid-back attitude, her constant fretting about details. His refusal to look beyond the present, her obsession with planning and attempting to control the future.

As easy as it was for her to be with Zach, and increasingly with Tom, she still found it difficult to blend in with their close crowd of friends. Their recklessness worried her, their jokes sometimes eluded her and their interests seemed quite different from her own.

The women who weren't attached—and some of the ones who *were*—flirted almost shamelessly with Zach, right in front of Kim. He deflected it easily enough, didn't seem to take it all that seriously, which made Kim even more aware of how accustomed he was to such behavior. Zach was simply the type of man that women went after, sometimes aggressively, just as men tended to zero in on a certain type of woman.

There were times she thought the others might be secretly wondering what Zach saw in her.

Maybe it wasn't love, she told herself bravely. Maybe it was only infatuation. Maybe she wouldn't be devastated when it ended, only temporarily disappointed.

She didn't believe a word of it. Sometime during the past month she had fallen in love with Zach McCain. And, since Kim was not a woman who gave her love easily, and never lightly, she knew it wouldn't be that simple for her when the relationship ended, as she still feared it must.

But in the meantime, it was all she could do to keep up with him.

"Come on, Kim, try it. It'll be fun." Zach's voice was pure liquid seduction. He knew, darn him, that she had a tough time resisting him when he spoke in just that tone.

Kim looked at him and swallowed a sigh. The early-October afternoon sun glinted off his dark hair and sparkled in his bright blue eyes. He wore a blue-and-white-striped denim shirt rolled back on his forearms, and faded jeans that hugged his lean hips and long legs.

"I don't think so," she said, struggling to sound resolute.

"Kim, they're only go-carts. It's like riding a lawn mower, only more fun. If you can drive a car, you can handle one of these," he said enticingly, waving a hand toward the row of brightly colored little vehicles nearby.

She looked suspiciously at the go-carts. They seemed to her to be little more than a seat, a steering wheel and a very loud motor. She couldn't imagine that driving one would be as much fun as Zach seemed to believe.

"Couldn't we play miniature golf, instead?" she asked, waving toward the nearby golf course with its cute little waterfalls and windmills and other clever decor.

"Sure," Zach agreed with a shrug. "Right after we ride the go-carts."

"I'll play golf with you, Kim," Tom offered. He leaned

lazily against a blue-painted wrought-iron fence, watching the increasingly familiar verbal showdown between Kim and Zach.

Zach sent Tom a narrow look, then turned back to Kim. "If you listen to him, you'll never try anything new. Trust me. This is perfectly safe. And lots of fun. You can drive like a little blue-haired granny, if you want."

She looked doubtfully at the track, where a couple of teenagers were spinning around the curves with what looked to her like reckless abandon. What if they smashed into one another? What if one of the carts went out of control, sailed into the air, over the tires lining the track, and crashed into a wall or something?

Zach had assured her nothing like that could happen, but Kim was very good at imagining worst-case scenarios. "Well, I—"

"Great," Zach exclaimed, deliberately misreading her hesitation. "You'll love it."

This time she almost did sigh. How did he do this to her so easily? She found herself torn between her long-ingrained caution and the desire to please him. Not to mention the blow to her pride if she refused.

"Okay, I'll try it," she agreed reluctantly. "But I'm not promising to like it."

He chuckled and gave her a squeeze that nearly emptied her lungs. "Attagirl."

"It really is fun, Kim," Tom assured her with a smile. "I'll help you strap in, if you like."

"I'll help her," Zach said quickly, his arm tightening around her waist. "C'mon, Kim, let me show you how they work."

Kim had survived a big exam that morning and was taking the afternoon off, a break she well deserved because she'd worked double shifts at the diner for the past couple of days. It was a weekday afternoon and a school day, so the "family fun center," as the place was called, was nearly deserted. When the two teenagers finished their stint in the go-carts, Kim, Zach and Tom were the only ones waiting to take their place.

Zach helped Kim into the first cart. She felt as though she was practically sitting on the ground, her knees bent sharply upward. It was hardly a comfortable position. "Don't I need a helmet or something?" she asked nervously.

Waving off the attendant who approached to help, Zach helped her strap in. "You don't need a helmet. Surely you've noticed that the center of gravity is very low in these things. It's almost impossible to flip it over, and you have this nice, sturdy roll bar if anything should go wrong."

He gave her quick directions for the controls—which consisted of an accelerator pedal and a brake pedal. And then he stepped back. "I'll be right behind you," he promised.

She doubted that he would remain there long. Something told her that Zach wouldn't be content to drive at the speed of the "blue-haired granny" she planned to emulate.

The track attendant gave a signal for her to pull out. Taking a deep breath, Kim pressed the accelerator, and gasped when the cart gave a jerk and a roar as though it couldn't wait to speed away with her. And then she eased onto the track. Behind her she thought she heard Zach yell, "And they're off!"

When she climbed out of the cart some fifteen minutes later, she was windblown and winded, laughing so hard she could hardly stand upright. It had taken her only two laps to get into the spirit of the sport, especially since Zach and Tom shouted teasing taunts at her every time they passed her. Before she'd known it, she'd had the pedal to the metal, chasing after them as they'd sped away, laughing like the maniacs they were.

Zach leapt out of his own go-cart and caught her around the waist, grinning. "Didn't I tell you you'd like it?" he demanded.

She nodded. "Okay, you were right," she admitted, still trying to catch her breath. "That *was* fun."

"I'm always right," he reminded her smugly.

Tom snorted loudly, making Kim giggle again. And then he said, "Ready for that golf game now, Kim?"

She nodded eagerly, turning toward the appealing course. "I'd love to."

"Okay," Zach agreed without a great deal of enthusiasm. And then his eyes lit up. "But after that—laser tag!"

Kim didn't know what laser tag was, but it didn't sound like something she was in any hurry to try. "Well, I..."

Zach slung an arm around her shoulders. "Trust me," he said with a flash of white teeth. "You'll love it."

The radio in Zach's truck was turned down low, so it was hard to hear the sound from the film playing on the large screen at the 112 Drive-In. Kim didn't notice. She was too busy being kissed by Zach.

She lay against the back of the seat in Zach's arms. He loomed over her, his mouth on hers, his hands roaming restlessly over her. The windows around them were fogged over. Kim was dimly aware that she was making out in a public place for the first time in her life, but she pushed the niggling reprimand away. It was dark, after all. Zach had parked in a very secluded corner. And this was a drive-in movie. It was practically against the rules *not* to make out.

Zach had found it hard to believe when Kim had admitted she'd never been to a drive-in. Her aunt Pearl hadn't approved, she'd explained, and after her aunt died, there weren't many drive-ins left to sample. This was one of the few that had survived the national changeover to multiplex theater chains. Zach had insisted on bringing her here after their afternoon playing games at the fun center. He hadn't invited Tom along for this outing.

Zach finally lifted his head for a breather. "Well?" he murmured, his voice husky, his eyes glinting in the darkness. "How do you like the drive-in so far?"

She managed a shaky smile. "I couldn't begin to tell you what the movie's about."

He shrugged and spoke against her cheek. "So who comes to the drive-in to watch a movie?"

She caught her breath when his hand made a lazy foray down her side, stroking her hip and then her thigh. "You—" She stopped to clear her voice. "You sound as though you've spent a lot of time here...not watching movies."

She caught the flash of his smile in the shadows. "Me? Of course not. I'm just going by what other people have told me."

"Bull—"

He laughed and covered her mouth with his again. And then slid his hand upward to cup her right breast.

Kim trembled, but didn't resist. Zach's touch was the most incredibly thrilling experience of her admittedly sheltered life. The feelings he brought out in her when he kneaded her, when he rotated his thumb against her nipple, when he lowered his mouth to nuzzle her through her blouse, were indescribably arousing.

Again Zach was introducing her to something new. Exciting. Dangerous to her peace of mind.

He slipped a hand beneath the hem of her soft pink sweater, his palm warm against her bare side. She squirmed a bit when he raised the hand to cup her breast through her bra.

"Shh," he murmured, nibbling at her lips. "I just want to touch you."

"It's not that," she assured him shakily. "It's just—well, we're in your truck."

He chuckled and his fingertips slid beneath the lace edge of her bra, making her shiver in delight. "No one can see us," he murmured. "I promised you a real drive-in experience, didn't I?"

He was turning her spine to liquid. She clung to his shoulders to hold herself upright. "Er, doesn't *anyone* come to watch the movie?"

"Movie? There's a movie?" He lowered his mouth to her throat.

"Mmm—never mind." She tilted her head back and closed her eyes, letting her fingers tangle in his thick, dark hair.

Zach slid a hand slowly down her tummy, tickled her navel with one fingertip, then moved very slowly lower. She felt herself tensing when he stroked her thigh, then ran his fingers lightly between her legs. Again Zach murmured reassurances, kissing her until her ears buzzed.

By the time he gave her a chance for air, he had her cupped in his hand, and his fingers were doing things to her that made her squirm in a combination of pleasure, frustration and discomfiture.

"Zach." His name came out on a gasp. She was embarrassed to think he might feel her heat and dampness through her jeans. "I—"

"I know," he murmured, taking a deep, ragged-edged breath. "We have to stop now. This isn't the place—or the time."

"No." She wondered if he heard the regret in her voice.

He shifted uncomfortably on the seat, then helped her straighten her clothes. "Man," he said with a rough laugh. "I think I'm getting too old for this."

She knew her face was flaming, and was grateful for the darkness that hid her fiery blush from him. All of a sudden she was feeling slow and awkward again. Zach might have had experience at this sort of thing, but she had not. She was twenty-four years old and had just had her first "make out'' session at the drive-in. And while it might have just been a lark for Zach, it had meant all too much to her.

She wasn't naive enough that she didn't know where this relationship was headed if things kept going at the pace they had been. True to his word, Zach hadn't pushed her into anything she wasn't ready for—other than the occasional go-cart ride or laser tag game, of course—but she knew he would soon grow impatient with her dithering. As he'd said, he was too old to be content for long with kisses and caresses. He would want more.

And so would she. But did she really have the courage to take this further? To become Zach McCain's lover?

She stared grimly at the big screen where Sylvester Stallone seemed intent on blowing up yet another terrorist hideaway.

Zach seemed to sense her sudden change of mood. ''Kim? You okay?''

She nodded. ''Just tired, I guess,'' she said. ''It's been a busy day.''

''Would you like me to take you home now?''

''You wouldn't mind?''

He shook his head. ''Of course not. I've seen this movie, anyway.''

She managed a smile and tried for a teasing tone. ''What, did you bring someone else here last night?''

He didn't laugh. ''You know better than that.''

An awkward silence fell in the wake of her flat jest. And then Zach reached for the ignition. ''I'll take you home.''

She couldn't even joke like the rest of his crowd, Kim thought with a touch of sadness. She should have known better than to try.

Zach and Tom were in the parking lot outside Zach's apartment building a few days later, their heads under the hood of Tom's classic red MG, backsides in the air as they worked on tuning the temperamental engine. Zach nearly smashed his head on the raised hood when someone suddenly patted his butt.

He swiveled his head around to find a well-built blonde in a form-hugging sweater smiling at him, her red-nailed hand still resting on his hip. "Hi, Zach," she said, her voice low and liquid. "I thought I recognized you."

He straightened nonchalantly, causing her hand to fall to her side. "Hi, Lisa. How's it going?"

"Fine. Hey, Tom."

Tom stood, wiping his hands on a shop towel. "Hey, Lisa. It's been a while."

She nodded, her gaze turning immediately back toward Zach. "A long time," she murmured, just a hint of accusation in her voice. "Lose my number, Zach?"

"You know how it goes. Been busy." He thought he'd made it clear to her some time ago that there was never going to be anything between them, but apparently she hadn't quite got the message. Lisa didn't like to think there was any guy who could resist her.

She gave him a look that had made stronger men than Zach melt. "I see. So, maybe you'll have an evening soon when you aren't busy?" The little smile and flutter of lashes that accompanied the suggestion had been perfected through diligent practice. Some of it on him.

"I don't think so. I'm sort of seeing someone now."

She lifted an eyebrow. "Seeing someone? Steadily?"

He nodded. "Yeah. We've been going out for over a month."

Lisa's expression combined irritation, disbelief and wry amusement. "I can't help finding this hard to believe. I thought you made it a practice never to tie yourself down to any one woman."

"That was before I met Kim," Zach replied with a smile and a slight shrug. "Things are different now."

"Kim?" Lisa sounded as though she'd never heard the name before.

He nodded, making no effort to further identify her. Kim was skittish enough about their relationship already. One thing he didn't need was Lisa Callahan stirring up trouble just for the fun of it.

Lisa shook her head. "How very interesting. And unexpected. Why don't you give me a call when you're free again? Shouldn't be long, I would think. Maybe I'll have an open evening to see you then. Perhaps."

"Hey, *I'm* not seeing anyone right now, Lisa," Tom piped up, a glint of mischief in his green eyes.

Lisa flicked him a vague smile. "Lucky you. Well, I have to be going. Bye, boys."

As soon as she was out of hearing, Tom made a sound of an airplane whistling into a crash landing. "Guess she shot me down neatly enough," he added.

"Count your blessings," Zach advised. "You know what a headache she can be."

"Yeah, but I've got a big stash of aspirin. It's been so damned long since I've had a, er, headache that I haven't needed *anything* out of my medicine cabinet."

Zach chuckled ruefully. "I know that feeling."

"Yeah, right. You and Kim have hardly been out of each other's sight for weeks now."

Zach cleared his throat and bent back to the car. "Where's the new oil filter?"

Tom propped his fists on his hips and cocked his head, looking at Zach quizzically. After a long, pointed pause, he said, "Don't tell me..."

"Tell you what?"

"You and Kim. You really haven't, er...?"

Feeling his face warm, Zach ducked beneath the hood. "Are you going to hand me that filter or not?"

"Well, I'll be damned."

"Drop it, Tom." Zach had no intention of discussing

his and Kim's sex life—or lack of one—with Tom, despite certain conversations they had shared in the past. Besides, what would he say? As fast as Kim's moods seemed to change, even Zach never knew quite where they stood from one date to the next!

Tom wasn't notably intimidated by Zach's growl. "So that's why you've been a bit surly lately. Not only are you in lo-o-ve, you're frustrated. Who'd have believed it?"

An attack of nerves kicked Zach squarely in the stomach in response to the L word, even so teasingly said. He still hadn't decided quite what it was he felt for Kim, though he'd had a sneaking suspicion for days now. He didn't need Tom to analyze his feelings for him. "This discussion is closed, Lowery. Now, either hand me the damned filter or finish this job by yourself."

Chuckling, Tom bent to pick up the filter from the pavement beside the car. "Don't get mad, Zach. I think it's sweet that you're giving Kim a traditional courtship."

Sweet? Now, that was carrying this too far.

Deliberately, Zach shook the dipstick in his hand. Drops of oil flew, most of them landing on Tom's gray sweatshirt. He jumped back, cursing fluently.

"Sorry about that," Zach murmured.

Tom swiped futilely at his shirt, succeeding only in smearing the oil stains. "Damn it, McCain, that was unnecessary. All you had to do was tell me to change the subject, and I would've."

Zach sent his annoyed pal a look of disbelief, but didn't bother to point out how many times he *had* asked Tom to change the subject.

Still grumbling at each other, they went back to work on the car. Tom very wisely didn't bring Kim up again and, to make up for his mild tantrum, Zach went out of his way to be in a better mood. They finished the tune-up in relatively good spirits, to the relief of both of them.

It occurred to Zach that no woman had been even close

to coming between him and Tom before. He assured himself that Kim wasn't doing so now, even unwittingly. But it was rather daunting to realize that if any woman could interfere with this close, twenty-year friendship, it would be Kim.

Which meant that he was getting in deeper than he'd admitted even to himself. And perhaps that L word was so unnerving because it hit all too close to home.

Chapter Nine

It wasn't one of Kim's better days. She'd awakened with a sinus headache that, even late in the afternoon, was still hanging around to annoy her. She was pretty sure she'd done a lousy job on a test she'd taken that morning. She simply hadn't been able to concentrate. She wanted to blame it on her headache, but she suspected that had little to do with her distraction.

She'd been held up in traffic leaving the campus—a fender bender at the intersection of Dickson and College had created a nasty jam—and had been late to work, earning herself a scowl and a few pointed words from Maggie, who wasn't in a particularly good mood today, either. A strong wind had blown all afternoon, leaving her hair a tangled mess that she'd tried to hastily smooth into a neat bun when she'd arrived at the diner. She knew she'd looked better.

And then she met the blonde.

The striking woman was sitting in a booth with an

equally attractive companion when Kim approached with her order pad. She noted automatically that she hadn't seen the women in the diner before; she wouldn't have suspected that this was the type of establishment they usually frequented.

"Would you like something to drink while you look at the menu?" she asked, pencil poised above her pad.

The blonde set her menu aside unopened. "Just coffee for me," she said. "Decaf."

The brunette on the other side of the booth nodded. "Same for me."

"I'll be right back," Kim promised. Maybe the women had needed a quiet place for a discussion, she thought idly. Other than to make sure their coffee cups remained filled, she wouldn't bother them while they visited.

She was filling their cups when the blonde asked, "Your name isn't Kim, is it?"

Kim lifted an eyebrow. "Why, yes. Have we met?" She usually had an excellent memory for faces, and this woman didn't look in the least familiar to her.

"No." The blonde studied Kim in apparent curiosity, then glanced quickly at her friend before explaining, "I'm a friend of Zach McCain's."

Of course she was. Feeling herself stiffen, Kim said, "Oh."

Brilliant comment, Kim.

"I'm Lisa," the blonde said. "This is my friend Camilla."

"Nice to meet you. Would you like pie or anything to go with your coffee?" Kim asked, rather hoping her ploy to change the subject would be successful.

"No, thank you," Lisa murmured a bit impatiently. And then she immediately returned to her own choice of conversation. "I'd heard through the grapevine that Zach was dating a waitress here. I have to admit, I was curious about you."

Kim heard the chill in her own voice when she replied, "Oh?"

"Apparently you hold some sort of record for keeping his attention. Congratulations."

Camilla smothered a giggle.

Kim lifted her chin and retreated behind dignified courtesy. "If you'll excuse me, I have other customers. Please let me know if there's anything else you need."

She turned and walked to the next table. She didn't think it was an accident that she overheard Lisa say, "Can you believe it? What on earth does Zach see in her?"

What, indeed? Kim had been asking herself the same question for weeks.

She tried not to let Lisa get to her. Fortunately, the women didn't linger long, nor did they request a refill on their coffee. Apparently they'd accomplished what they'd set out to do—check out Kim.

She told herself that Lisa was probably a woman scorned. She couldn't imagine Zach being interested in a snob like that for long. Zach was many things, but snob was definitely not one of them. So Kim wouldn't take the blonde's comments personally. She probably would have said much the same things to any woman Zach dated.

But the doubts remained at the back of her mind, ticking like a very quiet bomb waiting to explode into full-fledged paranoia if she wasn't very careful.

Kim thought it was entirely possible that her lungs were going to implode. She drew a burning breath into them, and released it in a series of panting puffs. Okay, so she was still alive. But she wouldn't put any money on that condition lasting much longer. Each time her bike tire hit a rock or rough patch of ground, her teeth slammed together and every joint in her body shrieked in outrage.

"Zach," she gasped, her voice thready, "I really need to rest now."

He immediately locked the brakes on his mountain bike. Since he was riding directly in front of her on a trail that was little more than a thin line up a mountainside, she almost ran smack into the back of him. Her borrowed bike fishtailed wildly before she put her feet down and brought it to a standstill.

"You okay, Kim?" Tom asked from his position in the rear as he expertly braked his own bike.

Trying not to wheeze, she nodded. "Just winded," she managed to say fairly coherently. "I guess I'm out of shape."

"Not that I can tell," Zach replied with a wolfish grin, giving her a teasing leer as he tugged his helmet off and ran a hand through his disheveled hair.

"Me, either," Tom put in promptly.

Zach sent his friend a frown, then turned back to Kim. "Let's take a break."

She almost wept in gratitude as she climbed shakily off the bike Zach had borrowed from his sister Elaine. When Zach had suggested a bike outing on this beautiful, warm autumn Saturday, she had readily accepted, pleased at what a relatively tame suggestion it had been, coming from him. Compared to skydiving or bungee jumping or some of his other bright ideas, biking didn't sound at all threatening. She didn't have a bike, but he'd waved off that single obstacle, assuring her that Elaine wouldn't mind lending hers.

Little had Kim known that Zach's idea of a relaxing ride was to go up the side of a mountain on a trail barely wider than a bicycle tire, a path that occasionally wound so close to a steep bluff that Kim had held her breath in fear of toppling right over the edge.

She noted in some resentment that neither Zach nor Tom was even breathing hard when they propped their bikes beside the trail and reached for their water bottles. Kim peeled off the helmet that seemed to have gained ten pounds since she'd strapped it on at the beginning of the ride. Her hair was damp and flattened against her head; she did her best to fluff it with her hand.

Her insulated water bottle had kept the water relatively cool; she chugged it gratefully. She sank to the ground beneath an oak tree that was in the process of going bald for winter; yellow leaves drifted lazily downward each time a breeze blew. She'd worn a white T-shirt and red-and-white windsuit, and had long since shed the jacket. The light breeze felt good on her bare arms.

She drew her legs up, tucked her sneakers in front of her and rested her forearms on her knees as she caught her breath and watched Zach and Tom argue over who could have ridden farther in the shortest time. Those two loved to bicker, she thought with a shake of her head. If they didn't have anything legitimate to quarrel about, they made something up. They were almost as bad as Maggie. But the bond between them was undeniable. She'd met brothers who didn't seem as close as Zach and Tom.

Both Zach and Tom were wearing black shorts and gray T-shirts with the fire department logo printed on the left breast. She knew they hadn't planned the matching outfits, since they'd teased each other about their choices when they'd first met at her apartment early that morning before making the long drive into the mountains. Still, she couldn't help noticing how much alike they were, in overall appearance as well as temperament.

Though Zach was dark and Tom sandy haired, and Zach an inch or two taller, they were both broad shouldered, slim hipped and long legged. They made an attractive pair, and Kim certainly understood why they both got so much attention. Yet, as much as she'd grown to like Tom, and as good-looking as he was, it was Zach to whom her gaze was drawn again and again.

Abandoning the good-natured argument with Tom, Zach folded himself onto the ground beside Kim, one arm propped behind her. Not quite touching, but close enough to make her feel the warmth radiating from him. Even that was enough to make her pulse jump.

He smiled at her. "Your cheeks are red."

"I'm not surprised," she said ruefully. "It's been ages since I was on a bike. When you suggested a bike ride, I thought you meant through a nice, flat park or something. I didn't realize you wanted to scale a mountain."

"Honey, when I scale a mountain, I do it with ropes and cleats. This trail isn't all that steep."

There were several things in that statement that made her frown, but she found herself dwelling on the casual endearment. No man had ever called her "honey," before. She didn't know if she liked it or not.

She had a sneaking suspicion that she did.

"Hey, Kim." Tom knelt beside her, holding something in his hand. "Look what I found."

At first she thought it was just a small, pinkish rock. Then she looked more closely and saw the streaks of glittering quartz embedded in the stone. In the sunlight the rock looked as if it had been dusted with diamonds.

"Pretty," she said with a smile.

Like a boy offering a tribute to his favorite teacher, Tom held the rock out to her. "For you."

Hiding her amusement, she accepted the gift gravely. "Why, thank you."

Zach cleared his throat. "Damn it, Lowery, are you flirting again? We have got to find you a woman of your own."

Tom sat cross-legged on the ground and grinned at them. "Why? I like yours."

Kim blushed.

Zach growled, then turned pointedly to Kim. "As soon as you're ready, we'll go on up the trail. There's a mountain stream ahead that falls about six feet into a deep, clear pool. It's a pretty spot, especially now with all the fall colors. I think you'll like it."

She almost groaned at the thought of getting back on the bike, but the waterfall intrigued her. She'd always liked waterfalls. "How much farther?"

Zach shrugged. "Just a little way. And it's mostly level ground. We've gone about as high as we're going today. Once we pass the pool, the rest of the ride is downhill."

She didn't entirely trust him on that. A little way for Zach might seem to Kim like a very long way, indeed. Still, she wouldn't mind seeing that waterfall. And she particularly liked the sound of that downhill part.

She drew a deep breath and pushed her protesting body upright. "Okay. Let's go."

They'd left their bikes in the order in which they'd been riding, Zach first, then Kim, and Tom at the back. Kim strapped on her helmet and swung herself onto her seat while the guys were still fussing with their bikes. Tom had already mounted up and Zach was just about to get on his bike when he glanced over his shoulder and frowned. Kim wondered what had suddenly bothered him.

"Hey, Tom," he said, pulling his bike over to the side, "why don't you take the lead this time. You know where we're headed."

"That's okay, Zach. I don't mind riding back here," Tom assured him, sounding suspiciously bland.

Wondering what was going on between them now, Kim looked from one to the other in question.

Zach leveled at Tom a look that should have made him blanch. "I'll take the rear this time," he repeated firmly. "You lead off."

Tom exhaled gustily and shrugged. "Okay. If you insist."

"I insist."

Tom flicked a grin at Kim, who was still watching them curiously, then pedaled past her. "Stay close, kiddies," he called over his shoulder. "Wouldn't want anyone getting lost on the trail."

Deciding there was simply no understanding these two, Kim swallowed a moan and kicked off, bending low over the handlebars as she told herself that she *could* do this.

Zach eyed Kim's sweetly curved backside in front of him and wondered grimly why he hadn't realized before just what view Tom had been enjoying at the beginning of the ride.

He knew his buddy was only teasing with his flirting with Kim, but it was starting to get on Zach's nerves a bit. Maybe because he was becoming just a little insecure about his relationship with Kim.

It didn't seem to be progressing as quickly as he'd hoped. In fact, he thought it was fair to say that Kim seemed to be backing away. It was a subtle change in her attitude, one he'd wondered if he was imagining...but he knew he wasn't. Since their date at the drive-in, there was definitely something different about Kim.

He only wished he knew what it was.

He'd been on his best behavior. He hadn't complained—much—when she'd suddenly become so busy with schoolwork and her job and other obligations that she'd hardly had time to see him during the past ten days. He hadn't pushed when she'd silently made it clear that their dates, for now, would end at her doorstep. He'd even included Tom today because she seemed to relax more with Zach when Tom was around.

He suspected that her experience with men had been limited, to say the least, and he considered himself nobly waiting until she was ready to carry their relationship to a new level. He'd thought of carefully bringing the subject up, letting her know that he was interested in moving on, but was willing to wait. He'd hesitated because he wasn't sure exactly how long his patience would last.

He wanted Kim. Wanted more than kisses and the occasional stolen caress. He wanted to make love with her. To spend the night with her. To watch her wake in the morning sun. Though he'd always been discriminating in his practices, he wasn't used to having a long-term platonic relationship with a woman he desired.

Ahead of him on the trail she shifted on her narrow bike seat, and he nearly groaned when her bottom gave an enticing wriggle. They really were going to have to have that talk soon, he thought. He'd like to at least have an idea of where they stood.

He wasn't accustomed to being this uncertain with a woman. And he didn't care for it. Maybe he'd become rather spoiled—okay, he *had* become spoiled—but he'd never even considered the possibility that he would finally give his heart to a woman, and she wouldn't be entirely certain she wanted it. In the past, Zach had been as lucky in love as he had in everything else, and he didn't want that record to end with Kim.

He wasn't sure either his heart or his ego could take it.

Deliberately shaking off the uncharacteristic attack of nerves, he called out to Kim, pointing out the widening stream along which the bike trail now ran. "This is the stream I was telling you about," he said. "It twists and turns a few times, gets wider and deeper, then falls into the pool."

She glanced over her shoulder. She had a rather glazed expression on her face, as though she'd gone beyond exhaustion into near catatonia. He felt a twinge of guilt. He hadn't meant to cause her discomfort. He hadn't realized what a challenging ride this would be for someone who hadn't been on a bike in a while. It was only a few miles, and on mostly level ground—well, somewhat level. And Kim looked as though she was in great shape.

"How much farther?" she asked.

"Not much. Do you want to stop and rest again?"

She shook her head, her sleek, aerodynamic, black-and-purple helmet glinting in the sunlight that broke through the autumn leaves overhead. Her cheeks were still red and there was a sheen of perspiration on her upper lip, but her mouth was set in determination. "I can make it," she called back.

"Attagirl," he said, promising himself he would take her for an elegant dinner or something to make this up to her. He would even put on a tie again, though the last time he'd worn one for her the evening hadn't turned out exactly as he'd hoped.

Still swollen from the autumn rains, the stream began to run faster, louder, tumbling over rocks, splashing against the banks. Kim sent Zach a smile over her shoulder, letting him know that she appreciated the beauty of the scene, which made him feel somewhat better about bringing her up here despite the effort required.

The waterfall was just ahead. He could already hear it, noisy despite its relatively short drop. The trail had taken a downward turn, making riding easier, though faster. Kim was clinging to her handlebars, but handling the rough trail well. For an amateur, she'd made a darned good showing today, he thought with a touch of pride Tom probably would have mocked.

Zach thought Kim would enjoy seeing the pool. It was a nice place, particularly at this time of year and in the spring, when the dogwoods in the surrounding forest were all in bloom. He and Tom had taken dips in the pool a couple of times after riding up here. It was cool and deep, more than twelve feet at the spot where the waterfall poured into it. The water ran off into the underground streams that formed so many of the caves hidden within the Ozarks.

Tom brought his bike to a stop at the edge of a line of small boulders that marked the beginning of the waterfall. Knowing Kim would be pleased that they had reached another resting place, Zach called out encouragingly, "This is it, Kim."

She glanced over her shoulder to say something in response. And then suddenly her bike skidded and jerked, and Kim went sailing over the handlebars.

To Zach's horror, she tumbled straight over the side of the embankment at the end of the trail.

The impact of the six-foot fall knocked the breath out of Kim's already burning lungs. And then the cold water closed over her head and she was sinking into the dark depths.

She couldn't swim. She'd never learned. She could feel her shoes and clothing and the suddenly heavy bike helmet dragging her down toward the bottom of the pool. Stunned from the swiftness of the accident, it was a very long moment before she could force herself to react, to kick upward.

Or was she headed upward? Still dazed, she was disoriented, not quite sure where she should go. She began to panic, her lungs aching for air, her limbs growing heavier by the moment. The helmet on her head was beginning to feel like a block of concrete; she clawed at the straps, trying to free herself, her frenzy growing when the wet straps stubbornly resisted her.

Where was Zach?

Had there been air, she would have sobbed in relief when strong hands suddenly grabbed hold of her. Fighting down the panic, and remembering stories of drowning victims hurting both themselves and their rescuers by struggling, she forced herself to remain still while he towed her upward.

She and Zach broke the surface with gasps for air. Holding her with an arm beneath her breasts, he towed her to the side, where Tom waited to lift her out of the water and onto the packed dirt and autumn-brown grass at the side of the pool. Zach shoved himself out of the water right behind her.

Tom made quick work of taking off Kim's helmet. Zach, she thought, must have ripped his off before jumping in after her. His hair was plastered to his head as he knelt beside her, dripping and looking half-distraught.

"Are you all right?" he asked gruffly.

She tried to speak, then settled for a nod when her voice refused to comply. She'd begun to shake, so hard her teeth were rattling. It was partly because of the cold. The water had been icy, and the breeze that had been so welcome earlier now made her shiver. She was also trembling in delayed reaction. Everything had happened so quickly, and she'd been so frightened alone under that water, even knowing that Zach would be there for her.

Zach pulled her roughly into his arms. "I'm sorry," he said into her wet hair. "Honey, I'm so sorry. I had no idea anything like that would happen."

"I'm going to try to find something to dry her off," Tom said, giving Kim's shoulder a quick squeeze as he rose. "I think there's a hand towel in my bike bag."

"There's one in mine, too," Zach said. "Bring those and her jacket."

"Be right back." Tom started up the rocky embankment to where they'd left the bikes, climbing like an expert. Which, Kim thought dimly, he probably was.

Zach ran a hand over Kim's arms and legs. "Are you hurt anywhere? Are you in any pain?"

She shook her head against his shoulder. "No. Just…just scared. I can't swim."

"It's okay. I was right behind you."

"I know. But—it seemed like a long time." Her lips were quivering so hard it was difficult to speak.

Zach cradled her against him, sharing what warmth he had. "I know," he said again. "But everything's okay now."

She groaned. "I feel so stupid."

"No," he protested immediately, "don't say that. Your tire hit a rock. It could have happened to anyone. I've gone over a few handlebars myself."

That didn't make her feel much better. Zach probably hadn't fallen off a bike since he was a kid. She'd bet none of his adventurous friends would have fallen into a pool and have to be rescued during what should have been a pleasant outing.

Tom skidded back down the hillside in a miniature avalanche of pebbles, his hands full. He tossed one of the towels at Zach and used the other to swipe at Kim's hair and face. "We'll get you as dry as we can," he said. "At least those wind slacks you're wearing will dry quickly."

"I'm freezing," she admitted with another shiver.

Tom nodded sympathetically. "You must be. You can zip into this jacket and that will help. Er, would you like to take that wet shirt off first? Zach and I will look away."

She thought about it for a moment, and then realized how much better she would feel without the soggy T-shirt clinging to her skin. The windsuit jacket was lined with a soft cotton that would feel so much nicer. She nodded. "Yes, please."

It took her longer than it should have to pull the shirt over her head and zip herself into the jacket. Her hands were shaking too hard to manage the zipper. Just when she was about to give up, Zach's hands were there, helping her. Blushing, she gave him a grateful smile. He zipped the jacket to her chin.

He'd already shed his wet shirt and was now wearing nothing but his shorts and wet biking shoes. She knew he had to be as cold as she was. She bit her lip in misery at having caused all this trouble. All he'd wanted to do was show her a pretty little mountain pool. And then she'd had to go and fall into it.

What an idiot you are, Kim.

Reassured that she wasn't hurt, Zach gave her a smile that was obviously intended to cheer her. "Once again, I'm all wet around you, Kim."

She tried to return the smile. "Yes. I'm sorry."

He brushed a quick kiss over her mouth. "No apologies. Stuff happens. Now, come on, let's get you back to the truck."

Zach was so sweet and solicitous that evening that Kim thought she just might scream. It was only another indication of the way he thought of her as different from the rest of his crowd, she thought sadly. He wouldn't have hovered over one of them, offering to make soup or order takeout or brew tea or rub their feet or any of the other niceties he'd suggested to Kim. He'd more likely have teased them mercilessly about their clumsiness in falling into the pool.

Of course, none of his other friends *would* have fallen in, she thought, her melancholy and self-pity mounting. And if they had, they'd have been able to swim and rescue themselves, certainly not needing Zach to do so. They'd have crawled out the way Zach had, shivering but laughing ruefully, shrugging off the incident as a great story to tell and exaggerate at a later date.

She'd bet that Lisa, the snobby blonde who'd looked her over at the diner, would never have been caught in such a humiliating position.

By ten o'clock she'd had enough. "No, Zach, I don't need any more tea," she said firmly in answer to his offer. "Thank you."

"You sure?" He stood over her as she sat on her couch snuggled into an afghan he'd wrapped around her, though she'd been warm and dry for hours now. "A snack, maybe? I can make you a sandwich or cut a slice of that cake I saw in your pantry."

"No. Nothing, thanks. Actually, I'm rather tired. I think I'll turn in soon, if you don't mind."

Still looking uncharacteristically somber, Zach nodded. "Good idea. Can I help you with anything?"

"I'm perfectly capable of getting myself ready for bed," she replied a bit dryly. "I've been doing it for years."

"I know, but you had a traumatic experience this afternoon."

"I fell in a pool, Zach. I didn't drown, didn't even get a bruise. I'm fine, really. Just tired."

Looking uncertain, he shuffled his feet on her carpet. "You're sure you want to be alone tonight? I could bunk on the couch, if you want."

She had to fight to keep from rolling her eyes. "Zach. I'm fine. I don't really think the pool's going to come after me during the night since I escaped from it earlier, do you?"

He smiled crookedly. "No. It's just…well, you gave me quite a scare this afternoon," he admitted. "I suppose I'm overreacting, but I'm not used to rescuing anyone who means so much to me. I guess it made me even more aware of the consequences if I wasn't fast enough or strong enough."

She shook her head. "No danger of either of those. You're 'Super Zach,' remember?"

He grimaced. "Yeah, well, I wasn't feeling so super when you went over the side of that embankment."

"Neither was I," she said with a sigh. "But you didn't even hesitate. You jumped right in after me, and saved my life. In case I haven't made it clear enough, I really do appreciate what you did for me."

He waved off her gratitude with a slight frown. "Anyone would have done the same thing."

No, not anyone. Only someone who could swim. Someone who wasn't terrified of water. Or of a six-foot jump over a rocky ledge. Kim would hate to think anyone would have been dependent on *her* to do any of those things. If she'd been the only one around to attempt a rescue, a simple accident could well have turned into a tragedy.

She released a long, spent breath. "Good night, Zach," she said, not bothering to mask the hint. "Thank you again for everything you've done this evening."

He looked at her with a frown, then shook it off and bent to kiss her. His lips clung tenderly to hers for a long moment, but he didn't try to deepen the caress into anything more than a gentle good-night kiss. "Sleep well, Kim," he murmured. "I'll call you tomorrow, okay?"

She didn't quite meet his eyes. "Sure."

Zach hesitated for another minute, then turned on one heel. "I'll let myself out. Call if you need anything."

She only nodded, even though he had his back to her and couldn't see her.

She waited until she heard the front door close behind him before she allowed a small sniffle to escape her. She made no attempt to swipe at the weary tears that were slowly trickling down her cheek.

Chapter Ten

Zach hadn't frequented the diner much since he'd started dating Kim. For one thing, he found it frustrating to be so close to her and have to share her with so many other people. He liked having her full attention, he thought ruefully. Liked being able to touch her and kiss her, which he couldn't do at her workplace.

It also bothered him that his friends seemed compelled to watch him constantly when Kim was around, trying to read his expression, apparently, or gauge his reactions to her.

He didn't know why everyone was making such a big deal out of his relationship with Kim. They all agreed that they liked her, but no one seemed convinced that she and Zach were right for each other. Chris, outspoken as she was, still muttered occasional predictions that Zach was going to end up hurting Kim.

Zach found Chris's gloomy conjectures ironic. Little did she know that Zach was the one who was beginning to worry about getting hurt. Kim had been as elusive as a rare butterfly during the past week since their bike outing. He'd thought she'd been evading him before—now he knew she was. For the past few days he'd been lucky to get to talk to her over the telephone.

That was one of the reasons he joined a few of his friends at the diner after a fire department meeting one Thursday afternoon late in October. He just wanted to see Kim.

He was watching her face when she spotted him. Something flared in her eyes, but she masked it before he could quite identify the emotion. He smiled at her. She nodded a greeting and finished taking the order of two elderly men at a table across the room from Zach and his friends.

"Kim's looking good today," Tom murmured, following Zach's glance.

Zach nodded. She was looking good. She'd pulled her hair back at the top with a clip, letting it fall to her shoulders in back. Her T-shirt was red—his favorite color on her—and her black jeans fit her snugly. She wore her lace-up boots again. For a woman who considered herself timid, she certainly favored bold colors, he thought with a slight smile.

"You still seeing her, Zach?" Mike Henry asked a bit too casually from across the table.

Remembering that Tom had mentioned Mike's interest in possibly asking Kim out himself, Zach frowned at the stocky redhead. "Yeah," he said in a near growl. "I'm still seeing her."

Mike blinked and swallowed. "Oh. Well, great. Y'all make a nice couple."

Zach nodded and looked back toward Kim.

Having finished with her previous customers, she approached their booth. "Pie break?" she asked lightly.

"You bet," Tom answered quickly. "Tell me you aren't out of chocolate."

"We aren't out of chocolate," Kim said obediently.

Tom made a production of wiping his brow in relief. And then he gave Kim a quick, searching look. "You doing okay?"

She acted as though she had no idea why he'd asked. "Yes, I'm fine, thank you," she said without looking at Zach.

He could have assured her that neither he nor Tom had mentioned her biking mishap to the others, but he hoped she knew they wouldn't have done that, anyway. Both he and Tom knew that Kim was a very private person, and wouldn't have appreciated being discussed behind her back. They hadn't turned her embarrassment into an amusing anecdote, as they would have done had it happened to either of them or probably one of their other friends.

Zach waited for Kim to give him a smile, a look, a touch on the shoulder—anything to indicate that she thought of him as different from the others. Special. And that she didn't mind admitting it in front of his friends. She didn't give him an inch.

"What can I get for you, Zach?" she asked when the others had all ordered. He grimly suspected she'd used much the same tone with the two old geezers across the room.

"Coconut," he said. "What time do you get off work tonight?"

She looked a bit surprised that he'd asked, but said, "Seven."

"There's a bluegrass concert downtown tonight at eight. I just heard about it today, and it sounds like fun. Want to go with me?" He knew he'd just chosen a rather Neanderthal method of staking his claim, asking her right in front of everyone this way, but he didn't particularly regret it. It was time for Kim to acknowledge that they had something going on between them—a courtship, Tom had called it. Zach had grown rather fond of the word since.

Kim hesitated only a moment before shaking her head. ''I'm sorry, I can't. I have plans.''

A sudden silence fell around the table. Zach cleared his throat. ''Er, plans?''

''Yes. There's a baby shower for someone in my Sunday School class. I promised I would help serve refreshments.''

''A baby shower.'' He didn't know why he kept repeating what she said. He supposed he was feeling a bit self-conscious about striking out like this in front of his friends. He wasn't sure it had ever happened to him before. ''Oh. Well, I'll call you later tonight, then.''

''Fine.''

She could have sounded a bit more pleased about it, but Zach figured he'd better settle for what he could get.

She moved away and Zach turned back to his friends. Chris was looking at him in open curiosity. ''You and Kim have a fight?'' she asked, as unsubtle as always.

''No, we didn't have a fight,'' Zach replied with a touch of asperity. ''She had plans for tonight. I certainly don't expect her to cancel her plans every time I suggest something.''

Chris didn't look convinced. ''She didn't exactly look overjoyed to see you.''

He felt a muscle twitch in his jaw. It took more effort than he would have liked to answer lightly. ''She's working, Chris. What's she supposed to do, forget her other customers?''

''No. It's just...''

''So, how's Burle?'' he asked, deliberately changing the subject.

Chris launched into a story about how grueling football practice had been for the past few weeks in preparation for a big game that weekend. Zach pretended to listen.

Kim was brisk and professional as she served their pies and coffees, then hurried away to take care of her other customers. Zach didn't try to detain her. As he'd told Chris, he knew better than to interfere with her work. Neither Kim nor Maggie would let him get away with that.

"You're sure Kim's not mad at you for some reason?" Chris persisted. She was frowning when Zach turned to her, after dragging his gaze away from Kim.

Chris had a reputation for not hesitating to butt her nose into her friends' business if she thought they were having problems. It was a combination of her youth, her utter lack of tact and her genuine desire to help anyone she thought needed her, but it could sometimes be annoying. Now, for instance.

"Chris, we haven't had a fight," he insisted. "Stop pretending to be Dr. Joyce Brothers for a few minutes, will you?"

She had the grace to look sheepish—for all of a second and a half. And then she went on, "I've got to tell you, Zach, I never thought I'd see you tumble like this. Anyone just has to look at you to know you've got a major thing for her."

Growing increasingly uncomfortable, Zach cleared his throat and looked across the table toward Tom. "You can jump in here any time," he muttered, broadly hinting for rescue.

Tom only shrugged and shoveled another huge bite of chocolate pie into his mouth as an excuse not to speak. Either he knew how difficult it was to derail Chris when she was on a tangent, or he was curious about what Zach would say.

Zach glared at him for a moment, then looked back at Chris. "Kim and I are dating, Chris. This isn't news to you."

"Well, yeah, but I thought—I mean, everyone's talked about how unusual it is for you to see anyone this steadily for this long, especially for the past couple of years or so, but...well, anyway, I just hope you don't get hurt,'' she finished cryptically.

Zach could hardly believe his ears. ''Wait a minute. Wasn't it just yesterday that you were warning me not to break Kim's heart?''

Looking across the room to where Kim was serving a plate of spaghetti to an active four-year-old, Chris nodded, her expression somber. ''Yes, I know. But that was before I...''

Zach couldn't leave it at that, though he knew he probably should. ''Before you what?''

''Before I saw you and Kim together today,'' she answered a bit reluctantly.

Zach scowled. So he wasn't the only one who thought Kim had erected invisible barriers between them. Even Chris sensed them.

He and Kim were definitely going to have to talk.

''One suggestion,'' Chris said, when it was obvious that Zach had no comment to make. ''Kim's sort of an old-fashioned girl. You might want to keep that in mind. You know, buy her little gifts, send her flowers, be romantic. Some women just can't resist things like that.''

Zach sighed deeply. ''Thank you so much for your advice, Patton, but I can handle my love life on my own, thanks.''

Chris looked doubtfully from Zach to Kim, who was all the way across the diner, talking to Maggie. ''If you say so.''

Perhaps taking pity on his friend, Tom finally changed the subject. Chris went along, apparently deciding she'd said enough.

Whatever their reasons, Zach was grateful. He wasn't ready to talk about Kim anymore. Not until he knew just where he stood with her, and why she was suddenly acting so cool. Chris thought he'd done something to make Kim mad, but Zach couldn't think of a thing. As far as he was concerned, he'd practically been a saint where Kim was concerned, he thought moodily.

When they'd finished their desserts and were ready to leave, Kim brought their checks. Zach stood as she approached, tossing enough money on the table to cover his tab and a tip that was generous, but not enough to embarrass her.

"I have to be going. I have things to do this afternoon," he said. "I'll call you this evening, Kim."

She nodded. "Yes."

Knowing he was taking a risk, he leaned over and brushed a firm kiss across her mouth. After all, he thrived on risks. And saintly behavior really wasn't something he could sustain for long. It just wasn't his nature.

He felt the others watching them in avid interest, and saw the color rush into Kim's cheeks. But he was grinning cockily when he drew back. "See ya," he murmured, and waved a farewell to the others as he sauntered out, his claim made clear.

He'd pay for that, he thought, then shrugged off the momentary concern. Kim would probably call his attitude arrogant or immature or possessively macho. But Zach hadn't liked the way Mike had been watching Kim. And Chris's warning was still bugging him. Whatever Kim would say was worth it as long as he'd made it clear that this woman was no longer available, and that no one needed to worry about him.

Where Kim was concerned, he could take care of himself, he assured himself confidently. Just as he did in every other situation.

Zach found himself at his sister Elaine's door that evening. He'd called on his way to make sure his visit was welcome, and Elaine had been surprised, but pleased. Zach and Elaine had always been close, probably because she was the closest to him in age.

"Come on in," she said, moving out of the doorway. "I just put on a fresh pot of coffee for us."

"Decaf for you, right?" he asked, patting her tummy, which was just starting to protrude a bit in her early pregnancy.

"Right. But I have regular instant, if you want."

"No. I don't need the caffeine this late, either."

She turned to head for the kitchen. He tagged at her heels, thinking it seemed awfully quiet in her house tonight. Usually her sons, ages six and ten, were ripping and romping through the place. Zach usually joined in when he came to visit, to Elaine's fond exasperation. "Where are Mark and the boys?"

"Clark's already in bed. His bedtime's eight o'clock, which, you might notice, was half an hour ago. Mark and Neil went to a high school football game. They should be home by ten."

"So it's just you and me, then."

She smiled over her shoulder. "Yes. We can have a nice visit. Seems like ages since we've had a chance to sit together and talk."

Inside her huge, oak-and-brick kitchen, Zach slung a leg over a stool at the bar, propped his elbows on the granite top and watched her pour coffee into two generously sized mugs. "How are you feeling?"

"Pretty good. I can't say pregnancy gets any easier with age," she added wryly, "but I'm taking it in stride."

He grinned at her. "Of course you are. Doesn't hurt that you've got a doctor in the house, either, does it?"

"Are you kidding? As brilliant a surgeon as he is, when one of his family is concerned, Mark's worthless as a doctor. You should have seen him when Clark fell onto a rock at the park and split his forehead open—remember?"

"I remember. Last summer, right? He looked terrible for a couple of days, all bruised and scraped. And he had a big bandage on his forehead. I thought it would leave a scar, but I haven't noticed one."

"Yes, well, when Mark saw the blood, I thought he was going to faint. I had to be the calm one during the crisis. Mark was practically hysterical."

Zach suddenly thought of the way he'd reacted after Kim had been thrown over the embankment during their bike outing. For just an instant he hadn't been a trained rescue worker. Hadn't gone into automatic response, the way he usually did. For the first time, emotion had interfered with his reflexes. When he'd gone into the pool after her, he hadn't been just rescuing *someone.* He'd been desperately trying to get to Kim. So, yeah, maybe he understood how Mark had felt.

Elaine shook her head. "It wasn't just a patient, you see. It was his baby. And he forgot that he even was a doctor. I'd like to think that if I hadn't been there, he'd have calmed down and handled everything."

Zach nodded. "I'm sure he would have." As shaken as he'd been, Zach had still beaten Tom into the water after Kim. When it had come down to the crunch, his instincts had kicked in, after all.

Elaine slid his coffee in front of him. "Want a cookie to go with that? I made a batch of oatmeal raisin this afternoon."

"Yeah, that sounds good, thanks."

She set a couple of the cookies on a dessert plate and handed it to him before taking the bar stool beside him with her own cup of coffee. "So, why do I have the pleasure of your company tonight, Zach? I would have thought you'd have plans."

He shrugged. "Kim's at a baby shower and Tom's having dinner with his mother. Everyone else was busy."

She laughed. "So I'm the last resort? Gee, thanks."

He grimaced. "I didn't really mean it quite that way.

Actually, I've been wanting to come visit, but I haven't had a chance."

"Yes, I hear you've been quite busy lately. You and Kim are still an item, hmm?"

He shrugged and picked a raisin out of his cookie. Popping it into his mouth, he muttered, "Yeah, I guess."

"I like her, Zach. She seems very sweet."

"She is. But..."

"But?" The word was said gently, encouraging him to talk if he wanted, rather than openly prying the way Chris had earlier. A family therapist by profession, Elaine was usually the first person Zach turned to when he had a problem, unless it was strictly a "guy thing," in which case he went to Tom.

"She's...elusive."

Elaine seemed struck by his choice of words. "Yes, I could tell that about her. She's very private. A bit shy."

"In a way, she is. But she'll speak out when something's important to her." He remembered the fire in her eyes when she'd chewed out the jerks who'd been tormenting the cat in the park. And she'd certainly put *him* in his place a few times, Zach thought ruefully.

Elaine smiled. "Good for her."

He assumed she'd correctly read his thoughts from his expression. He made a face at her. "You always said I should find a woman who wouldn't let me push her around."

"True. Still, Kim isn't exactly what I was expecting."

"Why not?"

"There's no need to bristle, Zach, I'm not criticizing her. She's just different from the other women you've dated."

He relaxed a bit and shrugged. "Yeah. I guess she is."

"The way you feel about her is different from the others, too, isn't it?" she asked, studying him perceptively.

He sighed. "Yeah."

Elaine cocked her head, looking fascinated. ''Are you in love with her?''

The L word again. He squirmed on his stool. ''Uh...''

Her eyes widened. ''You are!''

''Well...maybe,'' he said cautiously.

She leaned over and kissed his cheek. ''Zach, I'm thrilled for you.''

''Don't be,'' he said glumly. ''I have no reason to believe she feels the same way about me. Lately she seems to have pulled back.''

Elaine waved a hand in the air to dismiss his words. ''Of course she does. Why wouldn't she?''

His smile was wry. ''Think maybe you're just a tad prejudiced?''

She giggled. ''Maybe. But I still think she'd be crazy not to love you.''

''Maybe,'' he parroted. And then his smile died. ''But what if she doesn't?''

''What *if* she doesn't?''

He frowned at her. ''You're talking like a shrink again.''

''Can't help it. I *am* a shrink. What if she doesn't love you, Zach? Can you handle that?''

With his thumb he squashed a cookie crumb on his dessert plate. ''Yeah,'' he said firmly. ''Of course. It happens, right? People get over it.''

''Yes,'' Elaine said sympathetically. ''But it hurts. And you haven't had much experience with that kind of pain.''

''I can handle it, Elaine. If I have to.''

She patted his arm. ''I'm sure you can. But why are we being so pessimistic? You're young and in love for the first time. We should be happy.''

He groaned. ''Not so young. The big three-oh hits soon.''

''Yes, it does, doesn't it?'' Her grin was wicked.

Zach eyed her suspiciously. ''Elaine? You aren't planning anything, are you?''

She looked upward, her expression exaggeratedly innocent.

"Whatever it is, don't do it."

She snorted. "Yeah, right. I haven't forgotten what you did to me on *my* thirtieth."

He gulped. He should have remembered she had a memory like an elephant. And she *always* got her revenge. "Elaine..."

She only laughed and changed the subject. "Were you on duty last week when the frat boys got drunk and pulled the fire alarms at the campus several times in one night? I read about it in the paper."

He nodded. "Yeah, I was. Three wasted trips over there in the middle of the night. None of us got more than a couple hours' sleep."

"Did they catch the brats?"

"Yeah. Lot of good it'll do, though. Next big party, there go the alarms again."

"And of course you have to respond to every one, regardless."

"Of course. That's what the taxpayers are paying us for."

Elaine smiled, shook her head and changed the subject once more. To Zach's relief, she didn't bring Kim up again.

It was later that evening when Kim's doorbell rang. She'd been home from the baby shower for well over an hour and was sitting in her living room, poring over a textbook. She looked up with a frown when the bell chimed. She didn't even have to ask herself who it was.

Just to be on the safe side, she checked through the window before opening the door. Sure enough, Zach stood on the tiny porch.

"This is a surprise," she said when she opened the door.

He nodded. "I know. And I said I wouldn't drop by again without calling, didn't I?"

"Well, as a matter of fact..." She let her voice trail away.

He held out his hand. "I won't stay. I just wanted to give you this."

Automatically she closed her fingers around the little box he pressed into her hand. "What is it?"

"You can open it after I'm gone," he told her with a smile. "G'night."

Disoriented, she blinked. "Wait. Don't you want to come in?"

He shook his head. "Thanks, but I'd better go. It's late. You need your rest."

"But—"

He leaned over to kiss her, letting his lips linger just long enough for her to start to respond. And then he pulled back. "Good night, Kim. Sleep well."

He was gone before she could think of anything to say. Shaking her head in bemusement, she closed the door. Honestly, there were times when she simply didn't understand that man at all.

She looked down at the box in her hand. It was made of white cardboard and was about the size of a ring box. She hoped he hadn't done anything extravagant.

Cautiously she lifted the lid.

And smiled.

The box held a tiny metal snail with a brightly colored cloisonné shell. Its little face wore a sappy smile that Kim couldn't help but return. Two ridiculously intelligent-looking stalk eyes gazed back at her when she held it up to study it more closely.

It looked just like something Zach would have picked out for her.

This was no shy, retiring snail, she couldn't help noticing. Its almost gaudy shell cried out for attention, as did those twinkling eyes.

"Oh, Zach," she murmured, cradling the gift in her hand. "What am I going to do with you?"

How could she possibly go on protecting her heart when he did sweet, crazy, irresistible things like this?

Zach sent Kim flowers a few days later. Long-stemmed roses. A full dozen of them, in deep, ruby red.

Kim was overwhelmed. No one had ever sent her a dozen roses before. And even though she was allergic to them—cats and roses were her only allergies—and sneezed at least once every five minutes after they arrived at her door, she displayed them proudly on her table in a crystal vase that had belonged to her aunt.

"They're gorgeous," Dawn breathed in palpable envy, touching one fingertip to a delicate, velvety petal. "These had to cost him fifty bucks, minimum."

Kim gulped. Fifty dollars for cut flowers? She knew roses were expensive, but...

"If a guy sent me a dozen roses, I'd be all over him like a duck on a June bug," Dawn pronounced. "I wouldn't let him leave the bedroom until he was too worn out to whimper."

Her cheeks flaming, Kim sneezed, then frowned. "They're just flowers, Dawn," she said, trying to downplay the gesture—to herself, as well as to her friend. "It was sweet of him to send them to me, but don't read too much into it. I haven't."

"Right," Dawn murmured, her disbelief clear. "Didn't mean that much to you at all, huh?"

"I said it was sweet."

"Yeah. Just a nice, sweet thing to do. Doesn't mean anything particularly to you. Which is why you haven't let them get six inches away from you, even though you're sneezing your head off because of them."

Kim cleared her throat, then sneezed again. "Maybe I should set them in the living room while we study," she admitted.

Dawn smiled. "Maybe so."

Chapter Eleven

"If I'd had any idea you were allergic to roses, I'd have sent orchids. Or carnations or daisies or something," Zach said repentantly the next evening. Kim had made lasagna for dinner and had used the roses, along with two lighted candles, as the centerpiece. She'd hoped the antihistamine she'd taken beforehand would let her get through dinner without sneezing. Her hopes had been in vain.

Fighting another sneeze—and a healthy dose of embarrassment—Kim shook her head. "The roses are beautiful, Zach. You couldn't have known about my allergy."

His grimace was disarmingly boyish. "I've never been very good at grand, romantic gestures."

She didn't believe that for a minute. And, besides… "I don't need grand, romantic gestures," she murmured.

"Maybe you don't need them," he agreed, smiling at her in the flickering candlelight. "But I can't think of anyone who deserves them more than you do."

And he'd called himself no good at romantic blarney. *Yeah, right.*

"Would you like some more lasagna?" she asked quickly.

He shook his head. "No, thanks. It was delicious, but I'm full."

"Cheesecake for dessert," she enticed him.

He looked tempted, but pained. "I can't," he said after a momentary inner struggle. "Maybe later?"

"Whenever you're ready," she agreed with a smile.

"I'll help you with the dishes," he said, pushing away from the table. "Want to watch some TV or something after dinner? Or maybe I can help you study. I'm really good at quizzing. I had the world's densest roommate when I was in college. If it hadn't been for me, he'd have flunked out first semester. Not that I'm implying you're dense, or anything," he added hastily. "Just thought I'd offer."

She laughed. "I refuse to take offense—no matter how it sounded. And, thanks, but midterms wrapped up this morning and I really don't need to be quizzed tonight."

His eyes lit up. "Maybe you'll sing for me again? I'd love to hear you."

She blushed and shook her head. Even the thought of sitting down and singing, knowing Zach was listening, made her voice catch somewhere in the back of her throat.

"We'll just watch TV," she managed to say. "If we can find anything interesting."

A few minutes later they sat side by side on her couch while Zach flipped through channels using the remote control. Kim didn't see anything that caught her attention. But that wasn't surprising, considering that Zach was in the room, sitting only inches away from her. How could any mere television program compete?

Zach finally stopped on the Discovery Channel, which was showing a program about an expedition up Mount

Everest. "Man, I'd love to do that," he said. "Tom and I have talked about going down to Mexico sometime for a climb, but there never seems to be time."

Kim looked doubtfully at the man being interviewed about his climb, which had ended in disaster. He'd lost his nose and ears to frostbite, and parts of his hands and feet. "This looks like fun to you?" she asked Zach in disbelief.

Zach waved a dismissing hand. "That expedition went bad. Hundreds of people make the climb successfully."

"And how many have died trying?"

"A few."

"More than a few."

"Maybe, but I'm always careful...."

"No one can be prepared for every accident, every natural disaster. That man's a physician, hardly lacking in intelligence. I'm sure he thought he was being careful, too. Now look at him. Look what he's put himself and his family through, just so he could say he'd climbed a mountain."

"Not just any mountain. Everest."

She exhaled sharply through her nose. "Look at his hands, Zach. He has no fingers. His career as a surgeon is over. All the good he could have done in that capacity is finished. Do you really think it was worth it?"

Looking a bit uncomfortable, Zach shrugged. "You can't live every day waiting for tragedy to strike, Kim, or trying to avoid every misfortune. If you do that, you might as well lock yourself in a room and spend the rest of your life in hiding. And what joy would there be in that?"

"All I'm saying is that there's no need to go looking for disaster, either. There are plenty of pleasant hobbies that don't involve putting yourself in mortal danger."

"Bridge, perhaps? Croquet?" Zach spoke just a bit too politely. "Or maybe bowling. No, that could be dangerous. You could drop that heavy ball and break your toes. I'm sure it's been done. So should everyone stop bowling just to keep their toes out of harm's way?"

"Surely you see there's a difference between bowling and climbing to an altitude where humans were never meant to live."

"If you go with that theory, we wouldn't have airplanes. You don't believe that old saw that if God had meant for us to fly, he'd have given us wings."

"No," Kim admitted slowly. "But there have been a lot of plane crashes lately. Maybe we've been taking flight a bit too much for granted in the past few years, getting careless."

Zach shook his head and pushed the channel button on the remote. "I won't ask you to climb any mountains with me."

"Good. I wouldn't have done it, anyway."

A stock car race was in progress on the sports channel. Ironically, one of the cars hit a wall just as they tuned in. The driver climbed out, obviously disgusted at being out of the race, but apparently unharmed.

"There's another hobby I'm sure you disapprove of," Zach muttered.

Stung, she lifted her chin. "I think it's foolish and reckless, but it's their business if they want to risk life and limb just to drive around in circles at breakneck speed."

"It's a little more than that. Driving at those speeds requires training and skill."

"I suppose you've tried it."

He cleared his throat. "I've been in a couple of local races."

"Ever crash?"

"Once."

"Were you hurt?"

"Broke an arm. But it wasn't my fault. Another guy rammed into me on a curve." He sounded defensive.

Kim nodded. "That's just my point. No matter how

careful or how well trained you are, you can't anticipate and prepare for everything that could go wrong."

Zach shoved a hand through his hair. "What the hell are we doing arguing about this? It's hardly important."

Kim thought it was more important than Zach would admit. They weren't arguing about sports, exactly, but about the fundamental differences between them. She just didn't know if she could afford to get any more deeply involved with a man who regularly took so many chances with his safety.

It wasn't his fire fighting or his rescue work that bothered her so greatly, though she worried about him during those activities. Still, they were important jobs, of great benefit to the community. But his choice of dangerous sports for mere entertainment *did* concern her. How far would he go in search of a new thrill?

Did he really believe he was invulnerable? Had he taken his nickname, Super Zach, too seriously? And wasn't overconfidence the leading factor in most serious sporting accidents?

But she really didn't want to argue. They'd been having such a nice evening. She wouldn't be the one to ruin it, she told herself.

Zach turned off the television. "I'm not really interested in this, are you?"

She shook her head, trying to tell from his expression whether he was still annoyed with her for challenging his interests.

He stood and walked across the room, where he turned on her inexpensive stereo system and tuned in a soft country station. He snapped off the overhead light, leaving the room illuminated only by the soft glow of the lamp on her end table. And then he returned to the couch, sitting closer to her than he had earlier, turned on the cushion so that he was facing her.

Self-conscious beneath his close scrutiny, she shifted her weight. "Are you ready for cheesecake?"

"No. Still not hungry."

"Um, we could play cards."

He stretched his arm along the back of the couch and scooted even closer. "I don't think so."

"Want to work on a jigsaw puzzle?" Her voice suddenly sounded half an octave higher, and more than a little breathless.

He grinned and leaned toward her. "No."

Automatically, her hands went to his shoulders. She couldn't have said whether she intended to pull him closer or hold him away. "So what...what do you want to do?"

His breath whispered against her lips. "Guess."

She swallowed. "But we were just having an argument," she protested inanely, as if that had anything at all to do with this.

"Mmm." His lips were moving against hers now. "Let's make up."

"Zach..."

"Kim..."

His mouth covered hers.

He kissed her unhurriedly, undemandingly. Without words he coaxed her first to enjoy and then to respond. His tongue traced her mouth, then slid inside to taste her. And she somewhat tentatively responded in kind, which seemed to please him a great deal judging from his encouraging murmur.

Who cared if they'd argued? His kisses made her feel things she'd only fantasized about before. He made her feel beautiful, desirable, special—even though moments earlier he'd made her feel like a fussy, nervous little old lady, apprehensive of everything he found exciting.

Her emotions were so volatile, so capricious when he was around that she hardly recognized herself. She felt like a yo-yo, plummeting from highs to lows and soaring back again in a matter of moments. Hopeful, then fearful. Shy, then bold. Happy, then gloomy. One moment convinced that she knew exactly what she was doing, that she was prepared for whatever happened, the next resigned to having her heart broken, her confidence crushed.

"You're doing it again," Zach muttered against her mouth.

"Doing what?" she asked, her voice reedy from lack of oxygen.

"Thinking."

"I can't stop thinking."

"Let me help you," he offered, and pressed her into the cushions, his hand closing over her right breast.

He helped her, all right. She found that it was almost *impossible* to think when Zach was holding her this way, touching her, nibbling at her lips, her earlobes, her throat.

A hint of five-o'clock shadow made his face just rough enough against her skin to be exotic, exciting. That, and the muscles rippling beneath her palms as she clutched at his back, reminded her that Zach McCain was all tough, virile male. He moved against her thigh, and she was made aware of an even more powerful indicator. He wanted her. And tonight he wasn't bothering to mask his desire.

She wanted him, too. Wanted to know how it felt to be loved by this man. Wanted to sample what she suspected would be an extraordinary experience, something she would remember and savor for the rest of her life—if, of course, she could overcome the heartache of having it end. As she knew it would, eventually. Inevitably.

How long could Zach be content with a woman who considered bowling an adventure?

Zach kissed the tip of her nose. "What's going on inside that beautiful head of yours?"

Beautiful? She wasn't beautiful. But she didn't want to argue with him again. "I, um..."

"You know I want you, don't you? That I want to make love with you?"

It was the first time he'd approached the subject so boldly. Kim swallowed and moistened her lips with her tongue before murmuring, "I..."

"I'm not trying to push you into something you aren't ready for," he said when her voice trailed away again. "I just wanted you to know. It's getting harder all the time for me to hold you and kiss you without wanting more. I can't even look at you without wanting to carry you to bed. Does that disturb you?"

It disturbed her, all right, but maybe not in the way he meant. Just hearing him say the words brought startling images into her mind, made her ache in a way she never had before. An ache she was sure Zach would know how to soothe.

"Zach, we—"

"I don't mean to embarrass you, or make you uncomfortable. But—well, do you think there's a chance that we'll be taking this relationship to the next level any time soon?" He injected just enough plaintive hopefulness into his voice to make her smile a bit, which had obviously been his intention.

"Will you let me finish a sentence now?" she asked him.

He smiled and nodded.

From the stereo, Vince Gill was crooning a song about a love affair that was destined to end in heartache. Kim had always thought that few singers poured more gut-wrenching emotion into a song than Vince. Right now, the simulated suffering seemed all too real. All too prophetic.

"Making love with you," she said, struggling not to blush, "would be a big step for me."

"I know," he murmured.

"A *very* big step," she said, wondering if it would be necessary to spell it out.

He looked into her eyes and touched her cheek, and she knew he understood well enough. "I know," he repeated. "And I'm not trying to rush you. But, er..."

She sighed. "I really am a coward."

He pulled her toward him for a hug. "You're Kim. And I..."

He hesitated.

She didn't want him to finish the sentence—not with anything that she wasn't ready to hear. Couldn't yet believe. "Are you *sure* you don't want that cheesecake now?" she asked quickly.

He drew back a fraction, searched her face—which she knew had gone pale—and then nodded slowly. "Yeah," he said. "Sure. I guess I am hungry, after all."

Relieved, she gave him a tremulous smile. And then pulled away from his embrace while she still had the strength to do so.

Kim got very little sleep that night.

She had a nightmare, the first one in years. In it, she and Zach were kissing, and he was stroking her bare skin, her breasts, her stomach, her thighs. She wriggled against the sheets and cried out with pleasure and the pain of frustration, begging him to take the ache away.

"I will," he murmured, drawing back. "If you'll jump with me."

"Jump with you?" The dream-Kim opened her eyes, frowning in confusion. "But..."

They were in an airplane. And the door was open. Zach stood framed in the aperture, dressed all in black. Kim stood in front of him, dressed in skimpy bits of lace and satin that had never graced her wardrobe in waking life.

"Jump with me," Zach said, and held out his hand. The wind whipped his dark hair around his face, drifted around her legs like a soft, invisible rope trying to pull her out of the plane.

Through the opening behind Zach she could see the ground, so far below them that it seemed inconceivable to even imagine jumping. And besides, neither of them was wearing a parachute. She tried to explain that to him, but he waved his hand as though her argument didn't matter.

"Trust me," he said. "Jump with me."

She backed away. "I can't."

His expression turned sad. "Goodbye, Kim." And he turned toward the opening.

"Zach, no."

"Goodbye." And he jumped, spreading his arms as he plummeted downward into an endless fall.

"Zach!"

She woke with a gasp, her heart pounding, her hand clutching the high neckline of her prim, brushed-cotton nightgown.

She told herself it was nothing but a stupid dream. That it was ridiculous for her to get all worked up about it. It had been so utterly ridiculous that she should be laughing.

Yet she couldn't laugh.

Knowing she wouldn't immediately get back to sleep, she got out of bed and went into the kitchen, where she poured herself a glass of milk. And then she just stood at the sink, holding the glass in her hand, untouched.

Something Tom had said at the football game weeks earlier came back to haunt her.

Zach's never been able to resist a challenge. The more difficult a task seems to him, the more determined he becomes, you know? And then, once he conquers it, he moves on to the next.

Tom had gone on to imply that he hoped Kim would be the challenge Zach wouldn't walk away from so easily. But she simply couldn't be as optimistic.

She wondered how long it had been since Zach had dated anyone on a purely platonic level. She couldn't imagine that celibacy would appeal to him much longer.

He was a very physical, very demonstrative man, and he wouldn't be satisfied to go home to cold showers. Somehow she knew that there hadn't been anyone else for him since they'd been dating, and she was both flattered and mystified by the endurance of his interest in her. It simply couldn't last. Could it?

She was an idiot, plain and simple, she told herself in disgust. For being such a pessimist, for denying Zach what they both wanted, for being afraid to take the next step, yet too weak to walk away. She wouldn't blame Zach if he took to his heels any day.

Which was, of course, exactly what she was worrying about during the middle of the night. And if he left, it would be her own fault.

"How did you ever get yourself into this, Kim?" she asked aloud.

Her question echoed, unanswered, in the empty kitchen.

Zach was getting surly. Chalk it up to sexual frustration, he thought. Or to insecurity, a condition that was so new to him he simply didn't know how to deal with it.

He'd done everything he knew to convince Kim his intentions were both serious and honorable. He'd been patient. He'd been understanding. He'd introduced her to his family, repeatedly assured her that he had only her best interests at heart. He'd even resorted to Chris's suggestion of sending gifts and flowers. And still he felt that for every step he took forward, Kim pushed him another two back.

He could understand her fear of dogs. Sort of. After all, some dogs were vicious. He supposed he could understand her fear of chancy adventures, though he couldn't imagine living one's entire life without ever taking even the slightest risks. What fun was there in that? Still, he'd never pushed Kim to do anything dangerous. He'd known Sherm's dogs wouldn't hurt her and, of course, he'd had no idea that she'd fall off the bike.

What he couldn't understand was her fear of *him.* Not only did it make no sense to him, but it was somewhat insulting. What did she think he was, a monster? A practiced heartbreaker, cruising for innocent virgins to despoil?

He sat in a booth at the diner, drinking coffee, watching Kim work the dining room. Was it his imagination, or had she changed in the past few weeks? She seemed more confident with her customers, more approachable. A bit too approachable, as far as Zach was concerned.

He watched with a scowl as she laughed at something a couple of good-looking college-boy types said to her. She said something to make them laugh in response and then turned to carry their orders to the kitchen. She even walked differently than before, Zach fumed, noting the gentle sway of her hips and well aware that the college boys were watching, too.

Zach had never thought of himself as a possessive man, but several of his beliefs about himself had changed in recent weeks.

"Need anything else, Zach?" Kim asked, approaching him with the same smile she'd worn for the college boys.

Irrationally annoyed that her expression didn't change just for him, he answered without stopping to police his words this time. "Yes. You."

Her eyelashes flickered, and her cheeks darkened just a bit. "Er, anything off the menu?" she asked.

"No. Those punks over there giving you any trouble?"

She looked surprised, then glanced toward the young men at the far table. "Tyler and Joe? No, of course not."

She knew them by name. And one of those names sounded a bit too familiar. "Tyler? The guy who asked you out?"

She was starting to frown now, obviously not caring for Zach's tone. The rational part of him didn't blame her. But his rational side wasn't exactly in command at the moment. "He invited me to dinner one evening, as you know.

And, if you'll remember, I turned him down. But we're still friends."

"Yeah, well, I—"

"Kim," Maggie snapped as she stalked past with a carafe of hot coffee, "quit flirtin' with your boyfriend and get back to work. Zach, don't be bothering my help during work hours, you hear? She's got other customers waitin'."

"I'm leaving," Zach muttered as Kim rushed off after giving him one last, searching look. He stood and tossed a bill onto the table. "I'll talk to Kim later."

"You and Zach havin' problems, Kim?" Maggie asked as Kim prepared to leave the diner a few hours later.

Rather surprised by the note of concern in her employer's gruff voice, Kim shook her head. "No. I think he was just in a bad mood today."

Or so she'd tried to tell herself. She'd remembered that Tom had warned her once that Zach could be a bit moody, but that his funks didn't usually last long.

"Hmmph. Seemed to me he was lookin' at you like a junkyard dog looks at his favorite bone. Don't you let him start pushing you around, you hear, Kim? I'm right fond of that boy, as you know, but his mama and his sisters have him spoiled rotten. You let him, he'll expect you to do the same. That ain't no way to start out. And this is coming from someone who learned through two bad marriages, you hear?"

"I hear you, Maggie," Kim answered with a weak smile. "And I have no intention of allowing Zach to push me around."

"Good. You've got more backbone than I thought you did when I first hired you," Maggie admitted grudgingly. "I think you can hold your own, even with Zach, if you don't let those pretty eyes of his get to ya."

Zach *did* have pretty eyes, Kim agreed silently. But she

heard the rest of Maggie's warning, too. And she took it to heart.

Zach was waiting on her doorstep when she got home. Her heart tripping in a combination of nerves, anxiety and excitement at seeing him there, looking so good as he leaned against the rail, she tried to greet him casually. "Zach. I wasn't expecting to see you here this evening. I thought you had a meeting with your rescue team."

He nodded. "Something came up. It's been rescheduled until next week. Want to go do something with me?"

"I'd like to, but I can't. My accounting club at school meets this evening."

"Accounting club?" he repeated dismissively. "You can skip it tonight, can't you?"

"No. I'm the secretary. I take the minutes of the meeting. It's a responsibility I accepted at the beginning of the school year."

"Couldn't someone else take minutes tonight?"

"No." She was frowning now, her heart hammering as she realized that this confrontation could be more important than it seemed on the surface. "Zach, you can't expect me to change my plans at the last minute just because you've found yourself at loose ends for the evening. Accounting club may not seem very exciting or interesting to you, but it's important to the career I've been working toward for a very long time. I would expect you to understand that."

He started to speak, paused, then ran a hand through his hair. "You're right," he said with a sigh. "I'm sorry. I guess I was just disappointed that we can't spend the evening together."

Softening a bit, she said, "Maybe we can do something tomorrow evening?"

"I'm on duty tomorrow."

"The day after, then."

"Yeah." His smile didn't look quite right. "The day after."

She nodded. "Want to come in for a few minutes? I don't have to leave for another half hour or so."

He shook his head. "I'd better go so you can change for your meeting. I'll call you from the station tomorrow, okay?"

"Of course." She lifted her face for his kiss, which was long, deep and a bit rough. Her voice wasn't quite steady when it finally ended. "Good night, Zach."

"Night, Kim." His tone was gruff. "Dream of me."

She thought of the last dream she'd had of him. Dreams like that, she thought wryly, she could do without. But she didn't say anything to Zach, merely nodded and tried to smile.

He left then, and she let herself in to her house—tired, confused, a bit depressed. For the first time in days she felt that old, familiar fear hovering at the edges of her consciousness, waiting to overwhelm her again.

Kim was going through her mail the next afternoon when she found a letter from one of her aunt's long-term friends in St. Louis. Minnie Overton had been a childhood friend of Pearl's, and the friendship had lasted until Pearl's death. "Miss Minnie," as Kim had called her growing up, was now a retired schoolteacher, living in a retirement home in Kirkwood. Though her body was failing, her mind was as sharp as ever.

Seeing the familiar handwriting, Kim was momentarily assailed by guilt. It had been her turn to write; she'd gotten so busy with her new life in Fayetteville that she'd neglected the few friends she'd left behind in St. Louis. She kept meaning to get back for a visit, but simply hadn't had the time or money to do so. Maybe soon...

She opened the envelope.

Minnie began the letter gently fussing about the length

of time that had passed since she'd heard from Kim and hoping that nothing was wrong. She then went on to sweetly rave about what a "dear girl" Kim was—increasing the guilt level, of course—and how kind and thoughtful she'd been to Pearl during those last, trying years.

"You brought Pearl much happiness in her life," Minnie wrote.

> After so many tragedies in her youth, losing her parents and her sister to untimely deaths, having her heart broken by that jughead, Wallace Dunworthy, seeing her dreams of playing piano professionally dashed, you were her consolation. You were the beloved child of her heart.
>
> She always wanted children of her own, you know. But Wallace so completely broke her heart that she was never able to offer it to another man after him. I tried to warn her about him. I knew he would use her and then leave her, but she was too besotted to heed my advice. Only a week before she passed away, she spoke to me of how she had never stopped missing that man, or wishing she could have held on to him. Please don't think I ever said "I told you so." I did not, of course. That would have been unkind of me.

Kim didn't believe that for a minute. As fond as she was of Miss Minnie, she suspected that the somewhat imperious woman had taken more than one opportunity to remind her longtime friend of her superior judgment.

Kim finished reading the letter, which went on to complain about the inconsiderate behavior of some of the other residents of the retirement home, then folded it and slid it back into the envelope. Lost in thought, she chewed her lower lip as she contemplated Minnie's artless gossip.

She'd always known there had been a broken engagement in Aunt Pearl's past, though her aunt had steadfastly refused to speak of it, other than to say that it simply "hadn't worked out." Kim had always suspected that Pearl had been deeply disappointed by the ill-fated affair. She hadn't realized that Pearl had spent the rest of her life grieving for her lost love.

Nor had she known that Pearl always regretted not playing the piano professionally. Had it been a lack of talent or, more likely, a lack of courage that had held her back? And just how much like Pearl had Kim become?

She spent the next half hour staring into space, thinking of nothing—and worrying about everything.

"You're about as friendly as a wounded bear today, Zach. What's your problem?" Tom complained.

They were in the back parking area of the fire station, working on Tom's car again after dinner, using a couple of drop lights to help them see. Zach was aware that he'd hardly spoken two words since they'd started. "It's nothing," he said, knowing his friend wouldn't believe him.

He was right.

"What's going on? You and Kim have a fight?"

"No, we didn't have a fight," Zach snapped. *Not exactly, anyway.* "Why does everyone keep asking me that lately, as though it's inevitable, or something?"

Tom looked a bit surprised by Zach's vehemence, but shrugged. "Well, it *is* inevitable that you'll have a disagreement sometime. All couples do."

That made Zach feel a little better. He nodded. "Yeah, they do, don't they? It's normal."

And it didn't necessarily mean the couple was breaking up, he reminded himself, thinking of all the noisy quarrels Burle and Chris had gotten into. And they were certainly a happy couple, on the whole. Even Zach's sisters had gone through heated disagreements with their spouses, and they were both very content in their marriages, as far as Zach knew. So, the fact that he and Kim had exchanged a few sharp words didn't have to worry him quite as much as it had ever since he'd left her house yesterday.

"So—did you have a fight?" Tom persisted.

Zach shrugged. "We had a minor disagreement. I'm sure it's nothing to worry about." His voice sounded a bit hollow as he tried to convince both Tom and himself.

"Want to talk about it?"

"No. But thanks."

Tom nodded and bent back under the hood of the MG. "This love stuff isn't as easy as it's cracked up to be, is it, buddy?" he asked casually.

"No," Zach answered grimly. "It's not."

In fact, it was a whole lot harder than anything Zach had ever encountered before.

Chapter Twelve

The split, when it came, was over something incredibly trivial. Utterly senseless. And horribly painful.

Zach had asked Kim to another party given by one of his friends on the last Saturday in October, making her remember Maggie's early warning that Zach ran with a "party crowd." Kim and Dawn made a shopping trip to the Northwest Arkansas Mall Saturday afternoon to find Kim something new to wear for the party.

Though Dawn's choice would have been a bit sexier, Kim finally found an outfit that pleased them both, a long, jewel-toned challis skirt with a berry-colored tunic sweater.

"It needs a scarf or something," Dawn mused as they walked past the busy food court area. "Maybe we can find one at..."

Kim suddenly stopped walking.

Dawn looked over her shoulder. "What?"

Her arms weighed down with packages, Kim tried to

decide whether to keep walking or to stop to speak to Zach and Tom, whom she'd just spotted having ice cream at one of the food court tables. They were surrounded by women, she noticed immediately. Young women. Attractive young women. Neither Zach nor Tom had noticed Kim.

"Wow. Who are those two?" Dawn asked, following Kim's gaze. "Popular, aren't they?"

"That," Kim said quietly, "is Zach. The lighter-haired one is Tom Lowery, his friend."

Dawn's dark eyes rounded. "*That's* Zach? Your Zach?"

Kim swallowed and nodded.

Both of them watched as one of the pretty young women teasingly ruffled Zach's dark hair. He good-naturedly smoothed it back into place, not looking notably annoyed.

"You want to go say something to them? I wouldn't mind meeting him," Dawn hinted broadly.

The whole group burst out laughing at something Tom, who looked quite pleased with himself, had said.

"No," Kim said, starting to walk. "Let's just go find a scarf. I'll see Zach later."

Dawn had to hurry to keep up as Kim quickly turned a corner that put her out of sight of the food court. "Hey, Kim, wait. You don't even want to say hi?"

"I wouldn't want to interrupt his conversation with his, er, friends."

"Uh-oh. You're jealous."

"I'm not jealous," Kim snapped, her arms tightening around her packages.

"Oh, yeah. You're jealous. Downright green. You don't like it that he's talking to all those women, do you?"

"Zach can talk to as many women as he likes." *Even though he practically breathes fire every time* I *so much as smile at a male customer.*

"Kim, he's a gorgeous male. You've gotta expect that women are going to be all over him. He looked like he was behaving himself, just enjoying the attention. Don't make any big deal of it, okay?'' Dawn looked worried.

Kim forced a smile. ''I just said it didn't matter, didn't I? Come on, Dawn. Help me find a great-looking scarf. I have a date with that gorgeous male in a few hours.''

''That's right, you do. None of those other women are going out with him, no matter how hard they might have been trying. And don't you let him forget it.''

But Kim hadn't quite forgotten the scene when Zach picked her up later. Even though he ogled comically and gave a low wolf whistle when she opened the door.

''Great outfit,'' he said. ''Is it new?''

''Yes. I just got it today.''

''Turn around. Let me see it.''

Obligingly, she spread her arms and did a model's turn. The long skirt swirled softly around her calves.

''I like,'' Zach said, reaching for her.

She returned his kiss, then stepped back. ''I saw you at the mall today,'' she mentioned very casually. ''I was there with my friend Dawn.''

He looked surprised. ''Really? I didn't see you.''

''I know. You were, um, busy.''

Looking a bit confused, he said, ''Tom and I just stopped by for some ice cream after we'd been to the auto parts store down the street. I wish you'd said something. I would like to meet Dawn.''

What? Half a dozen women aren't enough for you? You need two more?

Knowing she was being petty and unfair, Kim swallowed the sarcastic rejoinder. ''We were sort of in a hurry,'' she prevaricated. ''I'll get my purse, and I'm ready to go.''

The party was more fun than Kim had expected. Though she still had a tendency to go quiet in large crowds, she was learning, through Zach, to be a bit more gregarious.

She missed Tom, though. He'd had other plans for the evening. Still, she had a very nice time and felt that she'd made some new friends among Zach's acquaintances.

And then, just as the gathering was breaking up late that evening, someone suggested going en masse to the haunted house being run as a fund-raiser for a local civic organization.

"Hey, that sounds like fun. How about it, Kim?" Zach asked, turning to her with a grin.

She could have groaned aloud. Everyone looked thrilled with the prospect. She hated to be a wet blanket, but she utterly detested haunted houses, no matter how innocuous they might be. She told herself she could go along with the group and wait outside while they went through. Surely they would accept her decision, though she didn't expect any of them to understand her unreasonable distaste for such harmless entertainment.

It didn't work out quite that way. Everyone insisted that Kim really should go through with them.

"It's a lot of fun. You'll love it," someone said when they arrived at the abandoned-warehouse-turned-haunted-house. Even this late, the parking lot was crowded, mostly with groups of teenagers giggling and squealing as they either waited in line to go through or hung around outside afterward to tease their friends about being spooked.

"Yeah, come on, Kim," Zach urged. "It'll be fun. I've heard it's a great house."

"Really, Zach," she murmured, trying to send him a silent message to drop it, "I don't care for these things. I'll just wait out here while the rest of you go through."

"I'll wait with you, Kim," Mike Henry, who'd attended the party without a date, volunteered. "They're selling hot cider at the concession stand. My treat."

Zach immediately bristled. "Come on, Kim, it's just a bunch of guys dressed up in costumes. What's the big deal about going through with me?"

The others had fallen silent or moved away, perhaps sensing that there was more beneath the surface of Kim and Zach's disagreement than whether or not she would go through the haunted house.

She almost gave in, just to prevent a quarrel. And then she asked herself what on earth she was doing. She didn't like haunted houses. She didn't like being in the dark, or being crowded into narrow spaces, or wondering when someone in a gory costume was going to jump right into her face and startle her. She didn't like the smell of paint or rubber masks, or the musty odor of an abandoned old building. She didn't like the way the teenagers screamed and pushed, giggled and showed off once they went inside.

Zach had no right to try to talk her into something she didn't want to do. And she very much resented him putting her on the spot this way in front of his friends, embarrassing her and putting a pall on everyone else's fun.

"I have been in a haunted house before," she said calmly. "And I simply don't care for them. It's no big deal. I would just prefer to remain outside. Now, please, Zach, go with your friends. You go in, too, Mike. I'll be fine out here, watching the fun."

"I don't really like these things, either," Mike admitted. "I always start sneezing from the dust and have trouble stopping. I'd just as soon drink cider out here with you. If, er, it's okay with you, Zach?"

Kim lifted her chin, prepared to inform both of them that it wasn't Zach's decision to make. If she wanted to share a cup of cider with Mike, it was entirely her own choice. Neither of them had to ask Zach's permission.

Zach said pretty much the same thing, though he made the concession a bit grudgingly. "Kim can do whatever she likes, of course. You don't have to ask me if it's okay."

Mike looked doubtful. "But..."

Kim turned to him with a smile. "Hot cider sounds good. It's cooler than I'd expected tonight."

"I won't be long," Zach said.

"Take your time," she replied. And then she walked with Mike to the crowded concession stand, where the scent of hot apple cider wafted temptingly in the air.

Zach didn't say much during the drive to Kim's house. Neither did she.

He didn't wait to be asked inside. He simply followed her in when she opened the door, closing it sharply behind him.

"Would you like some coffee?" she forced herself to ask politely.

He lifted an eyebrow. "After all that apple cider?"

She didn't particularly like his tone. "It was a simple yes or no question, Zach. If you don't care for any, I won't bother to make any."

Careful, Kim, you're sounding snappish.

"I don't care for any."

"Fine." She tossed her purse on a table and wondered what she was supposed to do with him now.

"You've made a conquest, you know." Zach's light tone didn't quite ring true. "Mike Henry thinks you're pretty hot stuff."

Uh-oh. Here it comes.

"Mike is very nice," she said coolly. "As are your other friends."

"Mmm. But my other friends weren't buying you hot cider and standing a half inch away from you while you drank it, were they?"

She almost gasped in outrage. "Of all the—"

Careful, Kim. You know how you hate confrontations.

She drew a deep breath, trying to get her rare flash of temper under control.

Zach crossed his arms over his chest, looking dark and

sullen and more than a bit dangerous. "You have something you wanted to say?" he asked politely.

She tossed her head. "As a matter of fact, I do," she said, throwing both fear and healthy discretion to the wind. "You have a lot of nerve criticizing me for having an innocent cup of cider with your friend Mike, particularly after you and Tom were practically smothered by women at the mall."

His eyes narrowed. "What are you... You mean the girls who were talking to us while we ate our ice cream? Come off it, Kim, they were just a bunch of flirty kids. I don't even know them."

Those "kids" had been nineteen years old going on forty, Kim thought, seething. Zach made it sound as though she were resentful of a group of kindergartners! "The point is," she said, her tone icy, "you feel free to talk to whomever you like. And so do I."

"Is that right?" His voice had gone even softer, which didn't in any way lessen its effect.

She faced him down. "Yes."

"You're telling me that, as far as you're concerned, you and I have no commitment at all? That we're both free to date anyone we like?"

She blinked. *Date? Who'd said anything about dating?* They'd been talking about drinking cider and eating ice cream. "Well, I..."

But Zach was angry now, and making no effort to hide it. "I thought you trusted me. God knows I've done everything I know how to convince you that my intentions were serious. But you've been just waiting for an excuse to send me packing, haven't you? More than half hoping you'd find one."

"That is so unfair! I have not been looking for an excuse to break up with you. I thought *you* understood *me.* I thought you accepted me the way I am. I didn't expect you to embarrass me in front of your friends about that stupid haunted house, or to yell at me just for talking to another man. Who's really the injured party here, Zach? You or me?"

"Me," he snarled.

"Wrong answer," she snapped.

"You're trying to drive me away because you're scared. It requires a lot more courage to take a risk on a relationship than to make a clean break before it gets tough, doesn't it? And God knows Kim Berry takes such pride in her fear."

She felt the tears sting her eyes in response to his cruelty. She refused to allow them to fall, but motioned toward the door instead. "Please leave now."

He threw up his arms. "See? You're trying to send me away, rather than have this out."

Maybe he was right. But— "I just want you to go. Now."

"Fine. I'll go. You stay here cowering in your fear, afraid of dogs and bugs and haunted houses and serious commitments. You're choosing to be afraid, Kim, because it's such a comfortable old habit for you."

She marched past him and opened the door, her heart pounding in her throat, her tears threatening to explode like water through a broken dam. "Goodbye, Zach."

He moved past her, then turned, half in, half out of her door. His expression was suddenly weary, his voice defeated.

"I wanted this to work," he said. "I really did. But I can't keep taking all the risks alone. I can't be brave enough for both of us."

She bit her lip to keep it from quivering. She didn't trust herself to speak.

Zach turned without another word and walked away. Somehow, even his walk was different. Less cocky. Less energetic.

Kim closed the door quickly, before she could be

tempted to beg him to come back. And then she spent the rest of the sleepless night persuading herself it had been the wisest thing to do.

She'd known all along that no relationship could last between Kim Berry and Zach McCain.

"What do you mean, it's over?" Tom demanded at the station the next afternoon, as he and Zach sat in the kitchen, alone for the first time that day, mugs of too-strong coffee in front of them.

"Just what I said," Zach replied curtly. "It's over. Finished. She dumped me."

"Kim dumped you." Tom sounded as though he weren't entirely sure he'd heard correctly.

"She dumped me," Zach repeated very slowly. "Threw me out of her house."

"What did you do?" Tom asked, sounding disgruntled.

"I didn't do anything."

Tom only looked at him, his disbelief written all over his face.

Zach scowled. "Well, okay, I tried to talk her into going into the haunted house with us. That's hardly a major offense, is it? I gave in when she made it clear that she just didn't want to."

"You probably embarrassed her. Was that really necessary?"

"I just thought she'd get a kick out of it. And she probably would have, if she'd just tried it. You saw how much fun she had on the go-carts, and remember how hard it was to talk her into that?"

"Why are you always trying to talk her into doing things she doesn't want to do?" Tom asked reasonably.

"Because she needs to get over this ungrounded fear she has of life. She's too young and healthy to live like a little old lady. She should be out having fun, taking a few chances, trying new experiences."

"And this is your decision to make for her?"

"No, of course not," Zach said impatiently. "It's just..."

After Zach had gone silent for a moment, Tom asked, "What else?"

"What do you mean, what else?"

"I doubt that the haunted-house incident is the full story. What else did you do?"

"I simply let her know that I didn't think she ought to be encouraging Mike Henry. You and I both know he has a crush on her. It's not fair of her to lead him on."

Again Tom looked openly skeptical. "Kim was leading Mike on?"

"She drank cider with him," Zach muttered. Even he realized how lame that sounded.

Tom snorted.

"The point is, she was never willing to make a real commitment to me," Zach said defensively. "She always evaded the issue when I tried to bring it up, and backed away when I tried to move closer. From the beginning she expected disaster, and then it was as if she did her best to make sure it happened. How was I supposed to have a relationship with her when I was the only one making an effort?"

"I don't think you were the only one," Tom argued. "Kim tried, too, Zach. Remember the bike ride? Sherm's dogs?"

"It wasn't enough."

"No, apparently not. Maybe the two of you just couldn't get past your differences. Maybe it's best that it ended now, before anyone got hurt."

Zach almost gave a bitter laugh. Before anyone got hurt? What did Tom think *he* was going through? Damn it, it felt as though someone had kicked him in the gut and then stomped on him while he was down.

If he'd known it could feel like this, he never would

have tried to have a real relationship in the first place. He'd have stuck to the light, easy friendships he'd had in the past, having a good time while they lasted, moving on with no hard feelings or backward glances afterward.

"I mean, it's obvious that you and Kim were mismatched," Tom said, his expression bland. "A mistake from the beginning."

Zach didn't know why Tom's words annoyed him so much, when they were exactly what he'd been saying to himself ever since Kim had thrown him out. It really was better that it was over, he thought. Kim was never going to make up her mind about what she really wanted, and Zach had been just wasting time hoping she would come around.

He tried to remember what he'd been like before he'd fallen for her. Tried to regain a touch of the old arrogance. He was Zach McCain. Super Zach. Nothing went wrong for him. He laughed at fate and fear. He could have any woman he wanted, if he happened to want one.

He didn't need Kim Berry.

"Maybe Mike *should* ask her out," Tom murmured. "He's a decent guy. They probably have a lot in common."

If the fire bell hadn't rung at that moment, causing both Tom and Zach to spring instinctively into action, Zach might well have gone for his best friend's throat. Even the thought of Kim with another man made him go ballistic.

Okay, he told himself as he sprinted for the truck. So it was going to take a bit longer than a day or two to get over her. But he would get over her.

It wasn't as if she'd given him any other choice.

Kim didn't see or hear from Zach during the next two weeks. He didn't call, didn't stop by the diner. But she heard plenty about him from others.

"I knew it wouldn't last," Maggie pronounced sourly.

"I don't want to talk about this, Maggie," Kim said as she tied her tiny apron over her jeans.

"Tried to warn you, didn't I? You and Zach got about as much in common as a dog and a cat."

Kim tucked an order pad and a pencil in her apron pocket. "Yes, you warned me, Maggie. And you were right, okay? So let's drop it now."

"Shame, though. I sort of thought the two of you were going to work it out. His mama sure thought he was a goner this time."

Kim looked upward and prayed for patience. "I do *not* want to talk about this," she repeated slowly. And she didn't even want to think about what Zach's "mama" was saying about her now.

"If you ask me—"

"The whole point is," Kim interrupted flatly, "I'm not asking you. And when it comes to this subject, I *won't* be asking you. Now, if you'll stop yapping at me and let me get to work, I have customers to see to."

And with that, she turned on one heel and marched away, leaving Maggie openmouthed behind her. After a moment Kim heard her employer give a crack of laughter. One thing Maggie respected, Kim had come to learn, was someone who stood up to her.

It was something Kim had never been able to do effectively before. Funny, she didn't feel as afraid as she once had. Maybe it was because the worst had already happened, she thought sadly. She'd had her heart broken.

"You broke his heart," Chris Patton said a couple of days later, gazing at Kim with big, reproachful eyes. She didn't bother clarifying who "he" was. It wasn't necessary.

"I don't think so, Chris," Kim replied, struggling to hold on to her composure and her patience. "What would you like to order?"

Chris had come into the diner alone, which she'd never done before. When she'd seen her Kim had worried that the only reason Chris was here was to talk about Zach. Apparently she was right.

"Just coffee," Chris said. "Can't you sit with me a minute and talk about this?"

"Chris." Kim used every ounce of willpower she possessed to speak politely. "I can't take a break now—I have to work. And there's really nothing to talk about. I know you're concerned about your friend. Zach told me that you take everyone's problems to heart and that you always want to help when you can. But this time there's really nothing you can do, okay? It just didn't work out."

Chris looked dissatisfied. "Zach just seems so unhappy. And," she added, searching Kim's face, "so do you."

"Zach will get over it. And so will I." *Maybe. Like in a couple hundred years or so.*

"But—"

"Chris, I'm sorry, but I really have to get back to work now."

"Yeah, sure. But you'll call me if there's anything I can do?"

"Sure," Kim promised, knowing she wouldn't have to follow through. There was absolutely nothing Chris, or anyone, could do about her and Zach.

"He's going to break his fool neck," Tom pronounced flatly almost two weeks later.

Kim set his chocolate pie in front of him. "Who?" she asked, though she already knew.

Tom gave her a look that chided her for her deliberate obtuseness. "You know who."

Kim sighed. "What's he doing?"

"He's gone nuts. Getting more reckless than ever. He's not sleeping, and he's living on caffeine and sugar, which makes him jumpy. He's an accident waiting to happen, Kim."

The grim words made her throat clench, but she managed to say, "There's nothing I can do about it, Tom. He certainly wouldn't listen to me."

"He might. He sure as hell won't listen to anyone else."

Kim shook her head, blinking back an unwelcome rush of tears. Tears had been coming much too easily the past four painful weeks, but she'd managed to shed them only in private. She was determined not to change that now. "He won't."

Tom sighed. "Damn."

"What...what's he doing, exactly?" Kim couldn't help asking, anxiety making her voice tremble.

"Just pushing too hard," Tom answered with a grave shrug. "He's going to burn out or do something stupid if he isn't careful. And he's not letting anything any of us say get through to him."

Kim rubbed wearily at her throbbing temple. "He's still just mad. He'll get over it."

"It's more than mad, Kim." Tom's expression was both sympathetic and a bit accusing.

She reacted defensively. "Look, I tried, okay? I wanted it to work. But he expected too much. And I couldn't deal with his unreasonable jealousy."

"He was wrong about that." Tom sounded utterly convinced on that point, at least. "And I've told him so. I think he knows it, too. The thing is, he was feeling insecure—something Zach McCain's probably never felt in his life—and he didn't know quite how to handle it. I think it just came out as jealousy."

"Maybe," Kim agreed. "But whatever caused it, he was wrong."

"Yes. But maybe Zach needed to feel trusted, as well?"

Kim bit her lip. She wasn't trying to imply that Zach had been the only one at fault, she thought of saying. She knew she'd sent him too many mixed signals, knew her fear of taking risks with him had frustrated him.

The point was, it hadn't worked. Had probably been destined for failure from the beginning. And wasn't it easier to end it now while she was still able to go on with her life, hurting, but not completely devastated? Had she and Zach become lovers and then broken up, wouldn't she have ended up like poor Aunt Pearl, forever grieving for what might have been?

Wrapping her fear around her like a familiar, comfortable old robe, she looked down at her order pad and said, "I'm sorry, Tom. There's nothing I can do."

"I'm sorry, too," he said sincerely.

"Hey, Kim. You expect the customers to go to the kitchen and serve themselves?" Maggie demanded, raising her voice to be heard throughout the diner. "Get a move on."

Kim nodded, gave Tom one last, regretful look and hurried back to work. She actually welcomed the activity. It was easier to work than to worry about Zach.

The four-wheelers were earsplittingly loud as they zipped through the woods, bumping over rocks and fallen branches, flying over the tops of low hills, skidding on fallen leaves, stirring up clouds of dust.

Zach straddled one of the low-slung recreational vehicles, gunning the motor with his right hand. The knuckles on that hand were bruised and swollen. He'd told everyone he'd slammed his hand in a door. It was better that they mock him for that than to admit the truth—that he'd smacked his hand into a wall of his apartment during the middle of the night while he'd been missing Kim.

There weren't enough ATVs for everyone involved in this Friday-morning outing to ride at once, so Tom climbed on behind Zach. "Promise me," he said before mounting, "that you won't kill me."

Zach rolled his eyes. "I've driven these things before, Lowery. I know what I'm doing."

Tom didn't sound notably reassured. "Yeah, well, just keep your mind on your driving, you hear?"

Zach nodded. "Hang on, buddy. You're about to have the ride of your life."

Tom sighed gustily. "What I wouldn't give to hear those words from someone other than you. Someone tall, blond, leggy..."

"Shut up, Lowery."

Zach revved the motor, released the clutch and the four-wheeler shot forward.

The ride was rough, fast, exhilarating. Zach loved the feel of the power beneath him, and in his hands. For the first time in weeks he felt fully in control. In this, if not in his totally screwed-up love life, he felt confident, competent. Prepared.

Behind him, Tom was laughing, his shouts equally divided between warning Zach of approaching obstacles and urging him to go faster. They skidded around a curve on the well-worn dirt-bike trail, simultaneously shifting their balance on the wide seat.

If Kim were to see him now, Zach thought, she would believe that he was doing just fine without her. At the moment, with the wind in his hair and the dust in his mouth and the roar of a powerful motor beneath him, he could almost believe it himself.

Almost.

He shot around another corner and headed up a sharp incline, looking forward to flying over the top and hitting the trail again with a teeth-jarring thud. Man, this was great. Behind him, he heard Tom laughing his fool head off, and Zach had to laugh with him.

He gunned the motor, took the hill.

He never saw the other rider who'd just gone into a skid

on the other side of the incline and was now speeding in the wrong direction, trying to regain control.

The crash happened so fast that Zach had no opportunity to do anything to prevent it. One moment he was driving the vehicle, the next he was flying. Landing. Hard.

Dazed, he heard shouts. Frantic ones. Someone yelling for EMTs to be called.

"Zach! Are you all right?" One of the other riders, a guy Zach had met only an hour earlier, knelt beside him, looking worried.

He hurt all over, particularly his left arm, but Zach didn't believe he'd been seriously injured. He shifted his weight, winced, then nodded. "I think so. Everybody else okay?"

The guy—Zach thought his name was Steve—didn't immediately answer. Zach took one look at his grim expression and struggled to rise.

"Hey, you better lie still. You probably shouldn't be moving around," Steve—or whatever his name was—protested, reaching out to stop him.

Zach shook him off and limped toward a grim, silent group that had gathered around the tumbled ATVs. He saw the other rider first, the one who'd hit him. The guy was bleeding profusely from a cut on his head, and was holding one arm cradled in front of him. He was hurt, but nothing life threatening, Zach assessed with a practiced glance.

And then he saw Tom. And his knees weakened.

Someone steadied him. "We've called for help."

Zach couldn't answer. He could only stare in shocked disbelief at his awkwardly crumpled, ominously unmoving best friend.

He knew without having to ask that it was bad. He pushed past the men gathered around Tom and knelt shakily on the ground beside him. "Tom," he said, his voice not quite steady.

He knew even as he spoke that his friend couldn't hear him.

Maggie got the news first—as she so often did. "There's been an accident," she said to Kim.

Kim set the coffee carafe down with a thump that sloshed the hot beverage dangerously close to the edge. Somehow, she knew who'd been involved. "Zach?" she whispered.

Maggie nodded, her expression grim. "Him and Tom. Tom's hurt worse, I think. Word is, it's pretty bad."

Kim was already untying her apron. "Where are they?"

"You're leaving? In the middle of the lunch shift?"

The apron landed in a crumpled heap on the counter. "Where are they, Maggie?"

"Washington Regional. But—"

Kim was already racing to the door.

Chapter Thirteen

Acting on a growing sense of urgency, Kim drove faster than she should have to Washington Regional Medical Center. To avoid the parking deck, she found a spot in the lot across North Street from the hospital, then waited impatiently for the light to change so that she could hurry across the street and down the sidewalk toward the hospital entrance. She rushed past a couple of nurses in scrubs and photo badges who were walking toward the intersection, and she was aware that they looked at her curiously, obviously sensing her distraught state.

All she could think of was that Zach had been injured. She had to see for herself that he would be all right.

She'd almost reached the entrance when Zach walked out of the hospital, his sister Elaine hovering beside him. Skidding to a breathless stop, Kim studied him closely, assessing his condition. He was limping, she noticed, and his left arm was in a sling. There was a darkening bruise on his left cheek. His jeans and sweatshirt were dirty and were torn in a couple of places. Other than that, he seemed fine, if grim-faced.

Almost sagging with relief, she called out to him. "Zach."

He'd been looking down. Hearing her voice, he glanced up. The expression—or rather, the utter lack of expression—in his blue eyes chilled her.

"You're leaving?" she asked inanely, when it was perfectly obvious that he was.

Zach nodded.

"I'm giving him a ride home," Elaine offered, looking worriedly from her brother to Kim. "He wants to clean up."

"How is Tom?" Kim asked, trying to read Zach's inscrutable face.

Again it was Elaine who answered. "He's being airlifted to Little Rock. He's...very badly injured."

"Oh, my God." Kim covered her mouth with one hand, and reached out to Zach with the other. "Zach..."

He seemed to almost shrink into himself to avoid her touch. "I've got to go. I'm driving to Little Rock after I clean up."

She wanted to offer to go with him. She even opened her mouth to do so. But he looked so hard, so cold, so distant. She wasn't at all sure he would welcome the offer, or accept it. She closed her mouth and nodded, her throat going tight.

Zach hesitated for a long moment, looking at her, his eyes seeming to search for something—she only wished she knew what. His own face gave nothing away. And then he nodded and stepped past her.

"Thanks for coming," he said gruffly, speaking as though to a mere acquaintance. "Elaine?"

His sister watched him limp away, then turned to Kim. "He's hurting. And he's terrified that Tom's not going to make it."

Kim caught her breath. "That's—that's a possibility?"

Elaine nodded somberly. "Yes. I think Zach blames himself, though everyone who saw the accident said there was nothing he could have done."

Clutching her arms against a sudden chill, Kim looked after Zach, who stood at the intersection, waiting for the light to change, his stance stiff. Yes, she thought. He would blame himself. Zach had never truly learned to accept his own limitations.

He was having to learn the hard way now.

"Is there anything I can do?" she asked Elaine.

"Be there for Zach," Elaine said promptly. "I know you still care for him, I read it in your eyes when you were rushing up the walkway to him."

"Yes." Kim saw no need to lie about that. "I care for him. But you saw him. He doesn't want my help."

"I can't reach him now, either," Elaine admitted, her eyes worried. "But maybe..."

The light changed. Zach looked impatiently over his shoulder. "Elaine?"

"I have to go. I'll call you, okay?"

Kim nodded and watched her rush to her brother's side. Zach didn't look back again.

Kim waited until they'd climbed into Elaine's car and driven away. She thought of going into the hospital to ask about Tom, but she suspected that his family and friends would be gathered around him, that questions from a virtual stranger would be seen as more of an intrusion than a show of concern. Still holding her arms, she turned toward her car, her steps lagging.

She couldn't help feeling that she had just failed Zach again, even though he had all but pushed her away.

A week passed. Feeling very much the outsider, Kim was able to monitor Tom's progress only through the grapevine at the diner.

The first few days were touch and go, his condition grave. His friends from the fire department could hardly talk about him without choking up. Everyone loved Tom.

Kim waited and prayed. And then breathed a sigh of relief when word came that Tom would recover, though the extent of his eventual recuperation was still in question.

"And Zach? How is he?" she asked Chris, who'd just given her the report on Tom.

"You haven't heard from him?" Chris asked, her round face creased with concern.

Kim shook her head and swallowed a lump in her throat. "No. Not a word."

"Neither have any of us in the past few days," Chris said, motioning toward the two off-duty firefighters who'd accompanied her to the diner for a late lunch. "We'd been planning a big blowout for his thirtieth birthday this weekend, but of course that's out now. He sent word he didn't want us to do anything right now, not until Tom can join us."

Kim hadn't even known that Zach's birthday was coming up so soon, a thought she found vaguely depressing. And then she thought about Chris's odd wording. "Sent word? You mean he hasn't been working?"

Chris shook her head. "Not since the accident. He's on medical leave for a few weeks. He hit his shoulder pretty hard."

"I suppose he's been staying in Little Rock with Tom," Kim murmured.

"Not that any of us have seen," Chris replied as her companions shook their heads. "We've all been to Little Rock on our days off. Zach's not there. He's not at home, either—or if he is, he's not answering the door or returning his telephone messages."

Biting her lip, Kim wondered if Zach's family knew more about his whereabouts than his co-workers did. She was worried about him. She couldn't stop thinking about that bleak, lost look in his eyes when she'd seen him outside the hospital.

Somehow the next morning, Kim found herself on the road to Little Rock, a three-hour drive. The first part of the drive was over winding, hilly, narrow roads navigated for the most part by pickup trucks and sport utility vehicles, eighteen-wheelers and the occasional college student in a sports vehicle, many of them fond of taking the sweeping curves right in the middle of the road. It was easier once she hit the freeway outside Fort Smith, but it was still a long drive.

She didn't usually like to travel that far by herself, particularly to an area she'd never visited before, and it was the first time she'd done so since her move from St. Louis to Fayetteville. But this was a trip she felt she needed to make.

Once she arrived in Little Rock, she had to stop twice to ask directions to the hospital. Traffic was heavy, but she negotiated it well enough, focusing on her reason for being there. Surprisingly enough, her knuckles weren't even white around the steering wheel.

A man at the hospital information desk gave her directions to Tom's room on the sixth floor. Her heart was pounding when she reached the room, but she took a deep breath and tapped tentatively on the door with her right hand, a small potted plant clutched in her left.

A very tiny woman with an ash blond bob and intense green eyes opened the door. "Oh, hello," she said.

At five foot five, Kim wasn't accustomed to looking so far down. "Um, is this Tom Lowery's room?"

"Yes. I'm Tom's mother, Nina. Please, come in."

Kim could hardly believe the woman was Tom's mother. She looked more as though she should have been an older sister. Kim stepped past the woman, looking toward the only occupied bed in the room.

It was all Kim could do to hide her shock as she approached Tom, who greeted her with a shadow of his usual broad smile. He looked terrible. Though he was covered to the chest by a sheet, and wore a blue hospital gown beneath that, he still seemed to have lost weight. An IV needle was taped to his right arm. His eyes were sunken, his cheeks hollow.

"Hi," she said, suddenly shy, her eyes stinging with a hint of tears she wouldn't shed.

"Kim." Even his voice was weaker. "It's good to see you. Did you come all this way by yourself?"

She nodded. "I had a very pleasant drive," she fibbed.

"I'm flattered. Mom, this is my friend Kim Berry."

"Kim?" Nina repeated, cocking her head. "Zach's friend?"

"Zach's friend and mine," Tom corrected smoothly.

Kim set the plant on a table that was already crowded with plants and flowers and balloon bouquets and boxes of chocolates and get-well cards. "How are you, Tom?" she asked.

He made a face. "Oh, you know. Getting by," he answered vaguely. "I'll be back on my feet in a few days, as good as new."

Kim saw the expression that crossed his mother's face. It was quick, purely instinctive, swiftly masked. But very telling. Nina didn't expect her son to recover quite as easily as he'd made it sound.

"If you two will excuse me, I'd like to step out for a breath of fresh air," Nina said. "I'll let you visit in private for a few minutes."

"Sure, Mom, take your time," Tom bade her.

"Your mother looks very young," Kim commented when Nina had left the room.

Tom nodded against the pillow. Kim couldn't help noticing that his usually bronzed face was almost as white as the bed linens. "She was young when I was born," he explained, then changed the subject. "Have you seen Zach?"

Kim shook her head. "Not since the day of the accident, and that was only for a few moments outside the hospital. He wasn't being very communicative then."

"He isn't now, either," Tom said, his eyes shadowed with pain and concern. "He calls every day, but he'll only ask how I'm doing and then he makes an excuse to hang up as soon as I tell him I'm still alive."

Kim winced. "He, er, hasn't been visiting here?"

"He drove down the first day, after I was transferred here. He stayed while I was in surgery, just to make sure I'd get through it, I guess. He left before I came out of anesthesia."

"Chris said none of his friends have seen him in Fayetteville."

Tom's mouth tightened. "I know. They've told me. Elaine called this morning. He's not talking to them, either."

Kim couldn't imagine what was going on with Zach. Why wasn't he here, with his friend? Or spending time with his family?

Tom's pain-gaunt face was grim when he looked at her. "He blames himself, you know."

Kim frowned. "For the accident?"

"Yeah. It's stupid. It wasn't his fault. If it was anyone's, it was Roger's, the guy who crashed into us. But as I've told both Roger and Zach, it was just a freak accident. Neither of them intended for it to happen, and there was nothing Zach could have done to prevent us from being hit. Roger feels lousy about it, but Zach—well, Zach's sort of lost it."

"What do you mean?"

Tom turned his head away from her, staring toward the window that overlooked a wooded hillside view. Kim sensed that he wasn't admiring the scenery.

"There's a chance—a very slim chance—that I'm not going to recover completely from this," he said, his voice so quiet she had to strain to hear him. "It's possible—not probable, but possible—that I won't be able to move around as well as I did before. That...well, that my life is going to be a little different. Zach's been told. And it's eating him alive."

"Oh, Tom."

He shook his head, still not looking at her. "I'm not going to let this thing beat me. I've handled tough times before, and it left me stronger because of it. Zach—well, he's never had to face failure before, you know? Everything's always gone right for him. Everything until..."

"Until I came along," Kim said, reading his expression when he looked at her again.

"He fell hard for you," Tom admitted. "It's the first time it ever happened to him. He didn't know how to handle it, and he handled it badly. He knows it. And, despite his pretense of anger at you, he blames himself for that, too."

"And then you were hurt."

"Yeah. And then I was hurt. And he was driving. And, despite what any of us have said to convince him, he thinks it's his fault."

Though most of her sympathy was reserved for Tom, Kim knew that Zach's suffering was genuine. He hadn't developed defenses to handle failure, she reminded herself. He'd never had to before.

"Someone has to talk to him," she murmured, only half aware that she'd spoken aloud.

Tom looked relieved. "Exactly. So will you do it?"

Her eyes went wide. "Me? No, I—"

"You're the only one who can reach him, Kim."

She was shaking her head, holding out her hands as if to ward him off. "No. He wouldn't listen to me—he won't even talk to me."

"I think you're the only one he'll listen to."

"What about Elaine? She's a psychologist, she knows how to deal with things like this. And he's her brother. He loves her."

"She's already tried. She couldn't reach him. She agrees with me. We think you're the one who should talk to him."

"I don't even know where he is. Chris said he won't answer his door or return his calls or—"

"I know where he is. I can give you directions."

"Oh, Tom."

Tom held out his left hand. It wasn't quite steady, and his skin was cold when Kim placed hers in it. "You love him, don't you?"

She sighed. "Almost from the beginning," she admitted. "But there were so many strikes against us."

"Maybe. But I happen to think there was a lot going for you, too. Loving each other is a darned good start, isn't it?"

She bit her lip.

"Please, Kim. Try. Zach needs you."

She'd never imagined Zach McCain needing anyone. She still wasn't convinced that he did. But as she looked at Tom, lying pale and broken in his hospital bed, worrying more about his friend than his own uncertain future, she knew she couldn't say no.

"Tell me where to find him," she said with a sigh.

Tom squeezed her fingers. It broke her heart that his own were so weak.

Kim had thought the roads around Fayetteville were twisting and narrow. But that was before she followed Tom's directions to the McCain family's fishing cabin on the Buffalo River, some sixty miles east of Fayetteville, a two-hour drive north from Little Rock.

Concerned by Tom's urgency, she'd driven straight

from the hospital to the fishing cabin, stopping only for gas and soft drinks. She was too nervous to eat, especially when it began to rain just as she got within the last half hour of the drive to the cabin.

The sky darkened, the roads grew wet and slippery, and the wind began to blow. Creeping along the winding roads, Kim held her breath as she drove, until she became aware that her ears were starting to ring. She exhaled in a gust and tried to breathe normally after that. It wouldn't do her any good to arrive at the cabin hyperventilating, she thought wryly.

At the end of a long, narrow gravel driveway she found Zach's truck parked outside the redwood A-frame that Tom had described. It looked like a nice family getaway, she thought, peering through the curtains of rain at the cabin with its big porch and what was probably a nice view of the river, though she couldn't see that far through the rain and gloom. A barbecue pit was set up on one side of the cabin, along with a covered pavilion holding a picnic table, benches and chairs. She could easily imagine the McCain family gathering here for summer cookouts, quality family time.

The image caused a pang of envy to shoot through her, until she reminded herself that Zach wasn't here for a relaxing retreat. He was holed up like a wounded bear, and would let no one near enough to help him, not even his concerned family. What on earth made Tom—or herself, for that matter—think that *she* could reach him, particularly after the hurtful words she and Zach had exchanged the night they'd broken up?

She spent a long five minutes sitting in her car, staring at the lighted windows of the cabin and talking herself into going in. The rain pounded against the roof of the car, reminding her of the night Zach had found her stranded on the side of a road. The night he'd asked her out for the first time. The night she'd found the courage to say yes.

She needed all the courage she could gather now. She reached for the umbrella she always carried in her back seat, got out of her car and climbed the porch steps.

She was beginning to think Zach was simply going to ignore her pounding on the door, when he finally opened it. She was almost as shocked by his appearance as she'd been by Tom's.

Zach's hair was wild, his face covered with stubble, the large bruise on his left cheek having faded to a sickly greenish yellow. She didn't want to know how long he'd been wearing the ragged gray sweatshirt he had on, or the jeans with the rip in one knee. He still wore the sling on his left arm. His feet were bare except for a pair of gray socks, and there was a hole in the toe of the right one.

If he was trying to look pathetic, he'd certainly succeeded, Kim thought with a flash of unexpected anger at him for letting himself get in this condition. That was followed by a wave of sympathy, because only genuine depression could have caused Zach's uncharacteristic behavior.

"What the hell are you doing here?" he demanded, no visible welcome in his expression or his voice.

Anger returned. Kim set her wet umbrella aside and pushed past Zach out of the wet, cold air and into the relative warmth of the cabin.

"I've come to talk to you," she announced, turning to face him when he only stood there, holding the still-open door. "It's about time someone did."

"I don't need your sympathy," he snarled, not quite meeting her eyes. "You might as well head back home."

She removed her coat to reveal the knit pantsuit beneath, then tossed her coat over the back of a nubby plaid couch. "I'm not here to give you sympathy, I'm here to kick your butt. And I'm not going anywhere until I've had a chance to rest a few minutes and get something to eat. I haven't eaten all day and I'm starving, so you might as well close that door."

Kim almost blinked in surprise along with Zach. Had that really been *her* voice coming out so firm and aggressive?

"You..." He hesitated, looking lost and a bit bewildered, still holding the door in his hand. Her appearance had obviously caught him off guard, as had her attitude.

Sympathy tried to take over again, but she pushed it back. Zach didn't need pity right now. First she had to get his attention.

She looked around the large main room of the cabin. Beneath the clutter Zach had created during the past few days, Kim could tell that the place was simply but comfortably furnished. She suspected that it was usually neat as a pin, and that Nancy McCain would be appalled that Zach had made such a mess for Kim to find. She spotted the kitchen on the other side of a bar that was almost buried beneath paper plates, discarded wrappers and crumpled aluminum cans.

"I'm going to find something to eat. Are you hungry?" she asked, marching that way.

"Er..." He was still just standing there, watching her as though waiting for her to disappear or explode or grow another head or something, apparently oblivious to the cold, wet breeze blowing in from outside.

"Look at this mess," Kim scolded, shaking her head as she surveyed the chaos in the tiny kitchen. She picked up a half-full food can, sniffed it and shuddered. "I bet your mom would have a fit if she were to see this. What have you been doing for the past week—sitting up here eating cold food out of cans and staying drunk on..."

She lifted an aluminum can, frowned, and noticed that all the ones scattered around her bore the same label. Only Zach, she figured with a sigh, would escape into an orgy of SpaghettiOs and root beer when he was seriously depressed.

Shaking his head as though he were coming out of an odd dream, Zach finally closed the door. He glared at her. "Look, Kim, I know you mean well, but you—"

Kim had her head in the freezer. "There is a microwave under this mess somewhere, isn't there?"

"Yeah, but..."

She pulled out a package of frozen stew meat, studied it for a moment and decided it was relatively fresh. A bag of mixed vegetables joined the meat on the counter.

"Maybe you'd like to shave and shower while I make us some dinner," she suggested to Zach, opening the meat to thaw in the microwave. "I'm sure I can find everything in here."

"Damn it, Kim..."

She pressed the Start button on the microwave, then rummaged through cabinets until she found canned tomatoes. "I suppose you could eat like that, but you'd probably feel better after you freshen up."

She thought he was going to argue. It was entirely possible that he would decide to toss her out on her ear, rain notwithstanding. Without looking at him, she pulled out spices and pans, found an onion in a bin and a sharp knife in a drawer. Maybe it was the sight of the large knife in her hand that made Zach finally nod curtly and spin on one heel.

"Fine," he snapped. "I'll take a shower. You'd be doing us both a favor if you'd be gone when I come out."

He stomped upstairs, slamming doors behind him once he got there. Only then did Kim allow herself to sag against the counter, her knees suddenly giving way.

She wasn't going anywhere, and Zach knew it. But she wasn't nearly as brave about confronting him as she'd pretended to be—and she suspected he knew that, too.

* * *

The stew was ready, the kitchen cleaned and Kim was working on straightening the living room by the time Zach finally emerged from upstairs. She thought maybe he'd taken such a long time on purpose, hoping she'd lose her patience or her nerve and leave him in his funk. She was proud of herself for doing neither.

He looked better, she decided after a quick, assessing glance. He'd shaved, put on a clean gray sweat suit with the fire department logo on the chest, and clean white socks. The sling had been abandoned, though he still seemed to be favoring his left arm. He'd left his hair wet—but then, she'd always liked the way he looked wet.

He probably knew that, too.

"Dinner's ready," she said, walking to the round oak table in the dining corner of the multipurpose room. "Nothing fancy, just a quick stew, but at least it's hot and filling."

"I'm not hungry."

She shrugged, took a seat at the table behind one of the steaming bowls of stew and picked up her spoon. "Fine. Don't eat."

She took a bite of the stew, decided it was pretty good and reached for a cornbread muffin she'd made from a mix she'd found in the pantry.

Zach wandered around the room for a moment, went into the kitchen and pulled a root beer out of the refrigerator, and popped the tab. He took a long drink of it, his throat working as he swallowed. Kim watched him out of the corner of her eye.

After another moment he carried the drink to the table and sat down, glaring at the bowl of stew in front of him. Kim took a sip of her ice water, then spooned another bite of the stew into her mouth.

As though he was simply bored and had nothing else to do with his hands, Zach picked up his spoon. He toyed with the stew for a moment, picking through it as though searching for contraband. And then, without looking at Kim, he took a bite.

It didn't take him long to empty the bowl. He stared at it as though he wasn't quite sure where the stew had gone. And then he set the spoon down and looked up at Kim, who was watching him and trying to hide her satisfaction.

"All right," he said, "I've eaten."

As though the only reason he'd done so was to get her off his back, Kim thought with a sigh.

"Now," he added, "you can leave."

"No, I don't think so." She stood to carry her own empty plates to the sink.

"What do you mean, you don't think so?"

"Just what I said. I believe I'll stay for a while. It's nasty weather out there, and I've been in the car all day, and I'm not particularly anxious to make the long drive home just now."

A flash of anger darkened Zach's face. Even though it made her nervous, she almost welcomed it. At least he was showing *some* emotion.

"Did Elaine ask you to come up here?" he demanded. "If she did—"

"Elaine didn't send me here. Tom did."

The sound of his friend's name made Zach pale. He looked away quickly, but not before Kim saw the anguish that crossed his face. She took an instinctive step toward him, reaching out…

He turned away. "Tom shouldn't have asked you to come. He knows I'm okay."

"No, he doesn't know that. And neither do I."

He flicked her a glance over his shoulder, his eyes glittering. "I neither need nor want your pity. Tom's the one who—"

"Yes," she said gently. "Tom's the one who's hurt. And he needs you, Zach."

His jaw clenched. "If it weren't for me, he wouldn't be hurt. I was driving."

"It wasn't your fault."

"You don't know that. You weren't even there."

"No, but others were. Everyone said there was nothing you could have done. It was an accident."

He shoved himself away from the table, his chair clattering on the wooden floor, and began to pace. "If I'd just been more careful. If I hadn't been going so fast—"

"Zach." Kim stepped in front of him, gripped his forearms in her hands. "There was nothing you could do."

He winced. She realized that she'd grabbed his injured arm. Quickly, she released him. "I'm sorry. I..."

He caught her arm with his good hand when she would have stepped back. "Why did you come here?" he asked roughly. "Was it only because Tom asked you to? Because you've mistakenly decided I need your charity?"

"No." She spoke without hesitation. "I don't pity you, Zach. Never that. I just wanted to be with you."

He drew a deep breath, released it very slowly. "I wish I could believe that," he said finally.

She frowned. "I've never lied to you."

His expression had gone distant again as he let her go. "Yeah, well, if there's one thing I've learned lately, it's that there's a first time for everything."

"Zach..."

He moved away, both physically and emotionally. "I'm going up to bed. I haven't slept much lately. There's a bedroom and a bath through there," he added, nodding toward a door at the back of the living room. "You can sleep in there tonight."

She wasn't going to be able to reach him. He wouldn't let her, she thought sadly. "Maybe I should just go."

He shook his head. "It's getting late. It's dark and still pouring rain. You'd be a fool to set off for Fayetteville now. Stay here tonight and leave in the morning."

She wanted to think he was genuinely concerned about her. But she didn't allow herself to read anything special into his offer. She merely nodded. "All right. Thank you."

He was halfway up the stairs when he turned, looking as though there was something he wanted to say. "Kim?"

She held her breath. "Yes?"

"Er...thanks for the stew."

Vaguely disappointed, she nodded. "You're welcome. Good night."

He muttered something unintelligible and disappeared upstairs.

Kim released her breath and ran a hand through her hair, wondering if she had accomplished anything at all by making this trip.

Chapter Fourteen

Having thought she would stay in Little Rock overnight for a bit of sight-seeing, Kim had packed a bag before leaving Fayetteville that morning. She fetched it from her car after Zach went upstairs. She was shivering when she came back into the cabin. It was turning colder, she thought. Winter was on the way.

Somehow, the change in seasons seemed appropriate just now. A glorious autumn giving way to cold, barren winter.

In the downstairs bathroom she changed into the plain, unrevealing cotton pajamas she'd brought with her, and found clean bedsheets, a pillow and a blanket neatly stored in a linen closet. The bedroom was furnished with twin beds, a dresser and a wooden rocker. She chose one of the beds, made it up, then sat in the rocker, watching raindrops sliding down the window glass and worrying about Zach. She hadn't turned on the overhead light, so the only illumination came from a small lamp on the nightstand between the beds. The dim lighting suited her mood, as did the rain.

She didn't know exactly how much time passed before the knock came on her door. She knew it had been several hours since Zach had gone up to bed.

Clearing her throat, she rose from the rocking chair and padded barefoot to the bedroom door, her body stiff from sitting without moving for so long. She opened the door to find Zach standing on the other side, still wearing his gray sweat suit, looking as though he wasn't entirely sure where he was or what he was doing there.

That little-boy-lost look of his was breaking her heart. She had to do something about getting rid of it, even if it meant making him furious at her again. "What is it, Zach?"

He quickly took in her functional pajamas, her bare feet, the still neatly made bed behind her. He moved as though to put his hands in his pockets, then dropped them when he realized there were no pockets in his sweatpants. "I, er, thought I'd better check on you. Just in case the strange surroundings or odd noises or anything bothered you."

"In case I was afraid, you mean?"

He shrugged. "Yeah. I guess."

"Thank you. But I'm fine."

"Oh. Well...good." He didn't immediately move away.

She leaned against the door, studying his face. "Was there something else?"

She saw him swallow, saw a muscle jump in his jaw. She sensed that he was suppressing a great deal of emotion, and it was all she could do not to reach out to him. But she knew that if she did, he would only draw back again. Zach had to be the one to take that first step forward.

He looked at her, his bright blue eyes so dark, so deeply shadowed with inner pain that they looked almost navy. "Kim..."

His voice cracked, just a little. It was enough to bring

tears to her eyes. She blinked them back furiously, knowing that crying was the worst thing she could do right now.

"Come in, Zach," she said briskly, stepping aside from the doorway. "Let's talk."

He entered the room slowly, as though being pulled in somewhat against his will. His eyes never left hers.

She moved backward, wondering if she should sit on the bed and hope that he would choose the rocker, or take the rocker herself, leaving him one of the beds for a seat. While she was still trying to decide the least suggestive option, he reached out, pulled her unceremoniously into his arms and covered her mouth with his.

Her first instinct was to wrap her arms around his neck and lose herself in the kiss. It had been so long since he'd held her. Kissed her. She had resigned herself that he would never do either again.

And then she remembered his injured shoulder. She stiffened.

He immediately lifted his head. "You don't want me to kiss you?"

"Yes. But I don't want to hurt your shoulder," she answered candidly.

A shadowy semblance of his usual smile crossed his mouth. "Forget the shoulder."

And he kissed her again.

She didn't know quite why this was happening. Whether Zach was kissing her because he'd truly missed her during the past weeks, or whether he was just using her as an escape from the despair he'd fallen into since the accident. Though she knew the reason should matter more to her, somehow it didn't.

She could sense the genuine need behind the kiss. It meant a great deal to her that Zach needed her. She had never thought it possible that he would.

She couldn't resist him now if she wanted to—which she did not.

Pulling her even closer, he slipped his right hand beneath the top of her cotton pajamas, his palm warm on the bare skin of her back. She shivered in reaction.

"I've missed you," he murmured. "Missed touching you. Kissing you. Being with you."

"I've missed you, too," she whispered against his lips. "So very much."

"Kim," he groaned between long, hungry kisses, "send me away now if you're going to. I'm not—I'm not feeling very strong tonight."

"I drove all day to find you," she murmured, nerves and anticipation making her voice thready. "Why would I send you away now?"

He murmured something that might have been her name. And then he took her mouth in a kiss that brought her up on her tiptoes, straining against him.

She didn't protest when he reached between them to fumble with the buttons of her pajama top. Her only concern was that he would hurt his wounded shoulder. When she tried to tell him so, he only muttered that his shoulder was fine. That he wanted her, needed her, ached for her. And by the time her top was pooled on the floor at their feet, she'd almost forgotten what she'd been worrying about.

With her help, Zach shed his sweatshirt. She heard him bite back a moan when he lifted his left arm, but she didn't say anything, knowing he wouldn't want her to. Still, she couldn't stifle the gasp that escaped her when she saw the bruises.

His shoulder and part of his back were covered in them, still dark and mottled after just over a week. Apparently Zach's left shoulder had taken his full weight from the fall. She stroked gentle fingertips over the painful-looking discoloration.

"It's a wonder you weren't hurt more seriously," she said without thinking.

His expression darkened again for a moment—and she knew he was thinking of Tom. To distract him, she cupped a hand over his bruised cheek and rose on tiptoe to kiss him, her breasts brushing his sleek, bare chest.

The distraction worked even better than she'd hoped. A moment later she found herself on her back on the made-up bed, Zach's mouth on her breasts, his hands sliding beneath the elastic waistband of her pajama bottoms. A fleeting worry for his shoulder crossed her mind, but she dismissed it. She figured Zach would stop if it hurt him. And he showed no sign of stopping.

She thought of reaching out to turn off the lamp when he slowly began to slide her bottoms down her legs, baring her completely to him. She knew her face had gone red, knew he wouldn't protest if she asked for the cover of darkness. But then she saw the appreciation in his eyes when he looked at her, and noticed the way the light gleamed against his skin, and the way the muscles rippled in his chest and back when he moved, and she decided maybe she would leave the lamp on, after all.

He loved her slowly, thoroughly. Patiently. He eased her almost effortlessly from leisurely tenderness to writhing passion, and still he took his time. She tried to protect his shoulder as much as possible, but he gave her little opportunity to hold back. He worried about hurting her when he finally entered her, but by that time she refused to allow him to wait any longer.

Perhaps there was some discomfort for both of them. But Kim decided much later—when her mind was clear enough to function again—that it had been well worth it. Judging from the gasps of pleasure she'd heard from Zach, she thought he would heartily agree.

Zach was the one who finally reached out to turn off the lamp. "We'll talk tomorrow," he said, tucking her into his right side, the narrow bed barely holding them both.

She cuddled against him, having no complaints about

the small size of the bed. "Mmm," she murmured. She had just begun to breathe steadily again, and her pulse still hadn't quite returned to normal.

They would have to talk tomorrow, she thought in dazed exhaustion. It would take her at least that long to form a coherent sentence again.

To Kim's disappointment, Zach was nowhere to be seen when she woke Sunday morning. She bit her lip, pulling the sheet around her rather sticky-feeling body, blushing as she seemed to hear her own husky cries echoing in the little bedroom. It would have been nice if Zach had been there to kiss her good-morning, to tell her their lovemaking had been very special for him, too. Maybe even to love her again, she thought with a little shiver of remembered arousal.

Drawing a deep breath, she slid off the bed, still clutching the sheet around her, and padded into the bathroom for a quick shower.

She towel-dried her hair as much as she could, then pulled it back at the top with a barrette, a quick, no-nonsense style. She dressed in a red sweater—Zach's favorite color on her, she couldn't help remembering—jeans and sneakers. And then she wasted a few minutes working up her nerve to go looking for Zach, wondering what mood she would find him in today.

He wasn't anywhere in the cabin. She checked the living room and the kitchen area, then hesitantly climbed the stairs, softly calling his name. There were two bedrooms upstairs. One was neat as a pin, except for a thin coat of dust on the furniture. The other was a mess—bedclothes tumbled half off the bed, discarded clothing littering the floor, root beer cans in the corners.

Kim shook her head at the sight of those cans. At least she knew where he'd been sleeping before she'd arrived, she thought. But he wasn't here now. Nor in the bath that connected the two bedrooms.

She went back downstairs and, on a hunch, opened the back door that led outside from the kitchen.

Zach was standing on a large redwood deck that overlooked the river from the steep rock ridge near the edge of which the cabin had been built. The wooded bluffs rose high on both sides of the river, and were dotted with the occasional vacation home, such as this one. There was a sense of privacy here, Kim thought, stepping out to join Zach on the deck. Of peace.

No wonder he'd come here when he'd needed to get away.

He wore a black sweatshirt today, along with black denim jeans. The dark color seemed to match the mood he'd fallen back into. A cool breeze tossed his nearly black hair around his bruised face, but he seemed unaware of it. He was wearing his sling again, though she couldn't have said whether it was to ease his discomfort or to continue to serve as a reminder of the accident.

He didn't look around as Kim approached. She wasn't even sure he knew she was there until he spoke.

"The roads are still damp, but the rain seems to have passed. Looks like it'll be a nice day. You shouldn't have any trouble getting home today. You're welcome to stay for breakfast before you leave, of course."

Kim stared at the back of his head in disbelief. She had hoped for a good-morning kiss. Maybe even a smile. After what they'd shared last night, she'd foolishly thought they would spend the day together, talking about what had happened and making plans for the future.

She'd certainly never expected him to make it quite so clear that he wanted her to leave. He acted as though he'd been doing her a favor to allow her to stay long enough for breakfast!

"Before I leave?" she repeated tentatively. "Are you

saying we should both go back to Fayetteville this morning?''

He shook his head, still not looking at her. ''No. I'll be staying here for a while. I don't know when I'll be back.''

''But what about your job? Don't you have to get back to work soon?'' She really didn't think his bruised shoulder would keep him out of commission for long. She suspected that sprains and bruises were run-of-the-mill for Zach, with his physically demanding job and hobbies.

''I'm on medical leave for a few more days. After that...'' His voice trailed away.

Somehow, Kim suddenly knew the truth. ''You aren't planning to go back at all, are you? You're thinking about quitting!''

His silence was all the answer she needed.

She reached out to grab his right arm, her fingers gripping tightly. She'd have shaken him had she been big enough and strong enough. ''Zach, what is going on? Why are you acting this way?''

''Tom might never walk again. Did they tell you that?''

In response to his blunt, unanticipated statement, Kim's fingers loosened in shock. ''No,'' she whispered, distress flattening her voice. ''No one told me.''

''The doctors said it would be another few days before they can tell exactly what motor functions he has left. Maybe he'll end up in a wheelchair. Possibly, he'll have to get around with crutches or a cane. Or, if he's lucky, he'll just have a bad limp.''

''If he's really lucky, he'll recover completely.''

Zach's jaw tightened. ''I don't think that was one of the options.''

Kim closed her eyes for a moment, picturing Tom's broad smile. His easy, loping gait. His athletic grace. And then she forced her attention to the man at her side. The one who most needed her now.

"It wasn't your fault, Zach." Maybe if she said it enough, it would finally get through to him.

He didn't answer.

She sensed again that sympathy wasn't the answer now. It was going to take more than that to break through Zach's now somewhat more understandable grief.

"If you're going to take some time off from work, maybe you should go to Little Rock to be with Tom. He could probably use the moral support right now. The two of you are so close...you could help him through this."

Zach only shook his head. "I think I've done enough for Tom lately," he said bitterly.

He really had allowed himself to sink into depression. While Kim understood how badly he must feel for his friend, and how natural it was for him to feel vaguely guilty that he hadn't been as seriously injured, she knew he had to snap out of it before he allowed it to destroy him.

"This is ridiculous," she said, forcing herself to speak crisply. "Just how long do you intend to hole up here, licking your wounds and feeling sorry for yourself?"

His arm was like an iron rod beneath her fingertips. "I don't need your analysis. Or your very generous pity."

She frowned, wondering if he was really implying what it had sounded like just then. "That's what you think last night was about? Pity?"

He flicked her a glance that wasn't quite as detached as he'd probably attempted. "What else? You made it clear that you didn't want me before. I can't see that anything else has changed."

She dropped her hand from his arm as if it had been burned. If it had been physically possible, she would have kicked his butt right over the deck railing and into the piles of wet leaves beneath them.

"I did not sleep with you out of pity, Zach McCain. Good God, what kind of a woman do you think I am?"

"A woman with a very big heart," he admitted, his voice softening a bit. "I know you meant well, but—"

"You jackass."

His eyes narrowed in surprise and irritation. "Look, Kim—"

"No. *You* look." Kim didn't lose her temper very often, but as Zach had already seen for himself on one occasion, she was a force to be reckoned with when she did. And he had just set it off.

"I can't believe how self-centered you are acting right now. Your best friend is lying in a hospital bed. He's worried about you and he needs your support, but you're too busy senselessly blaming yourself for the accident to be there for him."

"Tom is lying in a hospital bed because *I put him there,*" Zach almost shouted in return, his expression turning from anger to anguish.

"The accident was not...your...fault." Kim stretched the words out, lingering just long enough to stress each one, wishing she could simply knock them into that hard head of his.

He only turned away again, stubbornly silent.

Kim drew a deep breath, struggling for the right words, trying to be understanding and sympathetic rather than angry and disappointed that he hadn't behaved as she would have liked this morning. "What do you think you will accomplish by quitting the department, Zach? So many people are depending on you to help them, to protect them...."

"Protect?" Zach scoffed. "The way I protected Tom? The way I protected you last night?"

"Last night? *Now* what are you talking about?"

He shot her a seething glance. "Damn it, Kim, I didn't use anything last night. You trusted me, and you were there for me when I needed you, and I didn't even think about protection until afterward. I've been standing out here this morning cursing myself for being reckless and selfish yet again. Because of my negligence, it's possible that you could be—"

"I know exactly what I could be," she snapped. She'd tried to be sympathetic, but this time Zach was going too far with his determination to be a martyr.

She planted her hands on her hips and scowled at him. "I am an adult, Zach. I don't need you making decisions for me, or protecting me from my own actions. I knew exactly what chances I was taking last night, just as Tom knew what he was doing when he got on the back of that ATV. For once in my life, I knew the risks—and I took them. And if there is an 'accident' that evolves from my actions, whether it's a baby or a broken heart, I'll deal with it, knowing that I walked into the situation with my eyes wide open."

Zach opened his mouth to speak, but Kim was on a roll now, her temper in full flare.

"God, but you're arrogant!" she breathed. "You really believe you're 'Super Zach,' don't you? Well, I've got news for you, pal. You're human. I hate to break it to you so bluntly, but I really have no other choice."

"Kim..."

She ignored his attempt to interrupt. "You're going to fail occasionally. You'll make mistakes. Sometimes you're going to screw up royally. Bad things will happen. People you love will die, and there will be nothing you can do to prevent it. How do I know? Because I've been there. Tom's been there. We've survived. We will survive again. And so will you, once you stop whining and feeling sorry for yourself because all of a sudden your life isn't quite so perfect."

Stung, he jerked his head in automatic denial. "I'm not whining."

"Well, you could have fooled me. You are being incredibly selfish, Zach McCain. Spoiled and scared and selfish. Tom needs you. Your co-workers need you. Your family is worried about you, but you've pushed them away. And now you're doing the same with me. Every darned one of us loves you, Zach—though at the moment I'm having some trouble remembering why—and you're hurting us by shutting us out this way."

She saw his jaw tighten. "You don't understand."

Which, of course, only made her more furious. "Don't say that. I *do* understand, which is why it's so very stupid of you not to let me help you now."

He opened his mouth, started to speak, then closed it with a snap. After a moment he turned abruptly and stalked toward the stairs that led down from the deck. "I'm going for a walk. I think it would probably be best for both of us if you're gone when I get back."

"Oh, great. Run away, Zach. Send me away. *That* will solve everything, won't it?" she called bitterly after him.

He didn't answer.

Kim watched him disappear on a path that led into the woods surrounding the cabin. She inhaled deeply and leaned for a moment against the porch rail, trying to replay the entire conversation in her head. Trying to remember what he'd said, what she'd said, what she *should* have said.

And then she slapped her forehead with the heel of her hand, convinced that everything she'd said had been wrong. *Stupid, stupid, stupid.*

But her self-castigation accomplished nothing more than Zach's had, she thought wearily, turning to go back into the cabin, out of the chilly loneliness of the deck.

This wasn't exactly the way she'd expected the morning to progress, after all that had passed between them during the night.

Zach was furious. And he didn't even know where to aim his anger as he stomped through the chilled, rain-dampened woods, his boots squishing in the wet leaves covering the narrow path.

He came to a stop at a high lookout point that had been his favorite retreat as a boy, a rocky overhang that jutted out over the river, granting a breathtaking vista of the mountains and the river below. The fiery tones of autumn had faded into the dry browns of early winter, surrounding the evergreens that retained the only touches of color in the woods.

As he had when he'd been a reckless teenager, he climbed over a couple of large boulders and walked out to the very edge of the point, his toes inches from the edge. A cool wind whipped around his body, tugging at him as though urging him to take wing and fly off the high point. The very nothingness surrounding him appealed to Zach just then.

He was still trying to decide where to direct the brunt of the hostility building explosively inside him.

Certainly he blamed himself, for many things. For the accident. For abandoning Tom when his friend needed him most. For hurting Kim so many times, not the least of which was this morning.

He should have been holding her, cuddling her. Thanking her, damn it, for the precious gift she'd given him last night. Instead, he'd continued to take his rage and grief and anxiety out on her.

She'd called him a whiner. And while the word had enraged him, he secretly suspected she was right. And he was even irritated with her for being right.

But most of all, he was angry at a twisted fate that had turned against one of the finest, gentlest men Zach had ever known. A grievously unfair fate that had cruelly, senselessly ripped away Tom's lifelong dream.

He wanted so badly to believe that Tom would fully recover. That he would return to the job he so loved. But

Zach had seen the doctors' faces. He'd seen the truth in their eyes.

And maybe—just maybe—he'd pushed Kim away this morning because he'd felt guilty about the sheer happiness he'd found with her last night while his best buddy had been lying in a hospital bed, his own future a gloomy question mark.

That flash of self-insight made Zach wince.

Damn, he thought, shaking his head. Maybe Kim was right on the mark. Maybe he was being a self-pitying fool. And maybe he *had* become the most spoiled adult around, expecting life to be his oyster just because it always had been until now.

Maybe Kim had been right about a lot of things.

Chapter Fifteen

Kim almost did leave. She gathered the things she'd brought inside and took them back out to her car. And then she spent a few minutes sitting behind the wheel, trying to make herself turn the key.

She'd failed with Zach. She should have known that she would, especially if his friends and family hadn't been able to get through to him. It would take more courage, more fire, more stamina than she had to reach him.

And then she remembered their lovemaking, when she'd been so certain that they'd finally made the intimate connection they'd been seeking.

Tears filled her eyes, but she blinked them back. She would rather hold on to the anger than give in to the grief, she decided. With her hand on the key in her ignition, she looked at the inviting cabin, then glanced toward the woods into which Zach had disappeared. And she scowled.

Darn it, she wasn't giving up this easily! This was much

too important...to her and to Zach. She slid purposefully out of the car, slamming the door behind her.

She followed the worn path through the woods, thinking that it reminded her of the bike trail she and Zach and Tom had followed on that beautiful morning that now seemed so long ago. She could so clearly picture Tom on his bike, the very image of health and vitality. She had to blink back tears as she pushed a low-hanging cedar branch out of her way and kept on, looking for Zach.

The trail wound along the bluff lines, revealing the river below and the rocky cliffs on the other side. Kim didn't like heights, but the boulders and trees between the trail and the edge of the high embankment gave her a sense of security. In several places she saw evidence that others had climbed out on the rocks jutting over the edge, probably for a better view of the river and the hills surrounding them.

She couldn't imagine having the nerve to walk out that far, with no fence or guardrail between herself and a terrifying plummet to death. She'd bet Zach and Tom and plenty of others in their crowd would climb out there without hesitation.

She'd always considered herself the coward in the bunch. She hadn't thought Zach feared anything. Now she knew that he was very deeply afraid of failing someone else. Even when the perceived failure was only in his own mind.

She finally spotted Zach standing out on the very edge of a rocky precipice that seemed to be hanging in space, with nothing but a sheer drop to the river beneath it. He was looking down, and his face could have been carved from the same rock as the cliff beneath his feet. Alone, dressed all in black, his left arm still in the sling, he was the embodiment of desolation.

She had to force her voice past the lump in her throat as she stepped as close to the outcropping as she dared, stopping just short of the boulders that lined the path, over which Zach must have climbed to get out to the point. She knew he was aware of her presence, though he was trying to ignore her. "You aren't planning to jump or anything stupid like that, are you?" she asked politely.

He shook his head, making no effort to push the wind-tossed strands of hair out of his face. "I'm not planning to jump."

"Good. Because for a minute, I thought I was going to have to come out there and try to save you. And you know what a coward I am about things like that."

Zach drew a deep breath. "I stopped believing that a long time ago."

She took some encouragement from his tone, which was marginally warmer than it had been earlier. "What did you stop believing?" she asked, not quite understanding.

"That you're a coward." He turned to look at her, his movements as easy and casual as if he'd been standing safely in the middle of his own living room. "I'm beginning to think you're the bravest person I know."

She reached out to touch the trunk of a small tree growing beside the path, close to the edge of the embankment, but far enough away to make her feel safe. "You're wrong, you know. I really am a coward. I'm terrified of heights. Just looking at you out there scares me all the way to my toes. And yesterday? I hate to admit it, but I was terrified about confronting you. I didn't think you would want to see me. I thought you would be angry with me for invading your privacy, for taking it upon myself to come after you."

"And yet you came, anyway. None of my other friends had the nerve to try. Even my family stayed away, because I'd asked them to, and because they were afraid I'd get mad. But you came. Because you knew something they didn't."

She moistened her lips. "Which was?"

He spoke so softly that the wind almost whipped the words away before she could hear them. "You knew that, for the first time in my life, I was the one who needed to be rescued. And I just didn't know how to admit it."

Her knees weakened. She gripped the tree so tightly that the bark cut into her palm, but she was oblivious to the pain. "Do you need to be rescued, Zach?" she asked, her voice no louder than his. "Do you really?"

"Yes." He met her eyes, and allowed her to see the torment inside him. "I need help."

Knowing how hard it must have been for him to make that confession gave Kim the nerve to let go of the tree. "Then you're lucky I came along, aren't you?"

His face softened a bit more, and what might have been a smile tugged at the corners of his mouth. "Yes. I am."

She took a step toward the boulders, her eyes locked with his. "I've never rescued anyone before. I was always afraid to try. But for you..."

Realizing what she was planning to do, he took a quick step toward her. "Kim..."

She climbed carefully over a slippery boulder, still a bit damp from last night's rain. "Stay right where you are, Zach. I'm rescuing you."

"You don't have to do this."

She took a step out onto the precipice. "Yes," she said, her voice not quite steady, keeping her eyes focused intently on his face. "I do."

He nodded and held out his right hand. He didn't try again to stop her. And she realized that Zach really did understand her better than anyone ever had before.

The next three steps were the longest walk she'd ever made. She was all too aware of the jagged edges of the outcropping, which seemed to draw closer to her with every step she took away from more solid-looking ground. Her knees were shaking so hard that she was afraid she would topple right over the side. The breeze that had seemed light and playful before now felt as though it was trying to push her over.

She didn't stop until her hand was in Zach's. And, even though she knew he must be aware of the tremors running through her, she read the pride and approval in his eyes.

"I love you," he said.

At that moment she knew she'd made the right decision to walk out onto this high ledge. It had been worth any amount of terror just to hear those words from him. "I love you, too," she whispered.

Pulling his left arm from the sling, he drew her closer and locked both arms around her. There, standing on what could well have been the edge of the world, as far as Kim was concerned, he kissed her. And she knew her rescue mission had been successful. Zach would walk away from this edge—and the emotional one on which he'd been teetering for the past week. Battered, scarred, somewhat chastened, but stronger for the experience.

He had learned what it was like to be a survivor rather than a legendary hero. And she suspected that knowledge would make him even better at rescues than he'd been before.

He finally lifted his head, giving them both a chance to breathe.

"You coming out here like this, when I know you're frightened of heights, was the bravest thing I've ever seen anyone do," he said. "And it means everything to me that you were willing to do so for me."

"Now that I've demonstrated the extent of my love for you, could we go back to the path?" she asked him with a shaky smile. "I'd hate to ruin my grand gesture by fainting."

His own smile made him look more like the old, cocky Zach than he had since she'd found him. "Since I'm not at all sure I can carry you with this banged-up shoulder, we'd better go back,'' he agreed. ''Before we both have to call for help.''

He kept her tucked against his side as they moved slowly toward the boulders and then safely onto the leaf-covered path. Kim let out a very long, gusty breath when they were on solid footing again. ''I feel like I should kiss the ground,'' she admitted.

He turned her toward him. ''Kiss me, instead,'' he suggested.

She willingly complied.

A long time later they sat side by side on a large boulder. The rock was damp beneath Kim's jeans and her red sweater was little protection against the breeze, but she didn't complain. As long as Zach was sitting so close to her, she was warm enough.

Zach was looking out over the river, his expression pensive again, but not as grim as before. When he finally spoke, his voice was hushed, grave. ''When Tom and I were kids, and people would ask us what we wanted to be when we grew up, I had a different answer every time. A cop. An astronaut. A country singer. A cowboy. President of a bank. You know what Tom always said?''

Though she suspected, she shook her head.

''A fireman,'' Zach answered sadly. ''Always, a fireman. From the time he was maybe four. No one ever knew where the idea came from. There weren't any firefighters in his family. But that was always it for him. There was never anything else he wanted to do.''

''Maybe he can still be a firefighter. There's always a chance that he—''

He silenced her with a shake of his head. ''He's out, Kim. Even if he's lucky enough to be left with a bad limp, he can't do the job anymore. Whether male or female, a firefighter has to be strong. Able-bodied.''

''But, maybe, with time...therapy...''

"He's out," Zach repeated flatly. "I know it. Tom knows it. It's over. And you know why?"

"Because of an accident."

"Because of a stupid, senseless accident," Zach agreed heavily. "We were playing on four-wheelers, going for the speed, skidding curves and jumping hills like there was no chance anything bad could happen to any of us. If he'd been hurt on the job, saving a life, doing something worthwhile...well, that would be different. I could have handled that. Maybe I've always half expected it. But this..."

He shook his head, his voice trailing off to heart-wrenching silence.

Kim rested her forehead against his uninjured shoulder, willing him to accept her understanding. Her sympathy. Her love.

"I'm so sorry," she murmured. "It isn't fair—of course it isn't fair—but blaming yourself doesn't change anything. And leaving the fire department isn't the answer, either. Maybe you didn't always have that career in mind, as Tom did, but you love your job. You and I both know you do."

"You know what I keep remembering?" His voice sounded almost detached, as though it were coming from a distance.

She shook her head. "What?"

"The night we saw the documentary on the Everest expedition that went bad. Remember what you said about the doctor who'd lost his fingers? You pointed out that his career was over, that all the good he could have done in it was finished. All because he'd wanted a thrill. And you asked if it was worth it."

"And you said that no one could live every day waiting for tragedy to strike. You asked what joy there would be in a life spent hiding in a safe room."

"And then you pointed out that there was no need to go looking for disaster, either. Tom and I have spent the better part of our lives gambling with danger. And this time, it beat us.''

''It didn't beat you. Either of you. You're both still alive.''

''Tom's facing the rest of his life in a wheelchair. The answer to that question you asked me, Kim, is no. It wasn't worth it.''

Kim sighed gustily, deciding that the only way to get through this newest wave of self-castigation was with a serious reality check. ''You were riding ATVs. You weren't climbing a mountain in a blizzard, or walking a high wire with no net, or leaping into a river of crocodiles armed only with a nail file. Maybe—just maybe—you were being a little reckless, but there was absolutely no way anyone could have predicted this. *I* wouldn't even have fussed if I'd known you were going out to ride four-wheelers, and you know I'm afraid of *everything.*''

His mouth quirked. Just a bit, but it gave her hope. ''You? I'm beginning to think you aren't afraid of anything. I just saw you walk out onto that ledge, remember? It took even more courage for you to let me into your room last night—into your bed.''

That wasn't all I let you into.

Kim swallowed the remark that would only have embarrassed her even if Zach found it amusing. She cleared her throat. ''That was actually one of the easiest decisions I've made in a long time.''

His face softening, he touched her cheek. ''You might well have saved my life last night,'' he said, and she was too touched to call him on the exaggeration. ''And I will always be grateful to you for it.''

She wrinkled her nose. ''That isn't exactly the reaction I was hoping for.''

He smiled, his eyes lighting with understanding. ''Last night was the most spectacular thing that ever happened to me," he said deliberately. "You made my head spin. I've never felt like that before."

She nodded in satisfaction. "*That's* what I wanted to hear."

"It's all true, you know."

She nestled against him. "For me, too. It was beautiful. And whatever happens, I will never regret it."

"Neither will I," he said, his voice a bit unsteady. "Ever."

"You have to go back, you know," she said, meeting his eyes. "You have friends and family who want to see you. And when your shoulder has healed enough you have a job to get back to. You're needed there."

"I haven't been feeling very heroic the past few days," he admitted.

"The world doesn't need mythical heroes, Zach. Just real people who care enough to try to make a difference. And you'll never convince me that you don't care."

He drew a deep breath and let it out on a sigh.

Kim touched his face, sympathy softening her voice. "Now it's time for you to take a real gamble, Zach. Knowing you're human, and fallible, you still have to go back and risk making more mistakes, having more bad things happen. It's called life. And I have a feeling that, as imperfect as it is, Tom would still tell you right now that he prefers it to the alternative."

He nodded. "I really have been a jerk, sitting here feeling sorry for myself when Tom's the one who's suffering."

"Tom won't want your pity any more than you wanted mine," she reminded him.

Zach nodded again. "He won't get pity. But I'm thinking about heading for Little Rock and kicking him out of that hospital bed. Someone's going to have to bully him into getting back on his feet. Nina will do a good job, but I'll be better at it."

Kim smiled. "That's what he needs from you," she agreed.

"I learned it from you," he admitted. "You kicked my butt pretty good this morning, didn't you?"

"Just be glad I knew I couldn't take you physically."

He chuckled, a beautiful sound in her ears. "Trust me, honey, you inflict enough damage with that smart mouth of yours."

She cleared her throat.

He hugged her closer. "You knew exactly what I needed, and you gave it to me. And I love you for it."

She sighed and leaned against him. "No matter how much you deny it, I have been a coward, Zach. I was afraid to love you, you know. I was afraid we were too different. That you would grow tired of me, or bored with me. That you would break my heart. That's what made me so defensive."

"And I was afraid you'd break mine. Which is what made *me* defensive."

"So we almost ended up breaking each other's hearts," Kim said with a rueful shake of her head.

"We've been a couple of idiots, haven't we?" he agreed pleasantly. "But I'm willing to take my share of the blame."

"Big of you," she said dryly, though delighted that he was beginning to tease her again. They really were going to get through this. Together.

Since it was still early, they decided there was no need to leave the cabin until after breakfast. Both of them were hungry, but the supplies in the kitchen were growing limited. Zach made pancakes from a just-add-water mix, then made Kim giggle when he poured the batter onto the griddle in whimsical shapes—the way his mother had when he was a boy, he explained. Only, his shapes didn't come out quite the same, he muttered.

"And just what is this one?" she asked gravely, poking tentatively with her fork at a pancake made up of bulges and angles.

"A teddy bear."

"Hmm. And this one?"

"A heart."

She fought a smile. "Very sweet."

"Are you saying pancake art is not my forte?"

"Let's just say it's nice that you have other talents."

"Very tactful," he said approvingly.

"Thank you. I try." She took a bite of the lopsided, sort-of-heart-shaped pancake and studied Zach surreptitiously across the table.

He looked better, she decided. He was making an effort to tease and smile like the old Zach, and he was almost succeeding. The shadows were still in his eyes, but they had lightened considerably. She knew he was still worried about Tom, as she was, but he was beginning to accept that it had been a tragic accident, and that there had been nothing he could reasonably have done to prevent it.

He glanced at his watch. "It's almost eleven," he murmured. "We'd probably better head back to Fayetteville soon."

She nodded. "I'm sure your family will want to see you and know you're all right."

An odd expression crossed his face. "Yeah. I guess they will want to see me today, especially."

She cocked her head. "What do you mean?"

"Er—we'll probably be expected to have dinner with the family tonight. Today's my birthday. They're likely to make a fuss over it."

Her eyes widened. "*Today* is your birthday?"

"Yeah." He grimaced. "I'm thirty."

"And I didn't even get you anything."

His expression turned abruptly serious. "Yes. You did."

She smiled at him. "I love you, Zach."

His chair scraped the floor as he stood. "We have a little time before we have to leave, I think."

Her heart beginning to pound, she rose more slowly. "Then let's not waste it," she suggested.

He reached for her.

An hour or so later Kim was lying snuggled against Zach's right side, bare and damp and breathless, her pulse still rapid but slowly returning to normal. This, she decided, could easily become an addictive pastime.

Zach brushed a kiss over her slightly swollen lips. "I love you."

"I know," she murmured contentedly. He'd just taken great pains to demonstrate his feelings in exquisite detail. This time he'd dug in his bag and found protection first, since neither of them was quite ready to repeat the risk they'd taken before. "I love you, too," she added.

"I know." He sounded both smug and bemused. "You proved that when you came after me yesterday. And again last night. And yet again when you walked out onto that rock this morning."

She wrinkled her nose at him. "I hope you're satisfied now. I'm not sure what further drastic measures I could have taken to persuade you." But as she brushed her fingertips over the angry bruises on his left shoulder, she secretly suspected that there was nothing she wouldn't have done to convince Zach of her love.

As though he'd read her mind, he propped himself on his right elbow, leaned over her with a grave expression and asked, "Are you willing to take a real risk for me, Kim?"

Thinking suspiciously of parachutes and bungee cords, Kim eyed him warily. "What kind of risk?"

"Will you marry me?"

Her eyes opened wide. "M-marry?"

His mouth crooked into a one-sided smile. "Apparently I've frightened you into a stutter."

She blinked up at him. "I'm just...I wasn't expecting this."

"Do you need more time?"

She bit her lip and thought about it for a moment. And then Kim Berry, once known as "Scaredy-Cat Kim," for the first time in her life took a bold leap into an uncharted destination. And she did it with her eyes wide open.

"I don't need more time, Zach," she said, surprisingly calm now that her decision had been made. "I'll marry you."

His beautiful blue eyes were very bright when he leaned closer. "Thank you," he murmured against her lips. "That's the best birthday present anyone ever gave me."

They had a lot to discuss, she thought as she wrapped her arms carefully around his bruised body. She'd like to know whether he had a long or short engagement in mind. She wanted to make it clear that she intended to finish her education and embark on the career she'd been working toward for so long. She should tell him that she wanted children but would like to wait until she'd earned her degree—unless, of course, their recklessness last night had already taken that decision out of their hands, in which case she would count it as a blessing and make a few adjustments to her schedule.

But, for now, she had more important things to concentrate on. "You ain't seen nothin' yet, birthday boy," she murmured, moving sinuously beneath him.

He was laughing in delight when he brought his lips down to hers. And she was very proud of herself for making Zach McCain laugh again—with her, not at her, she reminded herself a bit smugly.

They had both changed during the past weeks. They'd both grown up in some ways. And, together, they would face a future that held no promises except that they would never stop loving each other. And that was one risk Kim was more than willing to take with him.

Epilogue

They were married in June, a lovely but simple wedding in the little church Kim had attended since she'd moved to Fayetteville. Dawn Lester was her maid of honor, and Zach's sisters, Patrice and Elaine, were bridesmaids. Since her daughter was only three months old, Elaine had fretted about fitting into the bright red bridesmaid dress Kim had selected, but she'd made it into the loosely fitted gown, to her pride and everyone else's amusement.

Because it had seemed important to Zach for the wedding to be a traditional one, Kim wore a white lace gown with a low-cut, fitted bodice, a snug waist and a full skirt that swished around her when she walked up the aisle on Zach's father's arm. She carried a bouquet of red and white roses that Zach had personally selected for her. He'd always liked her in red, he'd explained when they'd chosen the colors for the wedding.

George McCain had seemed delighted when Kim had asked him to escort her, and very touched when she'd explained that she'd never known her own father and was looking forward to sharing Zach's. Later, Zach's mother would whisper to Kim that George had looked as proud escorting her up the aisle as he had when he'd accompanied his own daughters.

Looking utterly delicious in his formal clothing, Zach waited impatiently at the front of the church. Tom was beside him as best man, standing tall and proud despite the crutches that supported him. He still had months of therapy ahead of him, but he'd faced his new limitations with his usual courage and was already considering new career options. Two of Zach's other friends from the fire department were the other groomsmen.

It was a day for family and friends, for joy and anticipation. A beautiful celebration of love.

Someone asked them at the reception where they would be honeymooning. Zach smiled at Kim and explained that they were leaving in a few hours for a resort in Mexico.

"I'm taking her snorkeling," he said. His grin turned slightly wicked when he added, "And parasailing."

Standing close to his side, Kim smiled blandly. "I'll try snorkeling," she agreed pleasantly. "But, Zach—you aren't getting me into a parachute. You never have, and you never will."

He only laughed and kissed her.

And she knew she had found with Zach enough adventure to enliven the rest of her life.

* * * * *

If you liked IT COULD HAPPEN TO YOU, don't miss Tom's story. Coming to you in early 1998, only from Special Edition.

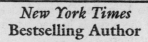

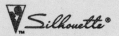